Katherine Roberts

THE OLYMPIC CONSPIRACY

An imprint of HarperCollins*Publishers*

THE SEVEN FABULOUS WONDERS

OF THE ANCIENT WORLD

THE GREAT PYRAMID OF GIZA

THE HANGING GARDENS OF BABYLON

THE TEMPLE OF ARTEMIS AT EPHESOS

THE MAUSOLEUM AT HALICARNASSOS

THE STATUE OF ZEUS AT OLYMPIA

THE COLOSSUS OF RHODES

THE PHAROS AT ALEXANDRIA

John G. Althouse Middle School

130 Lloyd Manor Rd.
Etobicoke, Ontario
M9B 5K1
(416) 394-7580

for Jerry

For more information about Katherine Roberts, visit
www.katherineroberts.com

First published in Great Britain by HarperCollins*Children'sBooks* 2004
HarperCollins*Children'sBooks* is an imprint of HarperCollins*Publishers* Ltd
77-85 Fulham Palace Road, Hammersmith
London W6 8JB

The HarperCollins*Children'sBooks* website address is:
www.harpercollinschildrensbooks.co.uk

1 3 5 7 9 8 6 4 2

Text copyright © Katherine Roberts 2004

Chapter quotations reprinted from *The Odes* by Pindar, translated by
G.S. Conway, Everyman Paperbacks, Orion, 1997, copyright J.M. Dent, 1972.

Illustrations by Fiona Land

ISBN 0 00 711282 3

Printed and bound in England by Clays Ltd, St Ives plc

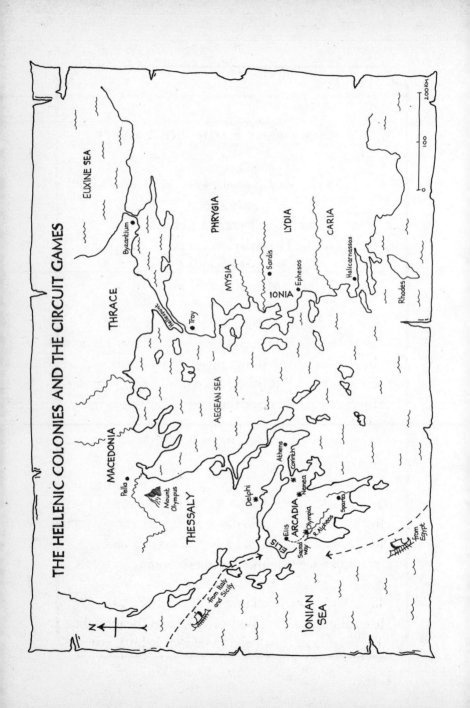

THE HELLENIC COLONIES AND THE CIRCUIT GAMES

EUXINE SEA

THRACE

Byzantium

PHRYGIA

MYSIA

Hellespont

Troy

Sardis

LYDIA

IONIA

Ephesos

CARIA

Halicarnassos

Rhodes

AEGEAN SEA

MACEDONIA

Pella

Mount
Olympus

THESSALY

Delphi

Athens

Corinth

Nemea

Elis

ELIS

Sacred
way

ARCADIA

Olympia

R. Alpheos

Sparta

from Italy
and Sicily

from Egypt

IONIAN
SEA

N

200 KM
100
0

CONSPIRACY

As THE FULL moon rose, Sosi began to shake. He took deep breaths. The last thing he wanted was his mother, and certainly not his brother, to realize he was scared.

"Hurry up," Lady Alcmena snapped. "We haven't got all night. You need to be in Theron's bed in the Blood House before morning if we're going to fool the judges into thinking you're him."

Theron smirked. "I bet he's forgotten how to do it."

Sosi squared his shoulders. "I haven't forgotten."

His curse meant he could change his shape every month. But for the past few years, he had not dared make more than minor changes to his appearance, having learnt from his mother's beatings that normal boys did not shed their skin like a snake every full moon. This wouldn't be easy.

He eyed his brother's body, exposed to the moonlight on their mother's bed, and couldn't help a pang of sympathy. Theron's muscles were as hard as marble, his skin brown from frequent oiling in the sun, his chin scraped clean of its first soft hairs. He had trained hard all year so he would be at the peak of his fitness when he came to Elis for the final compulsory month's preparation before the Games began – only to get injured on his second day. The bandage around his foot showed a sickly yellow stain. Sosi averted his eyes before his brother could accuse him of staring and wondered what to do about the wound.

"Well, little brother?" Theron said with a bitter twist of his lips. "Finished gloating yet? Make sure you copy my body exactly. Those puny muscles of yours aren't going to get you very far in the Olympic training camp, no matter how much you look like me."

"I'd better not copy you *too* exactly," Sosi retorted, their dependence on him making him bold. "Don't want to end up with a useless foot like yours, do I?"

It was a stupid attempt at a joke. A look of anger crossed Theron's face. But he seemed to remember that Sosi was doing him a favour and said nothing. Their mother frowned. "Just make it quick," she said. "I'll watch the door."

When she'd gone, Sosi stripped down to his loincloth and approached the bed. The night air raised goose bumps on his exposed skin as he perched on the edge of the bed and took his brother's hand. It was clammy with sweat. Could Theron's injury be worse than he'd thought? He darted a look at his brother's face, and caught an expression of curiosity mixed with disgust –

the sort of look people gave sacrificial animals when the priests took out their entrails on an altar to tell the future.

Sosi closed his eyes.

Theron needs me. This is my chance to show I can control my curse.

He imagined a scar on his foot in place of his brother's wound. Then he opened a door inside his head, and his curse surged through in a mass of dark scales and writhing coils. It was fiercer than he remembered. He was smothered by the darkness and far too hot. He had an urge to jump through the window and flee into the cool, moonlit grass of the Elean countryside.

"Breathe, you little idiot, breathe!" Theron's voice came from a great distance, as if he were shouting underwater. Sosi dragged his hand free. As he did so, the darkness tore, and the walls vibrated to a clap of thunder.

Sosi fell off the bed. He landed heavily, which surprised him until he remembered. Of course, Theron was much bigger than him these days. His skin felt tender, and his loincloth was uncomfortably tight. Embarrassed, he fumbled with the knot and retied it.

Theron was staring at him strangely. Their mother, who had rushed in at the sound of the thunder, stared too. Almost afraid to see the result, Sosi looked down at himself. Moonlight, flooding through the window, made his limbs glisten silver. Flakes of skin clung to him like a snake's discarded scales. He felt a bit sick. But he'd done it.

"Amazing," Theron breathed, the bitterness that had

clouded his words since the accident briefly missing from his voice. "You actually look handsome, little brother!"

"Sit down." Lady Alcmena picked off a bit of skin and prodded Sosi's scarred foot. Satisfied, she wound a bandage around it to match the one around Theron's, and sat back on her heels. "You'll do," she grunted. "Should be good enough to keep your brother's name in the Circuit lists, anyway. Don't kill yourself trying to win anything – you haven't a hope against the other boys."

"It's only until my foot's better," Theron reminded him, his smile dying. "Just so I don't get disqualified for not completing the compulsory training programme. Then I can take over again. I'll be fit to run well before the Games themselves, don't worry."

Their mother frowned. "You heard the physician, Theron. You've got to give that foot as much rest as you can! If your father were here, he'd say the same. Let Sosi complete the training for you. It'll ruin everything if you go limping about the place tomorrow and someone recognizes you. Sosi, you hurry on over to the Blood House – and no silly tricks! This isn't one of your childhood pranks. We'll be in a lot of trouble if the judges find out what we've done. I'm going to burn this before anyone sees it." She gathered up the tatters of Sosi's discarded skin and left the room.

Silence stretched in the moonlight as the two brothers, identical now, eyed each other. Sosi said awkwardly, "Where are you going to stay? Mother's right. We can't be seen together, or the judges will think you have a twin you didn't tell them about, and might guess what we're up to."

Theron grimaced. "I know that! I'm not stupid."

"Maybe it'd be better if you went back to Macedonia and concentrated on getting fit for the Isthmian Games? If you're not going to win at Olympia anyway, I could always compete in your place—"

"I'm not going to let you compete in my place at *Olympia*!" Theron said through gritted teeth. "Don't you understand? If I miss this year's Olympics, I won't get another chance. The other Circuit games don't count. There isn't another Olympic Games for four years, and by then I'll be too old for the boys' events. You heard what Father said. I have to show I'm good enough to win at the Olympics, or he won't let me be a professional athlete and I'll be conscripted into the army instead. The most running I'll get to do then is across some Zeus-forsaken desert pursued by a horde of barbarian horsemen! It's all right for you – no one's going to want a weakling with a curse like yours fighting at his side, least of all King Alexander. If you run in my place, you'll only lose." He must have seen the hurt in Sosi's eyes, for he looked away and mumbled, "Mother knows nothing about sports injuries. My foot will be fine in a few days, you'll see, and you can easily hide here in Elis until you get your own shape back again. If you hurry, you should make it to Olympia in time to see me crowned winner of the boys' sprint before the Statue of Zeus! I had a dream about it." Ambition shone in Theron's face, brighter than the moon.

"They'll disqualify you if they find out I trained in your place," Sosi said, realizing how much could go wrong. "You'll get whipped, which is bad enough, but what if the judges find out about my curse?"

Theron laughed. "It's a bit late to start having second thoughts now, little brother! Don't panic, you'll be fine. All you have to do is jog a few lengths of the stadium and throw your opponent once or twice in the wrestling trials. You don't have to win anything. All the boys are saving themselves for the Games. In fact, it'll be better if you are a bit slow, because then Trainer Hermon will remember my accident and be lenient on you. You won't last two days in the gymnasium, otherwise."

Sosi adjusted his loincloth with another lurch of nerves, remembering how the old trainer in charge of the boys yelled at them. He'd seen grown men crying with pain after a so-called practice bout in the wrestling pit.

"Shouldn't be too difficult for you," Theron continued, the bitterness back in his voice. "No one can train badly with a fine body like that. You'd better get going. At least you shouldn't have trouble getting into the Blood House. One thing you've always been good at is sneaking around where you're not wanted." He scowled at his foot, which was giving off a horrible smell, almost too much for Sosi's extra snake senses to bear.

Sosi eyed it doubtfully. "Theron...?"

"What now?"

"*Will* your foot heal in time for the Games? What did the physician really say?"

The length of his brother's pause frightened him.

"I suppose it might take a bit longer than a few days before I can run as fast as I could before... but we've nearly a month before the Games start." Theron's face closed. "What do you care, anyway? If you hurt yourself, all you have to do is wait until the next full moon and you can get another body, good as new! You've never really had to try, little brother, that's your trouble. One day, I'm going to be the best athlete in the whole world. Nothing's going to stop me. Not Father, not King Alexander and his army, and certainly not a stupid javelin accident!"

"You know that's not how the magic works—"

Sosi shut his mouth. His brother would not understand, just as Sosi could never understand Theron's need to be the best at everything. He might have copied his brother's body, but inside he felt the same as he always did.

Weak, slow, cursed Sosi. He'd been stupid to believe it might be otherwise.

PART 1

OLYMPIC TRAINING CAMP
ELIS

Ever are natural gifts the best,
but many a man struggles to win renown
by skills learnt from a teacher.

(Olympian 9)

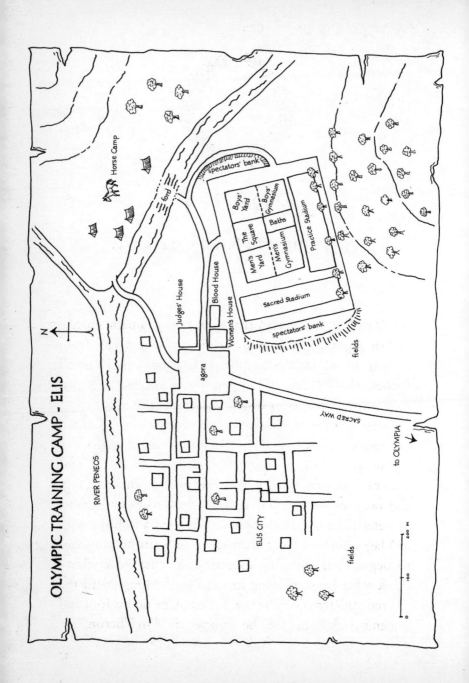

OLYMPIC TRAINING CAMP - ELIS

N

RIVER PENEOS

Horse Camp

ford

spectators' bank

Boys' Yard

Boys' Gymnasium

The Square

Baths

Men's Yard

Men's Gymnasium

Practice Stadium

Sacred Stadium

spectators' bank

fields

Judges' House

Blood House

Women's House

agora

ELIS CITY

SACRED WAY

to OLYMPIA

fields

0   100   200 M

Chapter 1

FITNESS

SOSI'S CURSE WAS always tiring, and the dramatic change of last night had left him feeling as if he'd run from Athens to Marathon and back like one of Theron's heroes, the legendary Phidippides, who had dropped dead immediately afterwards. What he really needed was to sleep late the next morning to recover. But no such luxuries were allowed at the Olympic training camp.

He woke from a confused nightmare of snakes and dark caverns to a trumpet blast that made his heart thump and sweat break out all over his body. Groans and grunts of determination filled the room as men and boys with bandaged limbs heaved themselves into sitting positions to begin their morning exercises. At first he couldn't think what he was doing in the Blood House with the injured athletes. Then he saw the bandage on his foot and remembered. "Theron," he whispered. "I'm Theron."

A nurse, working her way down the row of beds with a hydria, whipped off his blanket. "What are you mumbling about, young Macedonian? Up you get! No skiving for you today. It's time for you to report to the judges. Either you're fit, or you're out of the Games. What's it going to be?" As Sosi climbed shakily off the pallet, the nurse eyed his foot and her expression softened. "Don't look too bad to me this morning. I reckon you speared it yourself to get a rest! Some of you boys'll do anything to get out of a few days' training. Here – have something to drink. Don't suppose you'll have time for breakfast if the judges pass you fit."

Sosi gulped down the water and dressed quickly, watched by scowling boys in the neighbouring beds. They didn't seem pleased to hear that he might be recovered, and he wondered what his brother had done to annoy them. Surely even Theron couldn't have made enemies of the entire camp in just two days?

"Where do I go?" he asked, suddenly nervous.

"The Judges' House, of course!" the nurse said, giving him a push towards the door. "The physician's waiting for you there. Go on, get out of here – and I don't want to see you back again, so don't go running in front of the javelin targets next time!"

The other boys watched enviously as Sosi left the room. Outside, the rising sun had turned the mist over the river into a blanket of fire. Distracted by this, he forgot to check the road and spooked a racehorse passing the Blood House door on its way to exercise in the agora.

The jockey, riding bareback, grabbed the mane and shouted something as his mount galloped off. Noting his dark Persian skin, Sosi decided it was something rude. The Persian boy would be a slave. It was the owners of the horses who had to be of Greek descent like the athletes, since they were the ones who got the prizes if they won.

He waited until there were no horses near enough to smell him and retraced his steps of the previous night. His heart beat anxiously as he passed the Women's House, but there was no outcry to indicate his brother had been discovered hiding there. He crossed the ash track, avoiding the chariots exercising around it, and made it to the Judges' House without causing any further accidents.

Judge Demetrius, the man in charge of the ten Hellenic judges of the Olympic Games, waited for him between the marble columns that framed the entrance of the building. "You're late, Macedonian!" he snapped, and led the way into the shadows at a fast pace, his purple robe billowing around his ankles.

Sosi stumbled over the top step, regained his balance, and blinked nervously around the hall. But it seemed this wasn't to be a formal session. At the far end he could see only two purple-robed judges, talking in low voices to a man wearing a leather apron. They looked round when Sosi entered, and his cheeks grew hot. One of the judges gazed past him without interest, seeking out Judge Demetrius, and the two were soon deep in conversation.

The third judge was younger, with a clean-shaven chin. He gave Sosi a sympathetic smile, making him feel a bit better.

The physician motioned him over to a marble bench. Without a word, he went down on one knee, took Sosi's foot in his lap and unwound the bandage. He frowned, prodded the scar, told him to stand and balance on his left leg, then told him to sit down again while he ran his fingernail along the bottom of Sosi's foot. It tickled, and Sosi bit his lip to keep from jerking his leg away. All through this, Judge Demetrius and the old judge carried on talking in low voices. The younger one, however, watched the process carefully. When Sosi glanced up at him, he looked puzzled.

"The boy's foot seems to be healed, honoured sirs," the physician said, having to raise his voice to get attention. "In my opinion, he's fit enough to continue with the training."

Sosi let out a breath he hadn't known he was holding, and the judges broke off their conversation to frown at the physician.

"What? Healed already?" said the one who had so far ignored Sosi.

"Can't be," Judge Demetrius muttered. "The boy's foot was swollen bigger than a tyrant's head only yesterday morning!"

"I know, sir. I treated the wound myself. But I see no reason why this boy should not run in the Games. He appears to have made a miraculous recovery. The gods obviously favour this one."

Judge Demetrius came over to examine Sosi's foot himself. "I've had reports your bed in the Blood House was empty last night," he said. "Where were you?"

Sosi's heart thumped. What excuse would Theron have for leaving his bed? "I..." He remembered the physician's words. "I went to the shrine to pray, sir – for Zeus to heal me so I can win the boys' sprint." He had never seen his brother praying, but if Theron ever did turn religious this was the kind of thing he would pray for.

Judge Demetrius frowned some more. Then he sighed. "Perhaps they really do make them tougher up in King Alexander's country. All right, so it seems the boy's healed. Are we agreed to let him continue?"

With another smile at Sosi, the young judge nodded. The third one shrugged and nodded too.

"Congratulations, Macedonian!" The physician slapped Sosi on the thigh. "The gods obviously answered your prayers. May you dream of victory!"

It was a common athletes' blessing. But Sosi remained sitting, his legs suddenly weak, thinking of his brother saying, *I had a dream*.

"Well? What are you waiting for, boy?" bellowed Judge Demetrius. "Get on back to the gymnasium! You've two days to make up, so *run*."

Sosi fled before they could change their minds. At first he forgot he had copied his brother's body and just jogged slowly, concentrating on staying clear of the horses coming across the ford and expecting to get out of breath quickly. But as he neared the main camp compound, he realized he'd covered the ground a lot faster than normal. His body felt balanced and strong. He accelerated and took the long way round to the far gate for the sheer joy of it.

Shouts and the cracks of whips could be heard coming from the yards. Sosi made his way to the boys' yard and hesitated outside the low wall, watching the barefoot young athletes with strips of sweat-stained linen twisted around their waists. Some were running on the spot, others wrestling in the sandpit, others boxing stuffed goats' carcasses suspended from a post. Several boys were oiling themselves at the big communal urns near the entrance, laughing and joking as if they'd known one another for years. He'd watched Theron train from outside the enclosure with his mother and the other women who had sons and husbands competing in the Great Games, but inside the compound the noise and dust and smells were incredible. No one seemed to have noticed him. Each boy was concentrating on his particular exercise, watched over by Trainer Hermon with his whip ready to punish any breaking of discipline.

Not wanting to push through the crowd around the urns, Sosi hurdled the wall and landed as close to the trainer as possible. Someone muttered, "Show-off!" but he didn't care. For once in his life, he'd done something right. He'd got Theron back into the Olympic Games.

Whatever happened now, as long as no one found out about the trick, his brother could compete and chase his dream. Then maybe his family would no longer think him cursed, and—

The end of a lash flicked him across the arm. Sosi yelped, and some of the boys nearby laughed.

"Save your daydreams for the Games, Theron," said the trainer. "We already know you can run. Since you've obviously been passed fit, you're to practise wrestling this morning. Get oiled up, and get in the sandpit with Pericles. Let's see you do some real work for a change!"

Sosi looked where he was pointing and saw the blond boy who had called him a show-off waiting in the sandpit with his hands on his hips. Broad shoulders and large muscles marked him as a specialist wrestler. Sosi's stomach performed an uneasy turn. Pericles' smile didn't look particularly friendly.

The other boys melted away when Sosi approached, leaving him to oil up alone. He lingered at the urn, taking care to cover every part of his tender skin. He hoped his mother would put in an appearance among the spectators, but it was still too early for most non-athletes to be about. Some of the professional trainers, who had accompanied the richer athletes from their home towns, sat on the bank outside the enclosure watching their charges with narrow eyes. The only other spectator was a cloaked figure, standing so still in the shadow of the trees that Sosi had to stare hard to make out details. At this distance it was difficult to tell, but he had an impression of long black hair under the hood, and yellow eyes watching him.

An unlooked-for shiver went down his spine.

"Hurry up, Macedonian!" called Pericles. "Not scared, are you?"

Sosi was scared. But if he let the other boys know this, he'd be finished. "Sorry – I'm ready now."

The boy narrowed his eyes. "Sand yourself, then! I'm not grappling with you like that. You're glistening like a snake that's just changed its skin."

Sosi's stomach jolted. Quickly, he bent and scooped sand over the oil to cover his moment of doubt. Had Theron, in an unguarded moment, let something slip about his little brother's curse?

But the other boy simply stooped beside him and sanded himself as well. "Ready?" he asked, assuming the wrestler's classic stance.

Sosi swallowed and nodded, trying to remember what their father had taught them when he used to train with his brother. Stand balanced, weight forward, watch your opponent's feet... With a grunt, Pericles grasped Sosi's wrists and hooked his leg around the back of Sosi's knee. The next thing he knew, he was lying flat on his back in the sand, staring up at the blond boy's grin.

"Got you, Macedonian!" Pericles waited for Sosi to scramble up, before repeating the move with the other leg and throwing him flat again. Trainer Hermon watched with a little smile.

Sosi collected his breath – a little slower this time – and got to his feet again. The falls didn't really hurt. The sand was soft. But he was aware of the other boys grinning at one another.

Pericles threw him a third time, and that did hurt because his head missed the pit and bounced on the sun-baked ground beyond. Sosi closed his eyes and lay still. That was three throws. In a match, he'd have lost. He hoped the trainer would let them stop now. But when he opened his eyes, Hermon was tapping the handle of his whip against his leg, still smiling.

"Come on, Macedonian," Pericles said. "Get up and wrestle properly! You're not even trying."

There were a few chuckles. "Poor old Theron's hurt his footsie." ... "Maybe Macedonians are cowards, after all." ... "Look out, Macedonian – if you lie there too long, someone might throw another javelin at you!"

Sosi clambered to his feet, rubbed the bruise on his head, and tried to pick out the boy who had said that. The laughter stopped as Trainer Hermon finally flicked his whip at their audience. "That's enough," he said. "You boys get back to your own exercises. Pericles, well done. Good, clean throws. Theron, if you're still having problems with that foot, then for Zeus' sake say."

"It's fine," Sosi said, knowing his brother would never have admitted defeat. He took up the ready stance once more, imagining Theron's contempt if he got him disqualified now. It would be worse than if he hadn't tried to help in the first place.

Pericles stepped forward and grasped his wrists again, but did not immediately throw him. He frowned as they circled. "What's wrong?" he hissed. "If your foot's bothering you, you should say so. There's no point struggling on."

"It's fine," Sosi repeated through gritted teeth.

"Then throw me! I know you can do it if you try."

"We're only supposed to be practising."

"Yeah, yeah. You know why old Hermon matched you with me today, don't you?"

"No..."

"Oh Zeus, you must be dim, Macedonian!"

Pericles threw him again and whispered as he helped him up, "It's supposed to teach you a lesson, stupid! We're all fed up to the back teeth of you going on about that dream you had of victory, and how you're going to win all the time. So unless you fight back, I'm going to keep shoving your head in the sand till the sun goes down, whether you're having trouble with your foot or not. Slave-driver Hermon won't stop it. He's been told by the judges to test your fitness today."

Sosi felt sick. But if he had to eat sand all day to prove to his family that he could be useful, then he would do it.

"So fight me," Pericles said, backing off and waiting for Sosi to make the first move. He narrowed his eyes. They were blue, Sosi noticed, like the sky.

He did try to throw Pericles. He even forced him down on one knee once. But he hadn't wrestled for ages, he wasn't used to Theron's bigger body and the way it balanced, and he badly needed some food. Each time he fell it was harder to get up again. Pericles threw him nine, maybe ten more times... Sosi lost count. He had sand in his eyes, his mouth, his ears and his hair. Their audience had gathered again. Even some of the men were watching over the yard wall, silent.

Pericles grimaced as they clasped wrists yet again. "You're different today, Macedonian," he whispered.

Though he felt almost too weary and bruised to remain standing, Sosi's heart jumped. "I'm not different!"

"Yes you are. Before your foot got speared, you'd have accused me of cheating by now and stalked off with your head in the air. You seem to think you're something special, just because your king's off conquering Persia. Tell you the truth, no one was much upset to see you injured."

"How did it happen?" Sosi said, and knew he'd made a mistake when Pericles gave him another sharp look.

"You're plenty weird today, Theron," he said, shaking his head.

Sosi tensed for another throw. But Pericles backed off and climbed out of the pit, excusing himself for a call of nature.

Sosi took the opportunity to study the spectators' bank. But although some of the women had ventured over from town, there was still no sign of his mother. The mysterious cloaked watcher with the yellow eyes had vanished. Now that the wrestling show was over, the other boys and the men drifted in to lunch, but Trainer

Hermon stood over Sosi with his whip, so he dared not follow them. The sun beat down on the back of his neck, making the oil sizzle on his skin.

After what seemed an age, Pericles returned to the yard. Sosi braced himself for another bruising. But the boy was accompanied by the young judge who had witnessed Sosi's physical examination that morning.

"I think young Theron has had enough for today, don't you?" the judge said quietly to Hermon.

"I'm merely testing the boy's fitness as ordered, Judge Lysanias," Hermon replied stiffly. He scowled at Pericles, who gazed across the yard as if he had nothing to do with it.

"By matching him against Pericles?" the young judge said with a frown. "That's hardly a fair contest, is it?"

"Less chance of another accident that way," Hermon said, still defensive. "Pericles is the best wrestler here. He knows what he's doing. I'm in charge of the boys' training while they're in Elis. Judge Demetrius is usually happy enough for me to make the decisions."

"Judge Demetrius does not judge these Games alone." The young judge looked at the blond boy and back at Sosi. His expression said he knew exactly what had been going on. "How's the foot feel, Theron?" he asked.

"Fine, sir!" Sosi wiped sand from his eyes and stood straighter.

"Good," said Judge Lysanias with a smile. "Let's keep it that way, shall we?" He gave Trainer Hermon a meaningful look. "By the looks of things, you've both trained hard enough for a full day already, so you can have the afternoon off. Theron, you rest that foot, do you hear? Hermon, I'd like a word with you in private, please."

The young judge and the old trainer walked away, purple robe and white glowing brightly in the Elean sunshine. Trainer Hermon looked thunderous, but he had no choice but to obey. The Hellenic judges had the status of gods during the Olympic Games, and for another month their word was law.

Sosi glanced sideways at Pericles as they crossed to the oil vat and took strigils from the hooks. Pericles vigorously scraped the mixture of oil, sand and sweat from his skin with the metal edge, avoiding Sosi's eye.

"Why did you fetch the Judge?" Sosi asked, wincing as he followed the blond boy's example.

"Who said I fetched him?" Pericles grunted, scraping harder.

"You did, didn't you? Thanks, anyway."

Pericles stopped scraping and stared at Sosi. "*Thanks* now, Macedonian? What happened? That javelin hit your head on its way to your foot?"

Sosi realized he'd made another mistake. Theron would hardly have thanked someone who had spent the morning rubbing his face in the sand. "I... just... appreciate it, that's all. You didn't have to do that. I won't forget."

Pericles grunted again. "You'd had enough, and so had I. It's no fun fighting someone who doesn't fight back. Besides, I promised to meet my sister for lunch." He gave Sosi another frown and shook his head. "Here, give me that – you'll be all day at this rate!" He seized Sosi's strigil and scoured the sand and oil off Sosi's tender back, while Sosi bit his lip and tried not to yell. As he worked, Pericles leant close and lowered his voice. "Even though you're an arrogant idiot and you deserved a scare, I'm glad your foot's healed. That javelin wasn't an accident, you know."

Sosi stiffened. "What do you mean?"

"Keep your voice down! I saw it happen. I was on my way over to the Sacred Stadium with young Dion, to watch the preliminary heats for the pentathlon. The men were practising their throws on the strip beside it, just as they usually do. You were the only one still in the practice stadium, weren't you? You probably didn't see because you had your back to it, but that javelin came out of the trees. The only way a bad throw aimed at the practice targets could have hit you would be if javelins could fly around corners, which they don't. Looked to me like someone hiding in the woods threw it at you deliberately. Whether they actually meant to hit you, or just scare you, is another question. All I'm saying is, watch your back."

Sosi's breath wouldn't come. He leant against the urn. "It was thrown at Th— at me *deliberately*? But why?"

Pericles gave him a peculiar look. "Why do you think?

You go round bragging about having dreams of victory, and you're surprised when someone starts using you for target practice? I've told you what I saw, and that's the end of it. I can't afford to get involved in any funny business. I've got to win the wrestling this year. It's my last chance in the boys' events. I'll be competing against the men next Olympiad. Unlike you runners, we wrestlers are at a disadvantage when we're up against an older opponent."

"I know," Sosi said ruefully, rubbing his bruised back.

Pericles, of course, missed the significance of this. The other boys were coming out of lunch. Pericles handed Sosi back his strigil and ignored him. Sosi moved off a few paces and finished scraping himself down, listening to the boys' conversation. But no one else mentioned the javelin that had hit Theron. Was Pericles just trying to scare him? A sudden thought chilled him. What if Pericles had arranged for the "accident" himself? After all, he was entered in the boys' sprint as well as the boys' wrestling, and he'd said he was desperate to win.

He shook his head. No, Pericles had helped him, and he found it hard to believe anyone would do such a thing to a fellow athlete, even one as big headed as Theron.

Turning his back on the smell of fresh bread and cheese coming from the gymnasium, Sosi hung up his strigil and headed for the gate. He had to talk to his brother as soon as possible.

Chapter 2

WARNING

THERE WAS NO answer when Sosi knocked on the door of
Lady Alcmena's room. When he tried the latch, the door
did not open, though he thought he heard a muffled
scrape on the other side.

"Theron?" he whispered. "It's me."

The Women's House was the perfect place for his
brother to hide, because no self-respecting young athlete
would be caught dead visiting his mother during training
camp. It was bad enough that their mothers and sisters
were allowed to watch them train. They were prone to
shrieking at just the wrong moment and rushing to the
gate whenever it looked as if their offspring might get
hurt. Most of the boys couldn't wait until they made the
journey to Olympia, where married women were
forbidden to set foot on pain of death, but right now Sosi
wished their mother would show more concern. Where

had she been while he'd been getting his head shoved in the sand?

"Theron, open up! We have to talk."

Silence. Sosi wondered if his brother could be too ill to come to the door. His heart beat faster as he thought of the javelin thrower coming back to finish the job while his brother was helpless to escape. He took a run at the door, felt something give, and squeezed through the gap.

"What's going *on*, Theron?"

The room was empty. The bed had been used to block the door, its rumpled sheet spotted with blood. Sosi stared at it, suddenly not hungry any more. He didn't bleed when he changed his skin. What had happened?

He rushed to the window, surprised by the anguish that came over him at the thought of his brother in trouble. All seemed normal. The white houses of Elis clustered sleepily around the agora, where a few horses and chariots were still exercising. A breeze stirred the leaves of the plane trees that shaded the streets. He gripped the sill, leant out as far as he could and hissed, "Theron?"

The chest creaked behind him and his brother climbed out, scowling. "What are you doing back here so soon? Aren't you supposed to be in the gymnasium?" His gaze dropped to Sosi's foot. "The judges passed you fit, didn't they?"

Sosi didn't know whether to be furious with his brother for scaring him so badly, or to laugh.

"Judge Lysanias gave me and Pericles the rest of the

day off. What are you doing hiding in Mother's clothing chest? It won't do your foot much good."

Theron hobbled to the bed and collapsed on it with a groan. "No bars on the doors in this place, are there?" he muttered. "When I heard you knocking, I was sure it was someone come to see Mother. The other women just barge in, any time they feel like it. She said I'd better hide if anyone came – but you're right, that chest's far too small." He massaged his leg and winced.

Sosi's questions fled. "Gods, Theron! Your leg's fatter than a temple column! Something must be wrong. You ought to see the physician again."

Theron grimaced. "Think I don't know? Mother's gone to see if she can find some herbs. There's supposed to be a woman in Elis who knows about such things."

"A herb witch? You need proper treatment! I'll ask the camp physician to come—"

"Don't be such an idiot." Though he was obviously in pain, Theron heaved himself off the bed and gripped Sosi's shoulders. "I can't see the camp physician now, can I? If he passed you fit this morning, he already thinks I've recovered."

Sosi saw the sense in this. "Someone else, then. There must be another physician in Elis."

"Probably. But they all belong to the Brotherhood of Asclepius, don't they? They share medical information. That's how they know so much about diseases and things. If I go to see one of them about my leg, I might as well forget about running in the Olympics."

Sosi almost said his brother should forget about running in the Olympics, anyway, with his leg looking like that, but held his tongue. Theron looked upset enough, and if their mother was getting him some herbs, then it was probably all right. They had more important things to discuss.

"I wrestled with Pericles this morning," he said.

Theron scowled. "That over-muscled show-off!"

"He's not so bad. He said..." Sosi glanced at the door and lowered his voice. "He said that javelin was thrown at you deliberately, because you bragged about your dream of victory. Is that true?"

"Ha!" Theron said. "He would!" But he went a bit pale.

"Did you see where it came from? Pericles said the javelin came out of the trees."

Theron frowned. "He was probably trying to distract you, that's all. Forget it, Sosi. Go back and train. And don't you dare mention my leg to the physician or any of the judges, do you hear?"

"But—"

"Don't you *dare*, Sosi. These Olympics mean everything to me. Everything! If you let me down now, I'll tell the judges about your curse. No doubt they'll be most curious to know how I've suddenly produced a twin brother they knew nothing about."

Sosi froze. "You wouldn't," he whispered. "If you do, they won't let you go to Olympia."

"If I tell them about your curse, they won't let you go anywhere *near* Olympia. That's why you agreed to change your shape for me when I got injured, isn't it? Don't think for a moment I believe all that stuff about brotherly love and loyalty. I know you too well, little brother! You want to go to Olympia as much as I do. Your big chance to find out more about your curse, isn't it? Not that it'll do you any good. I reckon Father made the whole thing up to scare us, anyway, because he wants me to give up athletics and join the army."

Sosi bit his lip. His brother's words had struck close to the truth. According to their father, Sosi was cursed because twelve years ago their mother had broken the rule forbidding married women to visit Olympia during the Games, and the gods had punished her by causing her unborn son to shed his skin like a snake every full moon.

"I could just as easily have gone to Olympia without changing my shape," he said. "I did it to help *you*, so you could be a bit more grateful. You're not very popular in the boys' gymnasium, you know. Why did you have to tell everyone you had a stupid dream?"

"Because it's true! I saw Goddess Nike riding on an eagle, and she told me I'm going to win the boys' sprint."

Sosi wanted to tell him that dreams meant nothing, but every full moon he dreamt of snakes. His dreams had become more vivid since they'd arrived at Elis. Why shouldn't his brother dream of Nike, the Goddess of Victory? Probably all athletes did before their events – only most people had more sense than to brag about it.

"That was before you got injured, though, wasn't it?"

he said. "I think Pericles is right. Someone could have thrown that javelin at you to stop you competing."

It was pointless. Theron's face had closed, and his eyes stared inwards at some dark place where his poisoned leg and his dreams of Olympic victory were tangled hopelessly together.

Sosi took a deep breath, knowing he was taking advantage of his brother's pain but needing to know. "Did you notice anyone suspicious hanging around before it happened? This morning I saw someone in a cloak with the hood pulled up, standing in the shadows under the trees. I'm almost sure it was a girl, even though it was too early for the women to be about. She watched Pericles and me wrestle, and then she vanished."

Unexpectedly, Theron laughed. "Oh, that'd be Eretaia! She's Pericles' sister, quite a looker, too, with all that golden hair. She's always around when her precious brother's training. They're inseparable."

Sosi frowned. "But I'm sure the girl I saw had black hair."

Theron shrugged. "Someone else, then. Leave the girls alone, little brother. You might fool old Trainer Hermon and the other athletes into thinking you're me, but you won't fool a girl for very long!"

A chill crept over Sosi. "What if whoever threw that javelin at you tries again when they see me back in training and think that I'm you?"

Theron sighed. "I told you. Pericles was trying to distract you. Why would anyone go to so much trouble to take me out of the boys' sprint? It's not as if I'm running in the men's event and there's an Olympiad at stake, is it? It was a stupid accident. It happens." He managed a bitter smile. "If you've really got some time off, I suppose I'd better brief you on who's who in the camp. Relax, little brother! No one's going to throw anything at you. You're hardly going to look much of a threat in the practice stadium."

The encounter left Sosi feeling bad, but not because of his brother's taunt. Theron was right. Even with a copy of his brother's athletic body, Sosi hadn't been able to throw Pericles. So why should he be able to run as fast as Theron could? Part of winning was in the head, and Sosi's head was too full of his stupid curse.

He walked slowly back to the camp, struggling with his fears. A real brother would have helped Theron because he wanted to see him win the sprint and achieve his dream of becoming a professional athlete. He wouldn't have seized the opportunity to prove he could control the monthly shape-change, or because he desperately wanted to know the truth about his curse and was afraid their mother would take them straight home if Theron got disqualified through injury. He certainly wouldn't give up because he was scared someone might throw a javelin at him.

It was nearly supper time, but Sosi didn't feel ready to face the other boys yet. He walked on past the camp and the spectators' bank – no sign of the mysterious cloaked girl – and up into the wood. He might as well have a look to see if there was any evidence to support Pericles' story.

When he drew level with the stadium where Theron had been injured, a flicker of unease made him stop. Unlike the Sacred Stadium where the heats took place, the practice course was not bordered by a spectators' bank, and the trees reached right over the wall in places. Like all the other stadia Sosi had seen, it had been surfaced with a mixture of sand and ash. Two grooves scratched across its width served as start and finish lines, and a wooden post at the centre of each line marked the turn for the longer races. Four of the boys who had watched his wrestling bout this morning were out on the track raking the surface, stirring up clouds of dust in the last rays of the sun.

They didn't see him, being too engrossed in their work, which seemed to be an excuse for exchanging jokes interrupted by deliberately throwing rakefuls of sand. The strip where the men practised for the pentathlon was deserted. Sosi considered the distance and the angles. Pericles was right. A javelin cast at the targets from the throwing circle, even if it went wide, would have to turn a corner in order to hit someone running in the practice stadium. Whereas from the wood, if you were careful not to hit the trees, it was a straight throw over the wall... though surely too far, even for an Olympic athlete?

Sosi dropped to his belly and used the extra senses that were a part of his curse – the heat-sense that could detect a warm body in the dark, and the special part of his tongue that could taste things in the air – to search the undergrowth for clues. He didn't really expect to find anything. The rain since Theron's "accident" would have washed away any lingering smells or tastes. Then he saw a knotted cord snagged on a twig, camouflaged in the shadows.

At the same time, he heard a horse trotting slowly along the track behind him. He hesitated, torn between his curiosity to see the cord and the need to stay still. But it was already too late. The horse snorted as it caught his scent, broke into a gallop and burst from the trees, riderless, to the accompaniment of jeers and laughs from the stadium.

Abandoning further attempt at stealth, Sosi backed out of the bushes to see what he'd found. When unravelled, the cord was about the length of his arm, made of coloured threads plaited together for strength. He touched it with his tongue and grimaced at the bitter taste.

"It's been used as a throwing-loop," an accented voice said softly. "I've been looking for it all afternoon. How did you find it so quickly?"

His heart almost jumped out of his chest. Behind him, motionless as a tree spirit in the shadows, stood the young jockey who had shouted at him that morning. The Persian had green marks on his tunic, and his black eyes were wary.

As Sosi stared back, equally wary, the boys who had been raking the stadium ran into the clearing. Still laughing, they pointed to the Persian's tunic. "Told you they can't ride!" said a tall, skinny one who seemed to be the ringleader. "That's why they race about in chariots all the time."

The Persian boy glowered.

"What's the matter, slave? Lost your tongue?"

There was less laughter this time, because some people really had been known to cut out their slaves' tongues.

"Ah, forget it, he's probably too scared to talk to us. Better run after your horse quick, Persian, before your master finds out you fell off and whips you!"

"STOP IT!" Sosi shouted.

"Since when are you friends with the Persians, Macedonian?" The skinny boy raised an eyebrow at him. "Your King Alexander won't be very pleased when he hears. Or is that why you got yourself injured? Because you're too much of a Persian-lover to go to war?"

There was a tense silence while everyone looked at Sosi, as if expecting him to do something stupid, like try to wrestle all four of them at once, as Theron might have done. The Persian watched from the shadows.

"Oh, shut it, Agis," muttered a big, dark-haired boy. "You heard what Pericles said. Not Theron's fault he got speared by that javelin, was it? Besides, he's too young to join the army."

"Too scared someone will throw a real javelin at him, more like," Agis mumbled, but shut up when the others frowned at him.

"Is your foot really better now?" the youngest boy asked, after a pause. Sosi nodded, desperately trying to put names to faces. The young one who'd asked after his foot must be the Corinthian boy, Dion – Theron said he'd won the sprint at the Isthmian Games his first time out, when he'd only been eleven and a half, although he'd managed to fool the judges into thinking he was twelve. The skinny one, Agis, was obviously the Athenian boy Theron had told him to watch out for because he was sly. But he couldn't place the other two.

"I'm Samos of Elis," said the dark-haired boy, rescuing him. "I don't think we've been introduced. I've been sleeping at home since it's so close, but after your accident the judges ordered me to move into the camp because of security. I'm best at the boxing, really, though I've entered the sprint as well for a bit of fun. Kallias and Agis told me what happened to your foot – of course it's better, squirt!" He tried to ruffle Dion's curls, but the youngest boy ducked away with a skill that spoke of long practice. "The judges wouldn't have let him continue training otherwise, would they?"

"I'm Rasim," the Persian said.

Samos looked at the slave. "You still here? Shouldn't you go and catch your horse?"

"He'll be fine." Rasim said. "I've trained him to come to my whistle. Can I see that?" He was still looking at the cord in Sosi's hands.

Sosi handed it over reluctantly. But the Persian didn't run off with it, as he'd feared. He turned it over in his slender fingers and pulled the threads apart, frowning a little. "Could be... they use Ahriman's fire on the ends to seal the enchantment, see? And in here somewhere, they've probably put a—"

"What are you talking about?" Agis said, scowling. "Give that back! Theron found it." He snatched the cord from Rasim and dropped it with a yelp. "It burned me!" he said, sucking his fingers.

Rasim retrieved the cord and pulled out what looked like a human hair, before passing it back to Sosi. "I was afraid of this," he said, matching the hair against Sosi's sun-bleached curls. "I tried to warn you this morning when you spooked my horse. You should be more careful. All of you, but especially Theron and anyone else from Macedonia. The... men... who made this cord are very angry with your King Iskander for burning Persepolis the Beautiful."

"What are you going on about, Persian? Who's angry?" Agis raised his rake, forcing the boy back against a tree. "What's all this rubbish about magic? Do you know something about the javelin that hit Theron? Because if you do..."

"Let him go," Samos said. "You were the one who snatched the cord before he'd finished with it."

Agis' knuckles tightened on the rake. But he lowered it in favour of examining his "burnt" hand. Rasim rubbed his throat and glared at him. "Just like a Greek! I'm taking a big risk talking to you, and you thank me by attacking me! If you won't listen, that's *your* problem. I have to go and see to my colt now." He edged away.

"Wait!" Sosi said, recognizing the name Persepolis

from the letters their father sent home from Persia. "You mean King Alexander, don't you? I'm sorry he burnt your city." He held the throwing-loop gingerly. "You said you were looking for this. Why?"

Rasim hesitated. "Because after what happened to you, I suspected they might be here. And because…" He glanced over his shoulder and shuddered. "…I don't want to become one of them."

"You don't want to become one of *who*?" Agis demanded. "Speak sense, Persian, or we'll get Samos to box it out of you!" Kallias nodded and folded his arms, though the big Elean shook his head with a sigh.

Rasim looked as if he wasn't going to answer. But he glanced at Sosi's foot, looked over his shoulder again and whispered, "The Warriors of Ahriman. They follow the prophet Zarathustra like many of my countrymen, but they interpret his teachings in their own way. Ahriman's the evil one in our religion, so their ways are evil, too. When they die, their souls go to the House of the Lie where there is no hope, and they are condemned to serve Ahriman for ever. That's all I can tell you. But if I were you, I'd take that cord to your judges and tell them where you found it." He was backing away as he spoke. Before anyone thought to stop him, he gave a shrill whistle and dodged out of the trees.

"After him!" Agis said, giving chase. He kept hold of his rake, though it obviously slowed him down. Kallias followed.

"Idiots," Samos muttered. "They won't catch him once

he gets on his horse." He eyed Sosi. "I wouldn't take too much notice of what he said, if I were you. I expect he was just trying to scare us into leaving him alone."

"I *am* scared," Dion whispered.

"There's no need to be, squirt," Samos said. "If someone really is attacking the athletes, the judges will soon deal with them."

Sosi hoped Rasim would get away. The Persian's words had chilled him, but Rasim had seemed to be on their side. He touched the burnt ends of the cord. Had that really been one of Theron's hairs twisted into it? If the javelin had been hurled by magic, it would explain the impossible throw.

"Warriors of Ahriman," he repeated. "Who are they?"

Samos shrugged. "Some crazy Persian tribe, I expect. They're all crazy over there. That's why they make such good jockeys and charioteers – don't care about staying alive to race another day, do they? No wonder your King Alexander is conquering them like flies! Come on, Macedonian. If we're going to see the judges, we'll miss supper at this rate."

At the mention of food, Sosi remembered he'd missed breakfast and lunch, too. His stomach rumbled embarrassingly. Samos slapped him on the shoulder. "On second thoughts, put that thing in your pocket and we'll have supper first," he said. "Reckon you need it. I saw that marathon wrestling bout you and Pericles had this morning. It takes guts to let yourself be thrown so many times without fighting back, but it was the right thing to do. Slave-driver Hermon would only have kept you at it till you were both half-dead, otherwise. I'll be glad when we get to Olympia and can have a rest!"

Chapter 3

WARRIOR

WHEN SOSI AND Samos delivered the cord to the Judges' House, Judge Lysanias listened gravely to their account of where they'd found it and sent them back to the camp with orders not to spread the story around. He told them not to worry because everything was under control. Agis was the only one who ignored this advice. He went around telling anyone who would listen that a Persian terrorist had tried to cripple him with sorcery to stop him from winning, and only shut up when Judge Demetrius suggested he should drop out of training if his hand was giving him that much trouble. Since there was no physical sign of a burn, the other boys decided Agis had been imagining things.

Theron seemed a bit worried when he heard about the Warriors of Ahriman, but laughed at Sosi's story of the enchanted cord with his hair braided into it, which he claimed was typical Persian claptrap. Lady Alcmena warned Sosi to stay well away from the horse camp and let the judges deal with it, and Theron told him not to panic because he'd be well enough to take over soon. Sosi doubted this – his brother's leg didn't look any better to him. But getting into town to see Theron was made harder by the armed guards the judges had posted around the camp for their protection, following the discovery of the throwing-loop. So he had to be content with news of Theron's progress from their mother when she came to the spectators' bank to watch him train.

Sosi discovered a strange thing about fear. When you lived with it constantly, it dulled around the edges, and physical activity was a shield that could keep it out. He plunged into his training with such energy that not even Trainer Hermon could fault him, and his days settled into an uneasy routine. The young athletes were woken by a trumpet blast at dawn to begin their morning exercises, snatched a quick breakfast of bread and fish before training in the boys' yard under the supervision of Trainer Hermon, stuffed down a lunch of goat's cheese and fruit, and spent the afternoons working on their starts and running in the practice stadium. Then they had to rake the stadium and tidy up the yard before being allowed to use the baths, after which they fell asleep over supper and staggered to bed in the gymnasium dormitory.

Several times, Sosi thought he spotted the cloaked girl with the yellow eyes standing in the shadow of the trees, and experienced the same prickling sensation as the first time he'd seen her – a stirring of darkness that belonged to his dreams. He was convinced she was watching him, but when he plucked up courage to ask Pericles if he knew who she was, the blond boy laughed. "Oh, that's Nike! She's some minor priestess my sister got friendly with last time we were here. Because she's named after the Goddess of Victory, she likes to play this silly game where she tries to pick the winners of the Olympic events. She's always hanging around the training camp, eyeing up the athletes. Thinks she's something special because she has the job of tying on the winners' ribbons – as if anyone would look twice at an ugly great lump like her! Ignore her, Theron. We've got quite enough to worry about, as it is."

Nike wasn't watching him in particular. The relief was like a weight being lifted from his shoulders. The other boys, seeing the way Pericles and Samos had accepted Sosi, gave up taunting him about his Macedonian heritage and turned their energy to discussing why the Persians might be trying to sabotage the Games. The fear did not go away, but each day that passed with nothing more than the usual sports injuries of sprained ankles and bruises, Sosi breathed a little easier.

He began to think Rasim had been lying about the Warriors and Pericles must have been wrong about the javelin being thrown at Theron deliberately. Then one morning his mother didn't turn up at the spectators' bank, cutting off his source of news. And, four days later, Pericles' sister was attacked on her way across the agora.

That night, Sosi had another nightmare. He saw his mother lying senseless in some dark place, and his brother alone in the Women's House, tossing feverishly while a Persian terrorist, holding a cord threaded with a sun-bleached hair, crept closer...

He awoke bathed in sweat. In the shadows of the gymnasium, the other boys' bodies glowed orange to his heat-sense – all except Pericles'. His pallet was piled up with blankets as if someone slept there, but there was no sign of life. Still sweating from his dream, Sosi forced himself to feel under the covers. When he discovered a pile of rolled-up clothes, he almost laughed. He could guess where Pericles had gone. For their own safety, they were now forbidden to leave the gymnasium complex during the day without a guard, and Pericles must be as frantic about his sister as Sosi was about his mother and brother.

Quietly, he tied on his sandals and picked his way through the snoring bodies to the door. It creaked when he opened it, making him wince. But the boys were so exhausted after their day's training that no one woke. The moon was in its last quarter and covered by cloud, making the yard almost as dark as the dormitory. The guards were wary after the attack on Eretaia, but they were looking for people trying to get in, not out. Sosi waited until they were looking the other way and vaulted out of the yard. He worked his way around the back of the gymnasia and sprinted across the practice stadium. Safely in the shadow of the trees, he climbed over the wall.

The wood was easy enough to slip though unseen. But when he reached the field that separated the training complex from the town, the moon came out from behind the clouds, illuminating the white houses of Elis. The guards patrolling the bank would see him if he went that way. It would be safer to cut across the field to the Sacred Way, which would take him to the agora from the south.

The barley had been recently harvested, and the stalks poked through Sosi's tunic as he wriggled through them. Halfway across, he felt a vibration in the ground and heard the sound of hoof beats and rumbling wheels – some idiot driving a chariot. He swore under his breath and lay still, hoping the horses wouldn't smell him. Then he realized the chariot was not on the road but in the field, heading his way at a reckless pace. His heart thudded uneasily. By now, the men guarding the camp had seen the chariot, too. They shouted at the driver to stop and ran across the field to cut it off.

Sosi hesitated. Even after what had happened to his brother, he didn't realize the danger until he saw the driver, swathed in black robes so that only his eyes showed, crouched over the front of the chariot, whipping his horses towards the spot where he lay.

"*Run*, you idiot!" someone shouted.

He jerked round to see Pericles stumbling across the field from the direction of the Women's House. There was no time to wonder which of them was the intended target. Sosi took one look at the charioteer's eyes, glittering with triumph, then he was on his feet and running for his life.

Stalks snapped behind him as the chariot came after him. He felt real fear. Even Theron couldn't outrun a galloping horse. He trod on a sharp stone and his stride faltered. He heard the driver's whip crack... felt the horses' hot breath on the back of his neck... and heard the driver curse as they scented the snake in Sosi and shied. The chariot swerved around him, taking the turn on one wheel. Pericles gave a yell of fear. When Sosi next looked, it was heading straight for the blond boy.

There wasn't time to be scared. "Hey!" he shouted, picking up stones and running after the chariot. He aimed at the horses, and one of them jumped sideways as he scored a hit on its quarters. The driver managed to drag his team round in a circle, but unfortunately Pericles had dodged the same way and ended up in the chariot's path again. Sosi darted in front of it and waved his arms, trusting his curse to protect him. The horses shied again – this time in opposite directions, pulling the traces apart. There was a crunch as a wheel hit a boulder and disintegrated. Sosi threw himself against Pericles, carrying the bigger boy to the ground. The chariot leapt into the air as its shaft snapped. The offside horse plunged away across the field, trailing its harness. The other went down in a tangle of legs and broken wood, rolling its eyes at Sosi and kicking frantically. The driver was thrown clear, hit the ground hard and lay still.

"Zeus' thunderbolts!" Pericles gasped, white-faced. "I thought we were dead! Quick, help me with the horse." He dodged the flying hooves and pulled at the harness that trapped the injured animal. Sosi backed away.

The guards arrived, breathless. Two of them bent over the prone charioteer, while a third released the horse with a slice of his sword. The horse struggled to its feet and hopped to the extent of its reins, one foreleg dangling, obviously broken. The guards shook their heads, and the one with the sword cut the unfortunate animal's throat. It all happened so fast, Sosi barely had time to think.

He was still trying to decide which of them the charioteer had been trying to run over, when Pericles muttered, "Here comes Judge Demetrius. That's all we need."

The judge's sandals were unlaced. He wore his night tunic and carried a clay lantern. He took in the wreckage of the chariot and the unconscious driver, and listened to their explanations in silence. When the guards unwrapped the charioteer's scarf to reveal dark skin and a beard curled into ringlets in the Persian fashion and dyed crimson, he frowned and gave orders that the man should be taken to the Judges' House for questioning.

"Sir..." Sosi said, shivering. "Was that a Warrior of Ahriman?"

Judge Demetrius rounded on him. "Where did you hear that name?"

"We're not stupid, sir," Pericles said, which made the judge's expression darken. "Someone's trying to injure us, aren't they? A javelin was thrown at Theron, and Agis claimed he got burnt by that cord Theron found in the wood. We all thought he was making it up, but what if he wasn't? Then there's what happened to my sister, and now this chariot. Who's going to be next? Is someone trying to stop the Games, sir?"

Judge Demetrius glared at Pericles as if he'd suggested Zeus was not a real god. "Nothing and no one stops the Olympic Games," he said, slowly and clearly, as if explaining something to a small child. "That's why we have an Olympic Truce, and anyone who breaks it will be severely punished. You boys get back to the gymnasium before half of Elis wakes up and comes to see what all the fuss is about – and I don't want to hear another word about stopping the Games!" He sent one of the remaining guards with them, while he stayed to examine the broken chariot.

Sosi was glad to get away from the dead horse. *My fault*, he couldn't help thinking. *If it hadn't been for my curse, that horse would still be alive.*

And we might both be dead.

He shuddered, and Pericles gave him a sympathetic look. "All right?" he whispered, eyeing the guard, who walked a discreet distance in front of them.

"Not really," Sosi said, still shivering although the danger was past.

"I know." Pericles squeezed his shoulder. "Could be one of us lying there instead of that horse, huh? That Persian must have been crazy to drive his team across the field in the dark at that speed. Do you think he really was trying to run us down? I know it was a risk, but I had to see Eretaia. What are you doing out here?"

"I was worried about Th—" Sosi almost gave himself away. "I wanted to check on my mother," he mumbled. "She hasn't come to watch me train lately, and after the attack on your sister, I was worried something might have happened to her." He eyed the blond boy, hardly daring to ask. "Is... is your sister all right?"

Pericles nodded. "She's had a bad scare, poor thing, but she wasn't hurt. Luckily, Eretaia can run – almost as fast as you, Theron! She won the girls' race at the Games of Hera last time they were held. Her attacker can't have known that, because she managed to get away from him. But I don't know if she'll be coming to the spectators' bank any more to watch me train. Mother's worried. All the women are, and Eretaia's pretty shaken up. We've always discussed the Games, and now these stupid Warriors are keeping us apart!" He kicked a stone, making the guard look round. "Sorry, but it makes me so angry that someone should pick on a defenceless girl like that. My own sister!"

Sosi tried to make sense of it. Theron's injury, the throwing-loop he'd found in the wood, Rasim's warning about the Warriors of Ahriman, the runaway chariot... all these would make sense if someone were targeting athletes. But girls were not allowed to compete at the men's Games, so why had Eretaia been attacked?

He looked back at the Women's House, more

desperate than ever to talk to his mother and brother. But it didn't look as if he would get a chance tonight.

To punish them for their night escapade, Trainer Hermon matched Sosi and Pericles in the sandpit the next morning and told them not to bother coming in for lunch until they had completed twenty throws. "I'll leave it up to you to decide who gets thrown," he said, and went to supervise those boys training with the punchbags. By unspoken agreement, they took turns to fall, but their hearts weren't in it. They were both relieved when a messenger strode into the yard and summoned them to the Judges' House.

Wearing their ceremonial robes and hats, the ten Hellenic judges sat on benches arranged around three sides of a square in the hall where Sosi had been examined by the physician. Judge Demetrius had a chair to himself on the fourth side. In the centre, Elean soldiers guarded the charioteer they'd caught last night. The prisoner's black robes had been removed, his arms were bound behind him, and a rope around his neck tethered him to one of the columns. He knelt between the guards with his gaze fixed on the floor and his lips set in a stubborn line. Sosi saw blood encrusted in his crimson beard and felt a bit sick. He wondered if it was from his fall last night, or if his guards had beaten him.

As they entered the hall, the prisoner raised his head and fixed his glittering eyes on Sosi. "You won't win, Macedonian," he hissed. "Victory will be mine!" Straining against his tether until he choked, he spat as far as he could across the marble floor.

A ripple of unease went down Sosi's back. The guards dragged their prisoner back. Holding him firmly, they loosened the noose so he could breathe.

Pericles didn't notice Sosi's reaction. He was looking across the hall, where a tall, good-looking blonde girl stood in the shadows beside another soldier. "Eretaia's here!" he whispered. "Why did they have to involve her?"

The guards finally subdued the crimson-bearded man. He continued to glare at Sosi, but was thankfully quiet.

Judge Demetrius beat his staff on the floor for order. "So... it seems our barbarian friend can speak some Greek, after all. I ask you again!" he snapped at the prisoner. "What were you doing driving your horses through the barley field last night? Is this throwing-loop yours?" He dangled the cord Sosi had found before the prisoner's eyes.

One of the guards prodded the crimson-bearded man with his spear, but he refused to answer.

Judge Demetrius sighed and returned the cord to a pocket in his robes. "Very well, have it your own way. You will be flogged for breaking the Sacred Truce, and then you will be held in Elis until the Games are over and we can find someone who speaks your barbarian tongue.

We've more than enough evidence for now. You clearly recognize the boys you almost ran over last night, and the girl, Eretaia, has identified you as her attacker. Take him away."

As the guards hauled the prisoner to his feet, the blonde girl cleared her throat. "I told you I only remembered the beard, sir," she corrected. "The crimson colour... I can't be sure it's the same man."

Pericles frowned at his sister.

Judge Demetrius frowned at her, too. "How many men are there in the civilized world who dye their beards crimson, for Zeus' sake?" he said. "Of course it's the same man! You had a bad fright. I bet you didn't get a good look at him. Even if you did, it's understandable you wouldn't remember him clearly. You've had your chance to speak. The barbarian has been found guilty. We've other business to address."

Sosi's gaze was drawn back to the prisoner, whose eyes remained fixed on him with chilling hatred as the guards untethered him and dragged him out of the hall. The man might be refusing to answer questions, but it was obvious from his expression that he understood everything that was being said.

When he'd gone, the atmosphere relaxed slightly, and Judge Demetrius turned his attention to Sosi and Pericles. "Perhaps our sleepless young athletes would like to tell the court what possessed them to leave the camp last night? Well, come over here, then! We can't hear you from the door."

Judge Lysanias beckoned them into the square formed by the benches. They exchanged a glance, wondering how to begin.

"I just..." Pericles said.

"I wanted to..." Sosi said.

"One at a time, please," Judge Demetrius snapped. "You start." He pointed his staff at Pericles.

Pericles told the truth. When everyone turned to look at Eretaia, she blushed. But Sosi saw her smile in the shadows. He didn't listen very closely to Pericles' explanation of why he and his sister needed to discuss their training. He was too worried about getting his own story straight. If he claimed he was anxious about his mother, as he'd told Pericles last night, the judges might check her room and find Theron. But what else would they believe?

"Well?" Judge Demetrius snapped. "What's your excuse, young Macedonian? You haven't got a sister, so maybe it was a sweetheart? Or a midnight training run? Don't get enough practice under Trainer Hermon, is that it? I'll obviously have to ask him to work you boys harder."

No one laughed. After hearing about the chariot last night and seeing the prisoner's defiance, the judges were too worried. Pericles pressed his lips together. Eretaia looked at the floor.

"Speak freely, Theron," Judge Lysanias said gently. "We won't disqualify you for speaking the truth."

"My little brother!" Sosi blurted out. "He, er, wasn't

very well before we left Macedonia, and I wanted to know if Mother had found a cure..." At the side of the hall, Eretaia made an urgent noise in her throat. Sosi frowned at the girl. She had the same colour eyes as Pericles, he noticed, blue like the summer sky. The story he'd been going to make up about his "little brother" fled, and he couldn't think of anything to say. He closed his mouth.

Judge Lysanias leant across to whisper something to Judge Demetrius, who grunted. "Your father's fighting the Persian wars with King Alexander, isn't he?" he asked.

"Yes, sir," Sosi said, relieved that the subject had changed.

"I understand he's quite a high rank in the Macedonian army?"

Sosi nodded, unable to stop the pride creeping into his voice. "Commander, sir... Commander Sarapion." Pericles gave him a sharp look. It seemed Theron hadn't bothered to explain about their father.

Judge Demetrius nodded. "That might explain why these Persian scum are picking on you in particular. But since Eretaia has been attacked, too, and we can't seem to keep any of you boys inside the camp where you can be properly protected, I think to be on the safe side we'd better move the lot of you to Olympia early. Trainer Hermon tells me you're so busy watching for terrorists, it's affecting your training. Maybe being at Olympia will help concentrate your minds."

Whispers of surprise rippled around the benches as the other judges discussed this. Pericles and Eretaia exchanged an excited smile. Sosi's heart thudded. Going to Olympia early... they hadn't counted on that.

"Any objections?" Judge Demetrius demanded.

"The rest of the boys' training..."

"They can complete their training at Olympia easily enough. In fact, it'll free up the facilities here for the men and save us some timetabling headaches. There aren't that many boys entered this year. They shouldn't make too much of a mess of the Olympic Stadium before we get there."

"What about the procession and the ritual at the Fountain of Piera?"

"The boys will just have to do it early. One of us can go with them to see it's done correctly, and it'll be a good idea to send some guards to watch the fountain, anyway, after what's been happening in Elis. The rest of us can process to Olympia with the men and horses as usual, two days before the Games begin."

There was a short silence while the judges digested this.

"It makes sense," one of the younger judges said. "We can protect the boys a lot more easily at Olympia itself, and we ought to increase security there as soon as possible. The spectators will be arriving in their thousands soon."

"Enough of them are already there, by all accounts," grumbled another judge. "They come earlier every time."

"But the break with tradition! Won't someone question it? The last thing we want to do is alarm people.

And what about the journey? If someone's trying to get at the boys, then a smaller party will be vulnerable. They'd be safer making the journey with the men."

"They'll be well guarded," Judge Demetrius said. "And a small party can move faster. I suggest we commandeer some of the training chariots from the horse camp to transport them, so no one has to go on foot. We can always tell the owners of the horses that it counts towards their training. As for tradition, we're only talking about the boys' events. It'd be different if we were proposing to transfer the men to Olympia early."

"And are we quite sure no one's threatening the men?"

There was a longer silence.

"No one seems to be," said the old judge who had watched Sosi's physical examination, with a worried little cough. "Of course, once the boys are gone — "

"No one will be threatening anyone now we've caught the Persian terrorist!" Judge Demetrius said firmly. "I'm going to have him properly interrogated as soon as I can find someone qualified to do it."

Judge Lysanias stood and smoothed his robe. "I think it's an excellent idea!" he announced. "I always said it wasn't fair to expect the boys to undertake a two day march, endure the opening ceremonies when they're understandably overtired and overexcited, and then be expected to perform at their best before thousands of people that same afternoon. I vote 'yes'."

Pericles exchanged a smile with Sosi.

"We're not doing this for the boys' comfort," Judge

Demetrius snapped. "These two have been very foolish and put themselves and several others at risk. They should be punished, not rewarded. We're doing it because we want our visitors to feel safe during the Olympic Truce and to protect the integrity of our Games. Remember that. Any more objections to moving the boys to Olympia as soon as possible?"

There were one or two further grumbles from the older judges, but no one spoke out against the idea. One by one, the solemn men in their purple robes rose to their feet to join Judge Lysanias.

Judge Demetrius nodded gravely and struck his staff on the floor. "Then it's decided. I'll make the official announcement this afternoon, and the boys will set out for Olympia first thing tomorrow morning. In the meantime, I suppose they'd better be allowed to say their goodbyes." He gave Sosi and Pericles another scowl. "No training this afternoon, so make the most of it, but no going off on your own again! I'll arrange an escort to take those who want to visit their mothers across to the Women's House. For now, you're to go back to the gymnasium where you can be protected. The girl can go with you and have lunch there. We don't want rumours flying around the town before we're ready."

Eretaia's smile widened, and she and Pericles exchanged another excited glance. Sosi's mouth dried. Olympia! By tomorrow night, he could be at Olympia – the place that, according to Father, was responsible for his curse.

Chapter 4

NIKE

BACK AT THE gymnasium, the room where lunch was laid out grew noisy as the boys speculated about the judges' decision. The six of them entered for the sprint had gathered together, a little apart from the other competitors. Eretaia perched on the edge of the table behind her brother, swinging her long legs. Her presence drew sideways glances from the older boys, but she ignored them in favour of watching Sosi. She seemed puzzled. He felt himself colouring and avoided her eye. He wished he had his younger body back.

"I think it's a crazy idea, sending us to Olympia so early!" Agis said. "Why aren't the men being threatened? If someone's really trying to stop the Games, that would make a lot more sense. The judges must have some other reason for moving us. They're probably using us as bait to draw the terrorists out of hiding."

Sosi eyed the chunk of bread he was holding. He had drizzled olive oil over it and sprinkled it with poppy seeds, which were a luxury he didn't often get at home, but he had no appetite. The athletes' food was donated by rich Eleans and carried across from the town by their slaves – did any of them have crimson beards? He peered around the room, his neck prickling. The slaves had gone.

"I don't see why you're so worried," Kallias was saying. "We'll get to use the Olympic Stadium for training! I think it's brilliant."

"You would!" Agis grunted. "Won't make you any faster, though."

"I'll beat you easily once I get my start sorted out," Kallias said. "You'll see."

The others sighed.

Pericles said, "Forget about who's going to beat who for a moment, can't you? Let's try to think why someone's attacking us, but not the men. What's so different about the boys' events?"

They glanced at one another.

"They're always held on the first afternoon," Samos said. "And the men's events don't start until the second day. Second afternoon, really, since the morning's for the horse races."

"They've not got so many people in them," Dion piped up.

"That's only for this year," Pericles said. "The others probably scratched because the competition is so good. There's me in the wrestling, Samos in the boxing, and

Theron in the sprint, so you can see their point... though I expect you'll give our Macedonian friend a good race, squirt that you are."

Dion puffed up with pride, but Agis scowled. Even Kallias, who cheerfully accepted he was slow off the mark, looked annoyed. "Nothing's certain," Agis grumbled. "Any of us might win on the day, or there would be no point having a race, would there?"

Before Sosi could say anything, Eretaia leant across and whispered, "You weren't really going to the Women's House last night to see your little brother, were you?"

Sosi blinked at her, distracted. He had been trying to follow the others' conversation. Pericles and Samos were arguing about the various boys' events, and whether the Warriors of Ahriman might have entered one of their sons and were trying to fix it so he won.

"Barbarians can't compete," Kallias reminded them.

"The Macedonians have been let in," Agis pointed out with another scowl at Sosi.

"*Agis!*" Samos snapped. "Leave it, all right? We're all in this together now."

"Maybe they're only picking on us runners," Pericles said thoughtfully. "Have any of the others been got at, do you know?"

"I don't think so," Samos said.

"All right, then what's so different about the boys' sprint?"

"The sprint's the only foot race we do?" Samos said. "The men do the double-sprint and the dolichos, too."

"It's more likely to be in the timing," Pericles said, frowning. "We run on the first afternoon, and the men don't race until the third afternoon after the big sacrifice to Zeus. It must be something to do with the first day of the Games. Perhaps these Warriors want to disrupt them right at the start, to make people go home?"

"And the boys' sprint is the first event of all, which is why they're picking on us!" Agis said. "Those Persian *snakes*! If they mess up my chances of winning this race..."

"Shut it, Agis," Samos said, glancing at the door. "Why *us*? What do we do that the men don't?"

There was a silence while they thought about this.

"Nothing," Kallias said. "The boys' sprint is just the same as the men's sprint, except we don't get so much glory for winning."

"The winner of the boys' sprint carries the Sacred Torch," Eretaia said in her soft voice.

Everyone looked round in surprise. It was clear the others had forgotten she was listening. Sosi's spine prickled as Eretaia jumped off the table and smoothed her hair.

"It's obvious," she said. "Priestess Nike has to receive the Sacred Fire from one of you before she can light the fire on the Great Altar for the sacrifice to Zeus. Without the sacrifice, the Games mean nothing. If your race doesn't take place, there will be no winner to carry the torch around the altars, and no blessing from the gods."

"That's stupid," Agis muttered.

Samos frowned. "Your sister might be right, Pericles," he said. "Without the Great Sacrifice to Zeus there may as well not be an Olympic Games."

"But they could get someone else to carry the torch, surely?" Kallias put in.

Eretaia shook her blonde hair. "It wouldn't be the same. The whole point is that the winner carrying the Sacred Torch makes Nike strong enough to open the channel to the gods. I think that's why it's so important she chooses the winner of the boys' sprint correctly. She was pretty worried when Theron got hurt."

"Oh, not that stupid game of Nike's again!" Agis said. "I can't believe we're listening to this! You heard that slave boy Rasim, or whatever his name is. He more or less told us it was revenge for the Macedonians invading Persia."

Samos held up his hands for peace. "You've got to admit, it does rather look as if the Warriors are picking on us sprinters in particular. Maybe we should tell the judges our theory?"

"No." Agis scowled. "Or they might not let us continue training, and none of us will win. Besides, we don't know if it's the sprint they're targeting – Pericles, Theron and I are all in the wrestling as well."

Another argument broke out as to whether the judges would really cancel an event if they told them their suspicions, and whether the honour of carrying the Sacred Torch was greater than the honour of having a whole Olympiad named after you.

Eretaia, who had dropped out of the conversation after her input, took a slice of cold ox and smiled at Sosi. "I'm glad your foot's better," she whispered, "because I'm looking forward to watching you race."

Sosi blinked, caught off guard. "I thought you had to stay behind in Elis?"

Eretaia giggled. "Only the married woman have to stay here, silly. I'm not married – yet." She blushed as she met Sosi's gaze. "Don't worry, I won't tell anyone about your mother."

"What about my mother?" Sosi said, his neck prickling again.

The puzzled look returned to Eretaia's eyes. "You were the one who told me, Theron, remember? It's all right, I can keep a secret."

Sosi's mouth opened and, although he struggled to control it, his breath came faster. When had she seen Theron? "What did I tell you?"

Eretaia gave him a strange look and lowered her voice. "That she took your little brother to Olympia, of course, to find a cure for his curse. That's why I interrupted you in the Judges' House. I was terrified you were going to put your foot in it and make them realize where she'd gone. I think she's very brave. When I have children, I hope I'll be selfless enough to put my life in danger for their sake."

Fortunately, a detachment of soldiers arrived then to take the boys over to the Women's House, and in all the rush and excitement, no one noticed Sosi's reaction. He mumbled some excuse about a call of nature and rushed out, leaving Eretaia staring after him in bewilderment. Knowing what she did about his mother, though, she must have assumed he had no reason to go with them, and the visiting party with their armed escort left without him.

When everyone had gone, Sosi crept back into the deserted gymnasium, shivering violently. Theron had told Eretaia about his curse! And their mother had gone to Olympia, where married women were forbidden to set foot during the Games on pain of death! The "little brother" bit was obviously a lie, since it was unlikely Lady Alcmena would risk Father's anger and the wrath of the gods for his sake. More likely, she had gone to find a cure for Theron, which meant his brother's foot must have taken a turn for the worse.

He glanced out of the window, saw the other boys disappearing up the road with their escort, and turned cold. Theron! He should have thought... The Women's House would be turned upside-down when the visiting party arrived. The guards were sure to search it for lurking Warriors before letting their charges inside to say goodbye to their families.

He ducked past the men's yard, where the older athletes were warming up for their afternoon session, and slipped out of the side gate. Trainer Hermon had taken the afternoon off and most of the guards had gone with the boys, so no one challenged him. The road from the ford was busy with horses at exercise. A string of colts cantered past, their proud necks curved as they strained against their bits. Their jockeys rode bareback, showing off as they tried to stand up and do tricks, laughing when the colts shied and the tricks went wrong. Sosi looked to see if Rasim was among them, but couldn't see him. He wondered if the horse camp knew about the judges' decision yet.

Not wanting to get tangled up with the horses, he retraced his route of the night before around the back of the camp through the wood. In his imagination, every tree hid a crimson-bearded Warrior. He broke into a run, leaping roots and ducking branches, certain he was being followed. When he finally did hear feet stumbling along the path towards him, they were coming from the opposite direction. He froze as a dark figure with its face concealed by a scarf lurched towards him. He'd been stupid to let Eretaia upset him. Why hadn't he gone with the others?

But the intruder veered off towards the camp, jumped awkwardly for the top of the wall and fell back with a curse. The scarf fell aside to reveal bedraggled, sun-bleached curls, and a jolt of recognition went down Sosi's spine. "Theron!" he cried. Abandoning caution, he raced to his brother's side. "What are you *doing*?"

His brother curled on the ground, clutching his injured foot. Sweat beaded his forehead, and his skin was yellow. His leg was still swollen, the bandage filthy and torn – he obviously hadn't managed to squeeze his injured foot into a sandal. The branch he'd been using as a crutch lay on the ground beside him, snapped in two. He must have tried to use it as a vaulting pole to get over the wall.

"Is it true?" he demanded, seizing Sosi's arm. "Are you going to Olympia tomorrow?"

"Yes, it's true. What are you doing out of bed? I can't believe you walked across the field with that leg!"

His brother lay back with a groan. "Ran, little brother... I ran when I saw the soldiers coming. Had to see you. Warn you about Mother..."

Worry, for his mother and brother both, made Sosi's tone sharp. "I already know about Mother! What have you been telling Pericles' sister? Have you lost your mind?"

His brother merely sighed, which showed how sick he was. "It was all I could think of. We were seeing each other in Elis before I got injured, and she found out I'd gone to the Women's House to recuperate. She'd only have got suspicious if I'd suddenly broken things off. I knew she'd probably see you training in my place so I made sure she didn't see my swollen leg, and I only let her see me at night, when she'd think I'd sneaked out of the gymnasium dormitory. She kept asking where you were, so I told her you'd gone with Mother to Olympia. She already knew you had a curse – don't ask me how. I didn't tell her any details. I'm not that stupid."

"You should have told me you were seeing her," said Sosi angrily. "You could have blown everything. Mother could have too! Why did she go to Olympia, anyway?"

"I know." Theron shook his head. "She wanted to see one of the priestesses about my foot. She was worried it might need more than herbs after all the rumours that have been going round about Persian magic, and apparently this old priestess she knows has studied such things. She thought she had plenty of time to get there and back before the athletes arrived, but if you're going early she'll be in danger. You've got to warn her, little brother! She got let off lightly twelve years ago, but if the judges find her there again, they'll throw her over the cliff for sure."

Sosi's heart thumped. "It's hardly a secret! If Eretaia knows, then Pericles will soon enough. You might as well have told the whole camp!"

"Eretaia won't tell." Theron closed his eyes.

"How can you be sure?"

"She won't. She knows Lady Alcmena will be in danger if she does—" His brother's eyes snapped open, and he stared past Sosi into the wood. "Someone's watching us!"

Sosi whirled around, remembering his early uneasiness, and his heart missed a beat. In the shadow of the trees, not ten paces away, stood the cloaked girl he'd spotted so many times on the spectators' bank, the priestess Pericles had told him was named after the Goddess of Victory. Her yellow eyes, luminous under her hood, studied him and Theron in silence. Sosi could not move as she pushed past him, knelt beside Theron and laid a hand over his face. Her nails had been bitten short and had dirt beneath them. Black tendrils of hair escaped her hood and curled past her cheeks. Her nose was big and curved like a beak. As she touched his brother's eyelids, there was a blurring of the air, and Theron sighed. His tense body relaxed, the expression of pain disappeared, and his breathing slowed.

The priestess straightened and dropped her hood, revealing freckles and a determined set to her mouth. "Clever!" she said. "I thought you were his twin at first, but that's not your true shape, is it?"

Her words freed Sosi's tongue. "Get away from my brother! If you've hurt him..."

Nike laughed. "What do you think I am? One of those Persian terrorists? Quick, help me with him. Don't want all Elis seeing you two together, do we?" She put her hands under Theron's shoulders and lifted them easily. "We'd better get him back inside the Women's House. You take his feet – careful, there's quite enough damage already."

Sosi found himself doing as she asked. It was pointless to flee now that the priestess had seen them together. Besides, he couldn't abandon Theron, and she was right – they had to get his brother back into hiding before anyone else saw them together. He picked up Theron's feet, wincing when he touched the sticky bandage.

"What did you do to Theron?" he demanded. "Why

won't he wake up? Are you going to report us to the judges?"

Nike laughed. "Report you? Don't be dense! As for your brother, he must be crazy trying to run across a field with that foot and then vault over a wall! I've put him to sleep so his leg at least has half a chance of healing. We can only pray he recovers in time to run the boys' sprint. I suppose your clever little trick of taking his place in training means he still has a chance of competing, though it won't be enough to save these Games – you do realize that, don't you?" She didn't seem to notice his confusion. "Never mind. At least you're still around to look after the other athletes. I was a bit worried when Eretaia told me you'd gone to Olympia with your mother, but now I see it was all part of the cover-up. I must say, you're good at hiding what you are! Even had *me* fooled for a while. Twins... ha!" She chuckled.

A suspicion dawned on Sosi. "Eretaia told you about my curse, didn't she?" He wondered how many more of her friends Pericles' sister had told.

Nike gave him a peculiar look. "I might be a bit distracted with these terrorists picking off all the best athletes, but I'm not that thick. I knew you'd be back eventually. It was just a matter of when."

If they hadn't been carrying his brother, Sosi would have shaken the girl's mocking smile from her face. She was the one walking backwards, somehow finding the path without looking over her shoulder. Her hood was back up again. He hadn't noticed her lift it.

"Why did you do it?" she asked. "Take your brother's shape, I mean. You didn't have to."

Sosi was still trying to make sense of what she'd said earlier. "I did it so he can stay in the Games and become a professional athlete," he mumbled.

"Really?" Her knowing look made him uncomfortable. Her luminous eyes seemed to see past Theron's shape, past his own, directly into his soul.

He flushed.

The girl's lips twitched up at one corner. "It's not a bad disguise, actually. Seems to be fooling the terrorists for now. It might give us a bit more time to find out what's going on."

"What *is* going on?" he asked, becoming more confused by the moment. "Does it have something to do with this game of picking winners that you play?"

"Mmm, I was wondering that as well! I appeared to Theron of Macedonia on the first day. He was such an obvious choice for the boys' sprint. How was I to know some idiot terrorist would decide to throw a javelin through his foot? Pericles was lucky you were there last night. But just in case they are targeting my choices, I'm not going to choose any of the men until the last possible moment. If too many of them fail to win, I'll be in trouble."

"*You'll* be in trouble?" Sosi stumbled after her as they crossed the field where he and Pericles had been attacked, taking a wide detour around the wreckage of the chariot. Someone had removed the dead horse, probably because of the smell. Nike moved fast for a girl carrying a burden. He was finding it hard to keep up. "Don't you care about my brother? Have you got money on the Games, is that it?"

She frowned. "Look, let's stop this stupid pretence, shall we? You know better than anyone how serious this is. With these terrorists around, I need to be as strong as possible in case they try something during the festival. I know you'll do your best, but I can't rely on you, not after what happened last time. You just concentrate on looking after the boys on the journey. I need to go back to Olympia to check on a few things." She glanced over her shoulder. "All right, I can manage him from here. I'll make sure your brother's in good hands before I go, don't worry – I've as much interest in his health as you have right now. You'd better join the others before they miss you. Keep alert. There's something very odd about these terrorists."

Sosi's head was spinning. "What do you mean? And what 'last time'? I haven't even been to Olympia before! At least tell me how I'm supposed to look after the others!"

The girl had heaved his brother's body over her shoulder. At his desperate tone, she paused. "What's the matter? Have you lost your memory, or something? We'll talk again when you get to Olympia. I really shouldn't hang around here any longer."

"Wait!" he called. "Where do I find you...?"

But she was already running through the barley stalks

in the shimmering heat, bent low, her cloak fluttering around her. The air blurred, and an eagle flew out of the field into the sun. Dazzled, Sosi shaded his eyes. When he could see again, Nike and his brother had gone.

Sosi stood very still, his skin prickling. It was as if he'd dreamt the entire thing. He thought of Theron's dream of victory. But Priestess Nike was surely too ugly to be a goddess. And if it had been a dream, his brother's leg would not have smelled so bad.

The Women's House was in chaos. In the yard, mothers were hugging their sons, telling them to be careful, giving them good-luck charms, saying an Olympic wreath was not worth killing themselves over. The boys bore this in different ways. There were tears from the younger ones, patient smiles from the older ones, and angry words as the young athletes tried to explain that Olympic wreaths *were* worth dying for, and women just didn't understand.

As Sosi hesitated, still trying to work out how Nike had vanished so quickly with his brother in broad daylight, Pericles and Samos spotted him and rushed across. "There you are! We wondered what had happened to you. Have you heard?"

"Heard what?" Sosi's brain struggled to catch up.

"The charioteer, of course! The one with the crimson beard who tried to run us over last night? Don't say you've forgotten already."

Sosi turned cold. "What about him?"

"He's dead! The guards found his body hanging in his cell. The cord around his neck had burnt ends like the one you found in the wood. They think he must have hidden it in the waistband of his trousers."

Sosi didn't know whether to be glad or not. "Then he can't hurt anyone else... Are we still going to Olympia early?"

"Of course we are," Pericles said with a dark look. "The guards left the cell open while they went to inform the judges, and when they got back the body was gone. Eretaia was obviously right about there being more than one Warrior. The judges think one of his accomplices broke in and stole it."

PART 2

SACRED WAY
FROM ELIS TO OLYMPIA

Yet for the race of man
ever about his struggling thought hangs there a net
of countless riddles, whence indeed
is it most hard to tell
what fortune shall be best, or now
or in the final hour, for any man to win.

(Olympian 7)

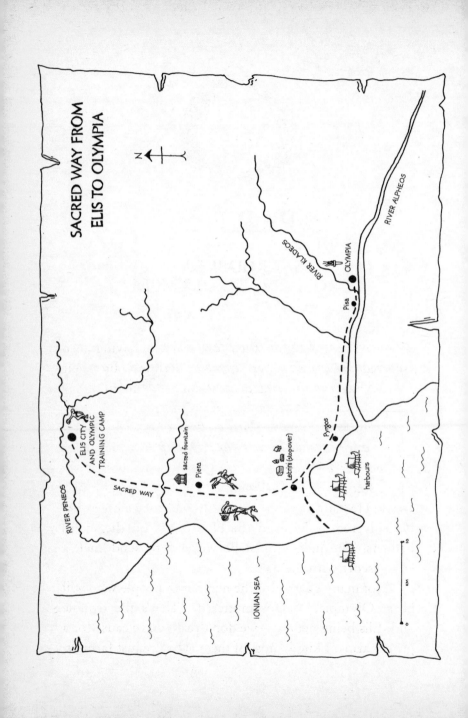

SACRED WAY FROM
ELIS TO OLYMPIA

N

RIVER PENEOS

ELIS CITY
AND OLYMPIC
TRAINING CAMP

SACRED WAY

sacred fountain

Piera

Letrini (stopover)

Pyrgos

harbours

IONIAN SEA

RIVER KLADEOS

OLYMPIA

Pisa

RIVER ALPHEOS

KM

Chapter 5

TROUBLE

THE BOYS ASSEMBLED in the agora at dawn, having been escorted from the camp in semi-darkness by their guards. Each young athlete carried a bag containing his spare clothes, personal strigil and skin oils. Most of them wore their cloaks, because the sun was not yet up. Waiting for them in the shadows were the chariots commandeered from the horse camp and about fifty Elean soldiers in full armour, which gave Sosi a bit of a shock. He hadn't even realized Elis had such a big army. He shivered as he eyed the blue crests on the men's helmets. The judges must be worried to send such a large escort with them.

"Not many guards for the number of people who will be at Olympia," Samos muttered. "That's the trouble with Elis being neutral – we don't really have cause for a proper army. I know most of them. They're just farmers, normally. Don't spread it around, but half of them can't tell one end of a sword from another."

Sosi looked closer at the men and noticed how awkwardly some of them were holding their spears, and how worried they looked. Farmers or not, they were only too aware of the seriousness of the occasion.

"That's not what really matters, of course," Samos added, noticing his expression. "People will feel better if they see them patrolling the site, and no one's likely to attack us on the road if we're accompanied by so many armed men, are they?"

Sosi wasn't so sure. If *he* could tell these men weren't really fighters, then surely the Warriors of Ahriman would be able to tell as well.

The judges filed out of their residence and formed a solemn line on the steps. Judge Lysanias stood a little apart from the others, a travelling cloak thrown over his purple robe. Relief rippled through the boys. Apparently, Sosi wasn't the only one who had been worried Judge Demetrius would decide to escort them himself. The chatter and laughter fell silent. The Eleans pushed back their helmets and stood straighter. Even the horses stopped fidgeting and champing on their bits.

Judge Demetrius used the formal address that identified them as young and privileged athletes rather than mere boys. "Ephebes!" he called. "These are unusual circumstances, but nothing has changed. Soon you will swear your Olympic oaths before the statue of Zeus Horkios. This is your final chance to escape his wrath. If you have trained diligently in your chosen events for the past ten months and are worthy to take part in the Great Games, you are free to go to Olympia with our blessing. If, however, you have neglected your training, or are not setting out with the olive wreath foremost in your dreams, then step forward now!" He eyed them sternly, as if he were trying to see into their hearts.

Boys shuffled their feet. There were a few nervous coughs. Kallias avoided looking at anyone, obviously thinking of his dodgy starts. But most of the boys were smiling, and Dion gazed at the judge in awe. Pericles nudged Sosi and whispered, "Don't know why they bother with that old speech. Do they honestly think any of us are going to back out at this stage? Young Dion's the only one impressed by it – look at the little squirt! He's going to be unbearable when we get to Olympia."

Sosi flushed as Judge Demetrius' stare reached him. *What if Nike's told him about me and Theron?* He felt as though his body must be changing shape for all to see. But the judge's attention moved past him without comment, and the agora filled once more with chatter and bustle as the non-athletes bound for Olympia joined them.

Judge Lysanias supervised the loading of a basket into the back of a chariot, where it rocked from side to side and emitted squeals that spooked the horses. There was a lot of arm-waving and shouting as the boys were assigned to the chariots that would carry them. Then the drivers had to persuade the excited horses to proceed out of the agora and along the first part of the Sacred Way at a pace to please the crowds that had gathered to see them off. Sosi found himself sharing a chariot with Pericles and his sister. It was obvious the driver was not the horses' usual handler, for they were playing up having caught Sosi's scent behind them, but he didn't want to draw attention to himself by getting out to walk. Sosi eyed Eretaia, wondering how much she knew about her friend Nike. Before he could ask, the chariot lurched forwards, making them stagger.

"Better hold on!" Pericles warned, putting an arm around his sister and gripping the side. Sosi was forced to do the same as the platform bucked under his feet. He hadn't taken much notice of the pair of horses drawing the chariot, but when he looked at their flattened ears and rolling eyes he recognized one of them as the grey colt Rasim had fallen off in the wood.

Pericles grimaced. "I bet I know why Judge Demetrius chose Rasim's colt to help transport us," he whispered. "He doesn't think much of Persians in the Games, does he? If Rasim's horse misses its proper training for a few days, it'll reduce his chances."

Eretaia, who had gone pale, whispered, "Rasim's got to win. Nike chose him for the horse race—"

She lost her hold as their chariot barged past the others, and fell on top of Sosi with a little scream. Seeing the road clear in front of them, the colts broke into a gallop, necks extended, manes and tails flying, hooves pounding the dirt as if they were already in the Hippodrome at Olympia. Sosi helped Eretaia up. There wasn't much room in the back of the chariot, and she clung to him in a whirl of blonde hair. His cheeks went hot, but there was no time to be embarrassed. Their driver hauled on the reins with grim determination, while his passengers sorted themselves out and crouched behind him, staying on board as best they could. A few Elean soldiers ran after them, but were soon left behind.

"Meet us at the Piera Fountain!" Judge Lysanias called.

Their driver was too busy trying to stop the chariot from overturning to acknowledge this, but Pericles managed a wave to show they'd heard. The boys further back in the convoy cheered them on. They obviously had no idea how out of control the colts were. Perhaps Judge Lysanias and Trainer Hermon didn't realise either.

Sosi shut his eyes so he wouldn't have to see the boulders blurring past their wheels. He was trying to pluck up the courage to jump out, when Eretaia gripped his arm. "Someone's coming!"

He squinted through the clouds of dust, his heart thudding. He'd been so certain she'd spotted a crimson-bearded Warrior, he laughed. A lone horse was slowly gaining on them, a slender figure crouched over its neck.

"It's Rasim!" Sosi cried.

Eretaia's eyes widened. "What's *he* doing here? He'll get disqualified!"

Their driver had seen the horse, too. He waved his whip at the Persian boy: "Stay clear!" he warned. "They're bolting!"

Rasim ignored him and urged his horse closer, his whole attention fixed on the grey colt. He whistled, and the colt's ears flickered in response. Sosi stayed as quiet as possible, though Pericles and Eretaia stood up to see what the Persian was doing.

"He's going to jump across!" Pericles exclaimed.

"At full gallop!" Eretaia breathed. Her hair whipped across her eyes as she turned her head. "Theron, you have to see this!"

Sosi saw only a blur of cloth, like the wings of a bird, as Rasim flew through the air and landed neatly astride the grey's withers. The horse he'd been riding shied away from the chariot and dropped back to a trot. Rasim braced one foot against the shaft and twisted his hands in the colt's mane. Their driver, realizing what the boy was trying to do, had the sense to drop the reins and use his weight to balance the chariot as it skimmed the edge of the track.

They held their breath as Rasim lay along his colt's neck and whispered in its ear. The colt arched its neck and snorted, and the pair slowed to a canter, then to a trot, and finally to a walk. Rasim slipped to the ground and went to the exhausted horses' heads. They drooped in their harness, streaming with sweat, as the Persian boy rubbed their ears and whispered to them in his own language.

Their driver jumped down to help, but there was little need. The colts were too tired to do more than flick an ear when Sosi climbed out on trembling legs and collapsed at the side of the road. Pericles and Eretaia joined him, casting glances at Rasim. Admiration shone in Eretaia's blue eyes, but Pericles' expression was one of distrust. Sosi's own feelings hovered between the two. This was the second time Rasim had turned up in the wake of trouble.

"They'd have stopped eventually," Pericles muttered. "He didn't have to risk his neck like that."

Sosi thought of the wreck in the field at Elis. "At least we didn't turn over."

"Wasn't he brave?" Eretaia said, giving Sosi a sideways look. "I wish I could ride like that."

Pericles scowled at her. "You can run, sis. Any fool can learn to ride. Shh, the driver's coming. Where are we, do you think?"

There was no sign of the convoy. The Elean plain stretched on either side of the track, shimmering in the heat. Sosi thought he could smell the sea.

Their driver looked from Pericles to Sosi and back again. "We seem to have taken a bit of a detour, young sirs," he said gruffly. "But I think I know where we are. If we continue along this track, it should lead us to the old ford across the river north of Piera. It should be passable at this time of the year, and it'll bring us out near the fountain. The alternative's to go back the way we came and pick up the Sacred Way again, but we'll be a long way behind the others, and the horses are tired, so we'll have to walk. Considering there's a young lady among you, we might be better going back to Elis and getting fresh horses and an escort. What do you suggest?"

He was waiting for a decision, Sosi realized. It made him feel very grown up, yet, at the same time, very inadequate. He thought of what Nike had said. *"Look after the boys on the journey."* How was he supposed to look after anyone when his curse had got them separated from their guards, and nearly killed them into the bargain?

He hoped Pericles would know what to do. Eretaia bit her lip, and her brother started to say, "I think we'd better go back to Elis—"

But Rasim interrupted: "No, it's too far. The horses need water. We'll go on to the ford."

Their driver nodded and headed back towards the chariot.

"Wait a moment!" Pericles said. "The Persian's not in charge! He's not even supposed to be here." He scowled at Rasim. "Did you arrange for your colt to run away like that? Someone tell you to make sure we were separated from the others, did they? Who are you working for? I bet he's got a crimson beard!"

Their driver looked confused. Eretaia pulled at her brother's arm as Rasim's eyes darkened. "Pericles, he rescued us..." she began, and then fell silent, obviously thinking of the man who had attacked her in Elis.

Rasim smiled at her, making her blush. "I knew Lightning wouldn't behave for anyone else and he hates being in harness, so I borrowed a horse and came after you to make sure his chances in the race weren't spoiled, that's all. His legs are bound to be sore after galloping over all those stones, though. What set them off?"

Sosi held his breath as their driver muttered something about the horses being overexcited and the convoy travelling too slowly for them.

"I don't mind walking," Eretaia said, stroking the neck of Rasim's horse. "You don't have to go back on my account."

Pericles considered the colts, their coats still dark with sweat, and frowned at Rasim. "We'll vote on it," he decided. "Who's in favour of going on to the river?"

Eretaia, the driver, and Rasim raised their hands. After a moment's hesitation, Sosi did, too.

Pericles took his sister's arm and pulled her away from Rasim's horse. "Fine," he said. "But no one's getting back in that chariot. We'll *all* walk."

Sosi was relieved to be back on his own two feet. Pericles and Eretaia seemed happier as well, for they started an argument about the merits of travelling on foot to Olympia in the traditional way over riding in a chariot. Eretaia said the girls were expected to walk there for the Games of Hera and it did them no harm, so she didn't see why the boys should get special treatment. Pericles pointed out that at the Games of Hera the girls had plenty of time to rest before they raced, whereas the boys usually had to compete straight away because there was such demand on the stadium for the men's events, and anyway there were the terrorists to consider.

They glanced round nervously, but there was nowhere for the Warriors to hide and ambush them out here on the plain. Sosi turned his attention to the question of his curse and his strange meeting with Priestess Nike back in Elis. He'd just decided that his imagination must have made Eretaia's priestess friend seem more mysterious than she was, when Rasim's voice at his ear made him jump.

"Horses are frightened of you, aren't they?" the boy said.

"What do you mean?" Sosi looked round anxiously for the colts, but Rasim had knotted their reins to the front of the chariot and left them to follow on their own.

"I know it was you who made them bolt. You spooked Lightning the day I tried to talk to you outside the Blood House. When I fell off in the wood, that was because of you, too. And when that chariot tried to run you and Pericles down in the field, you made it crash."

"What do you know about that?" Sosi said.

"I know a horse died that night." Rasim met his gaze. "These things cannot be hidden from the horse camp."

Sosi stopped, causing the colts to stop as well. They flared their nostrils at him as he seized the boy's arm. "If you know anything about the terrorist plot to stop the Games, you've got to tell someone," he hissed. "Do you?"

Rasim laughed. "Stop the Games? Is that what you think this is all about?"

"Then... what do you know?" Sosi tightened his grip, forgetting he had Theron's strength. The Persian boy winced.

Pericles and Eretaia realized something was going on and looked round. They and the driver were some way ahead, though. They couldn't have heard when Rasim dropped his voice to a whisper and said, "I know you're not who you appear to be. Let go of me before I tell your friends."

Sosi let go. They stared warily at each other.

"I'll tell you what I know about the Warriors of Ahriman if you tell me why my horse is so scared of you," Rasim continued, a challenge in his eye. "One secret deserves another."

Sosi let out his breath, relieved. Rasim didn't really know anything about his curse. "How should I know?" he said, making his tone light. "Maybe they don't like the way I smell?"

"Is everything all right, Theron?" Pericles called.

"Fine," Sosi said, eyeing Rasim. He couldn't forget the way the body of the crimson-bearded Warrior had disappeared from his cell. Rasim didn't look as if he had the strength to carry a grown man, but he had access to plenty of horses that did.

The Persian boy walked back to the chariot and unlooped the reins.

"Remember you're not supposed to be here, Persian!" Pericles called after him, scowling. "You'd better not be planning anything. We could get you in a lot of trouble when we join up with the others."

Rasim ignored him and whispered to his colt.

Pericles looked as if he wanted to wrestle the Persian boy to the ground. Sosi laid a hand on his arm. "Leave him," he said. "I think he knows something about the Warriors, but he's not going to tell us if we get angry with him."

Pericles scowled again. "I don't trust him. You'd be stupid to trust him, either, Theron. He could have come out here to lead us into a trap."

"He saved our lives," Eretaia reminded them.

Her brother grimaced. "Maybe... maybe not. Just keep alert until we're back with the others, and watch what you say in front of him. Never forget he's one of the enemy."

Chapter 6

FOUNTAIN

DESPITE PERICLES' DARK words, they reached Piera
without further incident. The village was nothing more
than a collection of mud and wooden built huts. The
convoy from Elis was drawn up around the fountain
beside the Sacred Way, where a grotto had been built
around a natural spring. The water bubbled into a basin
of pink marble shrouded in secret shadows.

The villagers had gathered at the edge of their fields
and were nervously eyeing the armed men. Some of the
women held flowers, which they seemed to be trying to
take into the grotto. The soldiers kept them back,
ignoring protests that they needed to decorate the Sacred
Fountain before the judge purified himself.

"We must have caught them by surprise," Pericles
said. "They weren't expecting us so early."

"They weren't expecting so many soldiers, you

mean," Eretaia said. "Why are the men keeping them away? What harm can a few flowers do?"

Rasim had gone quiet. The look on his face told Sosi he hadn't been expecting to see so many soldiers, either. He'd been walking at the colts' heads, chatting with their driver. But as they approached the fountain, he reached for the horse he'd ridden from the camp.

Pericles snatched its reins before he could take them. "Oh no you don't, Persian!" he said, pushing the boy away with one hand and dragging the surprised animal behind him with the other.

Rasim frowned. "I was only going to rub my horse down while your man unharnesses the colts."

"First, I doubt it's your horse," Pericles said. "Second, we're not going to let you ride off back to your terrorist friends. We're not that stupid."

Rasim sighed. "Think I'd trust Lightning in your care after what just happened? I could have left long before now, if I'd wanted to."

"The horses were tired. You wouldn't have got far. You knew that, which is why you didn't try."

They glared at each other. Sosi kept out of it. If he went near the horses, it would only make things worse. They had recovered from their mad gallop now and were neighing to their friends at the fountain. He didn't want to remind Rasim how much he scared them.

Eretaia bit her lip. "Oh, leave him alone, Pericles!" she said. "Judge Lysanias has seen us."

The judge hurried towards them, holding his robes

clear of his ankles. He'd taken off his travel cloak, and his purple robe glowed among the dusty clothes of the villagers and other travellers. Four Elean soldiers hurried after him, hastily putting on their helmets.

Lysanias checked Pericles and Sosi for injury, glanced at Eretaia, and frowned at Rasim. He waited until their driver had led the horses away before shaking his head at the slave boy. "What are you doing here, Persian? I hope you've got a good explanation, because I happen to know Judge Demetrius expressly forbade you to come."

"He knows something about the Warriors of Ahriman, sir—" Pericles began, but Judge Lysanias raised a hand.

"I asked Rasim to explain."

Rasim smiled and gave the judge the same explanation he'd given the others; that he'd come to make sure his colt was handled properly. He even offered to ride the grey in harness the rest of the way to Olympia. To Pericles' obvious disgust, after hearing Eretaia's account of how the boy had saved them, Judge Lysanias agreed.

The judge ran a hand through his hair and sighed. "I'd hoped to make Olympia today, but we've still got the ritual to perform. It looks as if we'll be forced to stop over at Letrini, like we usually do when everyone's walking. I only hope they're more prepared for us than the Pierans were." He gave them a distracted look. "You boys get to your places. We're running late enough as it is."

Eretaia looked away when they sacrificed the pig, and Pericles pressed his lips together. But some of the younger boys crowded round the grotto, trying to get a closer look. At a safe distance, Rasim stroked Lightning's nose and watched in silence.

Sosi shivered. The shadows inside the grotto seemed very dark. He watched, uncomfortable, as Judge Lysanias dipped a cup into the basin. The judge drank deeply and motioned the boys to form a line outside the grotto. As they jostled forward, Sosi found himself near the front. A strange odour came from the water, making him want to spit. His skin began to prickle.

Dion was first in line. Eyes shining, he stepped into the shadows of the grotto to receive the cup. Judge Lysanias said, "May you drink of the pure water of the fountain of Piera, as athletes before you have purified and refreshed themselves since the days of Hercules!" Dion took a solemn sip and passed the cup to Sosi. It had been a long walk since the river, and he was thirsty. But when the water touched his tongue, it burnt him.

The cup slipped out of his hand, and the boy behind snatched it from him. "Clumsy Macedonian!" snapped Agis. "There won't be enough for everyone at this rate. Depriving us of the sacred water won't help you win, you know."

Sosi saw Judge Lysanias stagger and grab the edge of the basin. Icy fear shot through him. He dashed the cup from Agis' hands. "No! Don't drink it!"

The skinny Athenian stared at him. "What's got into you, Macedonian? Now look what you've done. You've spilt the lot!"

Sosi watched the water seep away into the dust, his stomach fluttering. "The water! There's something wrong with it! I tasted it... I mean, I smelled it..." How could he explain? Normal people didn't have the extra senses he did.

Agis grabbed Sosi's tunic. The other boys pushed forwards, thinking there was going to be a fight.

Judge Lysanias came out of the grotto, shading his eyes from the sun. "What's going on out here? Agis, let go of him. Theron, you don't look well. Is it your foot again? It's not a good omen to spill the sacred waters of Piera—" He bent to pick up the cup, overbalanced, and fell flat on his face in the dirt.

Everyone stared at him in horror.

"Poison," Sosi whispered. "Oh gods, that's it, that's what I tasted in the water! The Warriors must have been here before us!"

The boys crowded forward, trying to see what was happening. "What's going on?" ... "Is Judge Lysanias sick?" ... "What happened?" ... "Is it a new part of the ritual?"

Their nervous giggles fell silent as the Eleans pushed through. Two of them helped Judge Lysanias into the shade of an olive tree, while the others formed a guard around the fountain. Suddenly, they seemed less like farmers and a lot more like soldiers. "Give him some air!" they ordered. "You boys, get back. Don't touch anything!" One of them picked up the cup and sniffed it. Another examined the marble basin of the fountain, while a third prodded the leaves around the grotto with his spear.

Sosi became aware of a struggle over by the chariots, where Pericles was pointing an accusing finger at Rasim. "That slave is with the terrorists!" he said.

Two of the Eleans dragged the Persian away from his colt and tied the boy's hands behind him. More soldiers surrounded the frightened villagers with drawn swords. Sosi saw Rasim's desperate expression and tried to think. Judge Lysanias was lying frighteningly still under the tree, but Dion seemed fine and he had drunk from the cup as well. Maybe he'd been wrong about the poison, and Judge Lysanias had merely fainted? Too late now. The news was passing through the crowd like flames before the wind, growing in destructive power as it went.

"The Persians have poisoned the fountain of Piera! Judge Lysanias is dying! The Persians are trying to kill our ephebes!"

Agis had gone quiet, staring at Sosi. "How did you know?" he whispered. Then he seemed to remember Dion had drunk from the cup as well, and looked hard at him. "Are *you* feeling all right?"

Dion's eyes were not shining any more. He stared at Judge Lysanias, very pale. "Are we all going to die?" he whispered.

"Of course not, squirt," Samos said, coming across and putting an arm around the younger boy's shoulders. "Don't worry, the judge will be fine. There's a healer in the village. The men have gone to find her. Let's worry about you. How much did you drink?"

"Not much... nothing, actually... I spat it back. I wanted to leave enough for everyone else..." Dion started to shake.

"Don't look like that, squirt!" Kallias said. "A little sip won't hurt you, especially if you didn't swallow it. Judge Lysanias drank a whole cup!"

Dion nodded. "It was meant to be sacred water..." He blinked and started to cry.

Samos gave him a squeeze and looked up at Sosi and Agis. "How much did you two have?"

"I didn't swallow any," Sosi said.

"I didn't get a chance," Agis grunted. "Theron knocked the cup out of my hand before I could even taste it."

"Just as well!" Kallias said.

Agis glared at him. "I wouldn't be surprised if the Macedonian and the Persian aren't in it together."

"Cut it out, Agis. Theron just saved your life." Samos glanced at Dion. The younger boy sniffed, trying to control his tears.

They moved off a short way, giving him a chance to regain his dignity.

"How *did* you know, Theron?" Samos said. "About the poison, I mean? You'd think if the water had tasted that bad, Judge Lysanias would have detected it himself." He eyed the grotto, where the soldiers were still searching the shadows.

"I... after everything that's happened, I was suspicious," Sosi said half-truthfully, and to his relief the others seemed to accept this. He frowned at the village, where the soldiers had taken Rasim inside one of the huts. "I don't see how it could have been Rasim, though. He was with us the whole time. How could he have got to the fountain and poisoned it, then ridden back in time to stop our chariot?"

"He was riding a racehorse," Agis reminded them.

While the others argued about this, Sosi shuddered at their near escape. If he hadn't stopped it, that poisoned cup would have been passed to every boy entered in the Games. Were the Warriors of Ahriman trying to kill them *all*?

"The Persian's going to talk, whether he likes it or not," Pericles said, joining them with a satisfied expression. "Even if he didn't actually poison the water himself, I bet he knows who did. The men are going to interrogate him as soon as they get permission. They've already started questioning the villagers."

Eretaia stared in dismay at the hut where Rasim was being held prisoner. "Judge Lysanias won't let them hurt him, will he?"

"Thanks to Rasim's terrorist friends, Judge Lysanias might not have a say in it," Pericles said.

Everyone looked at the olive tree, where the village healer bent over the unconscious judge, watched closely by the soldiers. The old woman with her basket of herbs reminded Sosi of how their mother had gone to Olympia to find a cure for his brother's foot. He closed his eyes, wondering what could possibly go wrong next. They must have been crazy to think they could get away with cheating at the Olympic Games.

Chapter 7

AHRIMAN'S FIRE

THEY DID NOT make it to Letrini that night. The village healer pronounced Judge Lysanias too sick to travel, and had him carried to her hut so she could treat him properly. The Eleans did not like it, but no one knew what else to do. They were relieved the judge was still breathing. After consulting with Trainer Hermon, the commander sent a man back to Elis with news of the poison attempt and a request for guidance, and the company made camp at Piera while they awaited his return.

Their narrow escape at the fountain had affected the boys in different ways. Some of them sat quietly with their arms around their knees, staring out into the darkness with sleepless eyes. Others were rowdier than normal, joking that there would be no competition at this rate. Agis and Kallias were at the centre of a muttering group that seemed ready to go over to the hut where Rasim was being held and "teach the Persian a lesson". The moon, which had been slowly shrinking during the training period at Elis, had disappeared altogether, leaving only starlight to struggle through the clouds. Normally, Sosi looked forward to this time of the month because it was when he felt most himself, but tonight he wished his curse had the power to make him as brave and strong as his brother, besides giving him Theron's shape.

The soldiers had lit up the camp for security, but the large number of fires only made the grotto harder to see. Sosi pulled his cloak closer and kept watch with his heat-sense, wondering what he'd do if a Warrior came. When he spotted a hooded figure creeping through the shadows, his heart missed a beat: But the figure wore a woman's cloak and beckoned urgently to him.

Trying not to draw attention to himself, he sauntered over to the grotto and ducked around the back. "Nike?" he whispered.

The girl he'd been following giggled and dropped her hood. In the faint starlight, her hair shone pale gold.

"Eretaia!" he said, disappointed. "What are you doing?"

"You've got to help me, Theron! Rasim's in trouble."

"It's his own fault," Sosi said, embarrassed he'd muddled the two girls. "He shouldn't have come after us."

"But he didn't poison the water! How could he have? He was with us all the time."

"Shh!" Sosi cast an anxious look at the men guarding the entrance to the grotto. "Calm down. I don't think he did it, either."

She gave him a grateful smile. "Pericles is hopeless! He won't help. He's afraid he'll get disqualified from the Games if he gets involved. Anyway, he's convinced Rasim's guilty."

"I don't see what we can do." Sosi eyed the hut where the Persian boy was being held.

"We can rescue him, of course."

He blinked at her.

"*Please* help me, Theron! They haven't given him anything to eat, and they've strung him up! It's not fair!"

Sosi frowned. "Strung him up? How do you know?"

Eretaia was carrying a bulging cloth that smelled strongly of cheese. It looked like one of her headscarves. She fiddled with the knot as she spoke. "I went over there and knocked a spyhole in the wall. The mud was crumbling, so it wasn't hard. But when I told Pericles what I'd seen, he just said it served Rasim right. He refused to come and look, even. He thought I was making it up to get him to help me. I tried to tell Judge Lysanias, but he hasn't woken up yet. That old witch is keeping him asleep with her potions."

Sosi looked doubtfully at the hut. He felt sorry for Rasim, but there was his brother to consider. "I might get disqualified, too," he said, hating himself.

Eretaia gave him a disgusted look. "You boys are all the same! Is winning the only thing that matters to you?

Don't you care *at all*? Rasim saved our lives, and now he's suffering! I thought better of you, Theron. I thought you were different, but now I see you were just passing the time with me in Elis. All right, if you won't come with me, I'll do it alone. *I'm* not afraid of getting into trouble." Her voice had risen and her cheeks were flushed. Before he could stop her, she strode off towards the hut.

Mixed emotions tumbled through Sosi. What had Theron and Eretaia found to talk about? Would Theron have risked getting disqualified from the Olympic Games to help her free Rasim? He knew the answer to that. But he wasn't his brother. He couldn't let Eretaia go over there alone.

"Wait!" he hissed, hurrying after her. "All right, I'll help. But we need a plan. We can't just go barging in. There are bound to be guards." He couldn't see how many, but movement around the door indicated at least one. Strange that he couldn't see their body heat from here, but his extra senses were often not as sharp at the dark of the moon.

Eretaia's face broke into a smile. "I've already thought of a plan. I've hidden Pericles' strigil round the back of the hut. You're strong, Theron. You can use it to make a hole in the wall big enough to climb through. I'll distract the guards while you free Rasim. He can ride. All we need to do is get one of the horses over there, so that when he's out of the hut he can escape."

Horses. Sosi's heart sank.

"Eretaia, I can't—"

"I'll get the horse while you're making the hole," she said. "I know you're scared of them."

"That's not why—"

"I'll go and get one now," she said, thrusting the bundle of food at him. "Take this over to the hut and wait for me. Don't start knocking your hole until I'm there to distract the guards!"

Sosi was left holding her bulging headscarf. *This is crazy,* he thought. Yet it would be a good opportunity to ask Rasim about the Warriors, and the boy might be grateful enough to tell them the truth. Even if he didn't tell them anything, Eretaia was right. They couldn't abandon him after he'd helped them.

Rasim's prison smelled of manure; obviously it was used for animals the rest of the time. As Sosi crept closer, he saw a man in Elean uniform slumped against the doorpost, his head resting at an awkward angle and his eyes closed. His sword was propped against the wall nearby. Fallen asleep on the job, Sosi thought with a smile. This might be easier than they'd thought.

He hid the food under a bush and started to look for Pericles' strigil, bothered by a horrible feeling he'd forgotten something. Then he heard low voices coming from inside the hut. He raised himself cautiously to peer through Eretaia's spyhole.

He thought he'd need his heat-sense to see the prisoner. But an eerie violet glow showed Rasim, strung up by his wrists to the roof beam just as Eretaia had said, his bare feet dangling above the ground. A shiver of sympathy went through Sosi as he imagined how painful that would be. A man wearing Elean uniform with his helmet covering his face knelt at Rasim's feet, holding a purple flame. He was chanting and moving his cupped hands in an intricate pattern. Each time the flame touched Rasim's toes, the boy jerked in his bonds and let out a whimper.

Sosi watched, frozen, trying to make sense of it. He couldn't seem to understand the words, but it took several more of Rasim's jerks and whimpers for him to realize why. The chant was in the Persian tongue.

He staggered away from the spyhole, his mind spinning. At the same time, he heard hoof beats and Eretaia's soft voice calling to the guard... the guard who didn't show up on Sosi's heat-sense, seemingly asleep... the other one in the hut, speaking Persian... Judge Lysanias still unconscious, so no one could have given permission for the prisoner to be interrogated...

"No, Eretaia!" he shouted, racing around the side of the hut. "Run!"

His sudden appearance startled the horse, which threw up its head and snatched the reins from Eretaia's hand. She whirled, and her eyes widened as the door flew open and the man who had been torturing Rasim leapt out. For an instant he stared at Sosi, his eyes glittering through the slits of his helmet. Then, swifter than Sosi would have thought possible, he grabbed Eretaia by the hair and jammed the sword that had been leaning against the door across her throat.

"Stay where you are!" he told Sosi, his accent the same as that of the Warrior they'd caught in Elis. "Do not call out, or your friend dies."

The other guard stayed slumped against the doorpost, and Sosi saw a smudge of blood on the wood under his head. Of course, dead bodies did not give off heat. He'd been stupid, stupid.

Eretaia's captor jerked his head at the loose horse. "Catch it," he ordered Sosi. "Tie it to that tree. Then get inside. Not a sound!"

He dragged Eretaia towards the door. She looked faint. The camp and the village were quiet. No one seemed to have noticed what was happening.

Sosi edged around the horse until he was between the animal and the camp. Eretaia's eyes followed him. Hoping she would realize what he was going to try, he mouthed "chariot" at her. As the horse caught his scent and backed away, he took a sudden run at it, flung out his arms and opened his mouth in a loud hiss.

The horse leapt towards the doorway in a desperate bid to escape him. The Warrior swung his sword at the crazed animal, and Eretaia ducked out of his grasp and darted into the hut. Sosi hissed again. The horse reared in panic. Its hooves caught the Warrior on the back of the head, knocking his helmet askew and revealing the crimson beard beneath. The sword slipped out of his hand and he stumbled to his knees, staring at Sosi through the twisted nose hole. "*What are you?*" he whispered.

Sosi didn't stop to question his luck. He snatched up the sword before the Warrior could recover and brought the flat of the blade down on the horse's quarters. The terrified animal fled back to the camp, neighing wildly. The Eleans who had been dozing around their fires jumped to their feet, seized their weapons and ran towards the hut.

Sosi left them to deal with the Warrior and hurried inside. Eretaia flung herself into his arms, sobbing.

"Rasim," he reminded her.

Together, they manoeuvred a bench under Rasim's feet so he could rest his weight on it, and Sosi used the sword to cut the knots that tethered the boy to the roof beams. Rasim slumped on the bench in relief and pulled off the bindings with a shudder. He'd been tied with a burnt-ended cord into which a strand of hair had been threaded, like the throwing-loop Sosi had found in the wood, only this time the hair was black. They stared at the smoking weals it had left around his wrists.

"I—" Rasim began. He was sweating, and his dark skin had turned green.

"Run, then!" Eretaia said. Snatching the sword out of Sosi's shaking hands, she began using the blade to enlarge the spyhole so that Rasim could climb through. "Or do you want someone to string you up there again?"

Rasim shook his head. "That Warrior, don't let him—" There was a cry outside, where the Eleans had been struggling with the crimson-bearded Warrior. They backed off as their captive slumped to the ground. The commander put his head through the hole in the back wall and frowned. He was holding the strigil Eretaia had hidden, and the bundle of food.

"What's been happening here?" he demanded.

Eretaia stared at Sosi and Rasim, her face pale. Sosi took deep breaths, trying to think of an explanation that would get them into the least amount of trouble.

Rasim rubbed his wrists. "Theron and Eretaia stopped that man from rescuing me," he said.

"*Rescuing* you?" Eretaia exclaimed. "He was torturing you!"

The commander climbed into the hut and dropped the food and strigil on the floor. He considered the Persian boy, then turned his attention to Sosi and Eretaia. "I won't ask what you two are doing here in the middle of the night, or why you hid food wrapped in a girl's headscarf in the bushes, or even why you were knocking a hole in the wall," he said. "That's for your judges to investigate. What I *would* like to know is how a Warrior of Ahriman managed to infiltrate my command, and what interest he has in a slave boy hired to race horses."

Rasim pressed his lips together, though Sosi noticed the way his eyes lingered on the cheese-smelling bundle.

The commander sighed and beckoned to his men, who were hovering in the doorway. "Have it your own way. We're expecting instructions concerning you from Elis tomorrow. Unfortunately, the Warrior we caught tonight won't be giving us any answers. He seems to have managed to fall on one of my men's swords. In the meantime, I'm doubling your guard. You two, take that strigil with you and get on back to camp. Try to get some sleep. There's been quite enough excitement for one day. Let me see your hands, Persian."

As Rasim extended his hands, Eretaia darted in front of him. "You can't tie him up again! Look at his wrists! It's cruel..."

"Get her out of here," the commander said. "And someone go ask that healer-woman for an ointment for this boy's wrists. That's the worst rope burn I've ever seen. Don't be so silly, girl. I didn't order him strung up there, did I? I had no idea this was going on. Thank Zeus we stopped it in time – you can leave the food," he added as Eretaia tearfully snatched up her headscarf. "I think the boy needs it. Someone better fetch him something to drink, too. Don't want him flaking out on us before we get our answers, do we?"

Rasim darted a look at the commander. As if fearing a trick, he ripped open the scarf and stuffed a piece of bread into his mouth. He chewed rapidly and closed his eyes. When he opened them, they looked just as haunted as before. But he squared his shoulders, put his feet back on the floor, and gave the Elean a level stare. "If you promise to protect me from the Warriors of Ahriman, I'll tell your judges everything I know," he said.

Sosi stiffened. *Including the fact I scare horses?*

The commander nodded. "We'll protect you. I apologise for what happened. The terrorist who broke in here is dead. They won't get so close again, don't worry."

Rasim shook his head, as if he didn't believe the commander. He swallowed another mouthful of bread and managed a smile for Eretaia.

"Thank you," he whispered. "I'm glad you came."

By the time the convoy moved on, late the following day, everyone was in a subdued mood. A feverish Judge Lysanias had been sent back to Elis in one of the village's mule carts for proper treatment, and Judge Demetrius arrived in person as the replacement to escort the boys onwards to Olympia.

Trainer Hermon seized the free morning to fit in some extra training, giving Sosi little chance to think about what had happened the previous night. Following a vigorous warm-up session, the six boys entered in the sprint had a race rehearsal between two lines scratched on the Sacred Way at a distance paced out by six hundred of Hermon's strides. The Elean soldiers and Pieran villagers lined both sides of the road to cheer them on. After the poison in the fountain and the discovery of a terrorist among them the promise of a race lightened the atmosphere, and the crowd got quite excited.

The race, however, was a joke. Pericles and Samos talked to each other as they ran. Kallias messed up his start as usual and gave up halfway. Dion was still quiet after his close escape at the fountain, and Sosi's head was spinning with questions about what the Warrior had been doing to Rasim with the purple flame, and why the crimson-bearded terrorists were so quick to kill themselves. Only Agis ran it like a real competition, so of course Agis won, and spent the rest of the morning telling them how he'd win at Olympia as well if they didn't snap out of it.

Meanwhile, Judge Demetrius spent the morning in the hut with the Elean commander and Rasim, emerging at midday looking thoughtful. Rasim was escorted out a little later with his wrists bandaged and his feet treated for burns. He limped over to the chariots and helped harness his grey colt for the journey, accepting a leg-up from the driver. Pericles scowled at the Persian boy, but said nothing. Judge Demetrius had brought another chariot with him from Elis, which Pericles and Eretaia laid claim to, leaving Sosi to travel with the guard posted to keep an eye on Rasim. Upon Judge Demetrius' orders, the dead Warrior from last night was to be transported with them as well so that the priests of Olympia could examine his hands, which had been charred by the purple flame, and the boys were arguing about when the next attack would occur.

The whole way to Letrini, Rasim stroked his colt's neck and whispered to the horse in his own tongue. When Sosi leant over the front of the chariot and asked, "What did you tell the judge?" Rasim glanced at the guard and said it was confidential.

The only time the boy's control broke was when Sosi asked what the crimson-bearded Warrior had wanted.

Then Rasim's bandaged hands tightened on the rein, making the grey colt snort and break into a jog. "He just wanted to scare me," he said.

Sosi thought of the purple flame. "But what was he *doing* to you, Rasim? That hair in the cord was one of yours, wasn't it? And that flame he was holding wasn't natural. Was he using his magic on you? What'll the other Warriors do if they find out you've talked to Judge Demetrius?"

Rasim smiled tightly and said with strange emphasis, "*They* won't."

"But what if they—"

"Leave me alone, please," the Persian boy said. "You're upsetting Lightning."

Sosi was sure the Persian boy knew something important about the Warriors that he hadn't told the judge, but dared not say too much in front of the guard. He decided his questions could wait until they reached Letrini, and started wondering instead about Nike's game, and how he was supposed to find his mother when they arrived at Olympia. He knew so little about the place. If only he'd thought to ask Theron while there had still been time.

Chapter 8

LETRINI

Upon arrival at Letrini, the convoy split up. The horses and their staff had separate facilities on the edge of town, while the boys were ushered into the guesthouse and told that, for their own safety, they must stay inside until the morning. Despite her protests, Eretaia was separated from her brother and sent with the other women to the inner quarters. The body of the Warrior was dumped in a storeroom where it would keep cool, and the Elean commander posted guards in the corridors and at every stair, window and door. On Judge Demetrius' orders, the guards were not allowed to wear their helmets. No one seemed to have considered the fact that crimson beards could be shaved off, though Sosi supposed any strangers among the Eleans would be spotted more easily if their faces were bare. He sighed. It didn't look as if he'd get a chance to ask Rasim about the Warriors' magic tonight.

There was a good spread for supper. All the best foods for stamina and energy – meat, fish, cheese, olives, fruit, and fresh bread – were sent to the large upper-floor room, which was as quiet as if the boys had done a full day's training under the whip at Elis. They ate out of duty to their training regime, not because they were hungry. A few half-heartedly smeared oil over their bodies and massaged one another's muscles. The rest settled down on the pallets, talking in low voices.

Pericles took the opportunity to examine his strigil. "Olympia tomorrow," he said, having satisfied himself it wasn't damaged after being used to knock holes in the wall at Piera.

"Do you think we'll be safe there?" Kallias asked.

"Of course we will!" Agis said. "Even those stupid Warriors won't dare attack us in the sacred Altis at Olympia! That's the whole idea of sending us there early, isn't it?" He sloshed water from one of the hydrias and peered into his cup. "More to the point, do you think this stuff's safe to drink?"

"Ask Theron," Pericles said, making Sosi start. "He seems friendly enough with the Persians. Tried to free Rasim last night, didn't you, Macedonian?"

Sosi didn't like the way Pericles was looking at him. "Your sister asked me to help. I couldn't let her try to rescue him alone."

"You nearly got my sister killed." Pericles' face hardened. Agis and Kallias glanced at each other. Samos had gone over to sit with Dion in an attempt to reassure the younger boy they were safe. He shook his head at Pericles' tone.

Sosi shook mumbled. "It was Eretaia's idea..."

Pericles, whose stillness must have been hiding a huge amount of tension, seized the front of Sosi's tunic and thrust him against the wall. He twisted the cloth into a tight knot and pushed his face close to Sosi's. "Just remember I can throw you any time I want, Macedonian!" he growled. "If my sister gets hurt because of some tangled Persian plot to do with your Macedonian king, I'll finish what that Warrior started when he speared your foot."

Sosi gave up trying to explain. He let himself go limp, which only seemed to infuriate the blond boy more. "Why don't you fight me, Macedonian?" he hissed. "You didn't try this morning in the race, either. You let Agis win."

"Hey! He did not!" Agis protested. "I was good enough to win on my own."

Samos shook his head again. "Shut up, Agis. Pericles, let him go. Theron was the first one the Warriors attacked, remember? It's not his fault King Alexander invaded Persia and upset them, is it? We should be using our energy to work out how to stop these Warriors from injuring any more of us, not squabbling among ourselves."

Pericles' fist tightened. But the anger ran out of him, and he released Sosi with a sigh. "Sorry," he muttered, backing off. "But I'm worried about Eretaia. Why did that Warrior attack her in Elis? It makes no sense."

"Maybe he thought she was someone else?" Sosi said,

thinking of the way he'd mistaken Eretaia for Nike in Piera.

Pericles pulled a face. "Are you suggesting my sister looks like a boy?"

"No, but you must admit she looks a bit like her priestess friend Nike in her cloak."

"Why on earth would the Warriors be after Priestess Nike?"

Samos said, "Theron has a point. It could have been a case of mistaken identity, in which case your sister's safer than the rest of us right now. Pericles has a point, too, Theron. You weren't trying to win this morning. You didn't even beat Dion, and the poor squirt had the runs from that Pieran witch's herbs. It's not like you."

"You weren't trying either, Samos," Sosi pointed out. "You and Pericles were *talking*."

Samos smiled. "Let's face it, neither of us are going to win the boys' sprint unless the Warriors poison everyone else in the race." Somehow, he managed to make a joke out of what was a serious possibility. "We're saving ourselves for the wrestling and boxing. But you're such a good runner, you could have won that race this morning going backwards with your eyes shut."

"I had other things on my mind," Sosi said, wondering what excuse Theron would have used. Something to do with his health, probably. "The Sacred Way's full of potholes," he added. "I didn't want to strain my foot before the actual event. The tendons are still a bit weak."

To his relief, the others seemed to accept this. Even Agis nodded. "It was a stupid race, anyway," he said. "What was the point of it? I didn't even get a prize wreath!"

Samos nodded. "I reckon Judge Demetrius only told Trainer Hermon to arrange it to take everyone's minds off the Warriors. Anyone had any more ideas why they're targeting us?"

There was a silence.

"Maybe it does have something to do with Nike and her game," Sosi said, remembering the strange conversation he'd had with the priestess back in Elis. "What if it isn't the boys' sprint they're trying to stop? They could be after those most likely to win their particular events – those of us Nike chooses. So far, they've had a go at me with a javelin, Pericles with the runaway chariot at Elis, and now Rasim. That would take care of the sprint, the wrestling, and the horse race. The only other boys' event is the boxing."

Everyone looked at Samos, who nodded. "It makes sense. Which probably means I ought to be extremely careful between now and Olympia." Again, he made it sound like a joke. No one laughed.

"They had a go at me, too!" Agis said. "Don't forget the throwing-loop that burnt my hand in the wood."

"Well..." Samos glanced at Sosi for confirmation. "That might have been a mistake. I doubt the Warriors would have been careless enough to drop that cord by accident, which means it was left there deliberately. Maybe, when they saw Theron's foot had healed faster than they thought, they left it for him to find knowing he would search the wood for clues – which he did, but you snatched the cord away before the magic could work on him."

Agis scowled. "Even if no one thinks I'm winning material, I could still win, you know. Especially if Theron's foot is still weak. I always thought it was weird, the way it healed up overnight like that." He glared suspiciously at Sosi.

"Rasim was in the wood that day as well," Kallias reminded them.

"Yes!" Samos brightened. "That would make even more sense. The throwing loop might have been left for *him* to find, only Theron got there first – he told you he'd been looking for it, didn't he Theron?"

Sosi nodded.

"That game of Nike's is only a silly amusement to give the girls something to do while we're competing," Pericles said. "But I suppose, if someone had a lot of money riding on the outcome, they might hire someone to make sure the right people win..."

Dion paled. "That's cheating! We should tell the judges."

Agis shook his head. "No, it doesn't make sense! Who in their right mind would trust a Persian to fix something they had a lot of money riding on? Besides, what about the poison in the fountain? That wasn't aimed at a particular athlete, was it? It could have killed us all!"

There was another worried silence.

Samos sighed. "Agis is right. The poison doesn't make sense. It only really affected Judge Lysanias, because he was the one who drank the most." He rubbed the back of his neck. "Zeus, but I'm too tired to think about it now! I vote we all get some sleep, and then maybe in the morning we can tell Judge Demetrius our suspicions. Rasim might have already told him the Warriors' plans, anyway."

"I bet he didn't. He's in with them up to his neck," Pericles said, scowling, which sparked off another discussion about the slave boy's possible connection to the terrorists.

Kallias yawned and stretched out on his pallet with a sigh. "You lot can stay up arguing all night if you want, but I'm going to get some sleep or I'll never get my start sorted out before the Games!"

Not even Agis made a comment about that, which showed how uneasy they all were.

"We'll have to make Rasim talk ourselves," Pericles decided. "It's probably best to wait until we get to Olympia. We should be able to get him on his own there. Meanwhile, everyone keep a lookout for each other, all right? That includes you, Agis! We might be rivals in the Games, but until then we have to work together, or there won't *be* any Games. Anyone sees anything suspicious, they tell the others. No going off on your own, like Theron and my sister did last night. From now on, we do everything together, the six of us. There's safety in numbers. Agreed? Are you listening, Kallias?"

The boy mumbled something and turned over with another yawn. It was catching. Dion yawned as well, and the apple he'd been munching rolled from his hand. Samos smiled, picked up the half-eaten fruit, and put a blanket over the younger boy. "May you all dream of victory!" he said, giving Sosi a friendly wink.

Sosi grimaced. If they were right about the Warriors picking on potential winners, dreaming of victory was the last thing any of them wanted to do tonight.

There was so much to worry about, Sosi was sure he'd never be able to sleep. But his head had barely seemed to touch his pillow before he was having another of his nightmares.

A man was creeping between the two rows of sleeping boys in the dormitory, picking his way through the leftover food and discarded clothes. He wore a long cloak with a hood pulled over his face. He paused at each pallet, parting his cupped hands to examine the occupant by the light of a purple flame.

Sosi lay rigidly under his blanket, unable to move. It felt too real for a dream. He and the other sprinters were at the far end of the dormitory. Dion had chosen the pallet next to the wall under the window. Samos was beside him, then Sosi. The pallet on his other side was empty, as if the other boys could sense his curse. Across the room, Kallias had the other pallet by the wall. Agis was next to Kallias, and finally Pericles slept on the pallet opposite Sosi, snoring. Sosi's heart beat faster as the intruder approached. He broke into a cold sweat as he glimpsed the crimson beard in the shadows of the hood.

The Warrior reached Pericles, crouched at his feet and lowered his flame until it licked the boy's leg. Sosi fought the invisible bonds that chained him to his pallet. He imagined himself leaping up and screaming at the Warrior to leave Pericles alone. He must have made a noise, or maybe the intruder sensed someone was watching him, because he spun round and stared at Sosi.

It was the terrorist they'd caught at Elis. The same one who had spat at Sosi in the judges' hall and later hanged himself in his cell.

The Warrior's lips curved into a slow smile. "So, the sleep magic doesn't work on you?" His accent scraped through Sosi's head like a strigil. "The poison in the fountain was too clumsy, and I should have realized your judge would drink it and give the game away. I think it's time to see what you are, and why I've been having so much trouble getting to your friends." He bent over Sosi and parted his hands.

The purple flame brightened as it touched Sosi's cheek, and the sudden fierce pain of it broke his bonds. He could move! He leapt off his pallet with a cry and launched himself at the Warrior. "You're the one who threw that javelin at my brother, aren't you?" he shouted, forcing the terrorist to the ground.

As soon as he touched the Warrior, he knew for

certain he wasn't dreaming. There was no time to wonder how a dead man was suddenly alive again. The Warrior writhed beneath him, reaching for something in his cloak. An acrid smell made Sosi's stomach heave. The flame fell to the floor and sizzled out.

"Pericles! Samos!" Sosi yelled, using a trick he'd learnt at training camp to pin the Warrior down. "Everyone wake up! There's a Warrior in here!"

As the flame died, the sleep magic died with it, releasing the other boys. Pericles groaned and sat up, rubbing his leg. He took in the situation with one glance and scrambled off his pallet to help Sosi hold the intruder. Further down the room, boys were sitting up groggily and asking what was happening.

"Keep the guards out!" Pericles instructed, applying a wrestler's hold to their captive and dragging back his hood. "Theron, keep a good hold of his arms, that's it! Kallias, you hold his feet. Samos, come over here."

Together, they managed to hold the struggling Warrior. His flesh was dry and hot. All Sosi could think was: *He hanged himself. He should be dead.*

"Talk!" Pericles hissed, squeezing the Warrior's neck with his powerful arm. "What are you doing here? What's the plan for the Games?"

The Warrior spat and struggled some more. Sosi grimly held on to his wrists, though they were almost too hot to hold.

"Punch him, Samos," Pericles said.

The boxer hesitated. Then he glanced at Dion, who

was trembling against the wall, and thumped the man twice on the nose. Surprisingly, there was no blood.

"Speak!" Pericles said. "We're not letting you go until you do. If you tell us the truth, maybe we'll let you out the window before the guards get here."

The Warrior's eyes glittered with hatred. He kept trying to turn his head to look at Sosi. "Release me," he breathed, "or you'll be sorry."

Pericles tightened his grip on their captive's neck until he choked. "What do you mean, we'll be sorry? Are you planning something for the Games? Talk, or we'll hand you over to the Eleans right now!"

The Warrior laughed. "Think that scares me?" he whispered. "I get stronger every time. How does your leg feel, boy wrestler?"

At first Sosi couldn't think what the Warrior meant. Then he remembered how he'd crouched over Pericles with his purple flame. "What did you do to Pericles?" he demanded.

The Warrior's lips twisted. "You'll find out soon enough."

Samos' face hardened. He thumped their captive again. "What were you doing in here? How did you get in, anyway?"

At the door there was a commotion as the guards arrived, alerted by the noise. The boys Pericles had told to keep them out tried to block their way, to no avail. Dion stared at their captive, still shaking. "Let him go," he whispered. "Please. He's not going to tell us anything. He'll only hurt someone else."

The Warrior laughed. "Your young one is wise."

Pericles frowned at his leg, which he'd wrapped around the Warrior's waist so he could lock his ankles together. Sosi clung on stubbornly. The Elean guards had drawn their swords and were advancing on the captive with grim faces. "Well done, boys," said one of the men. "We'll take it from here."

Pericles untwisted his legs and massaged one of his calf muscles. Kallias let go of the Warrior's feet. Samos backed off, rubbing his knuckles. Only Sosi still had hold of their captive. He knew that if he let go as well, the Warrior would escape.

Though their captive now had several swords pointed at his throat, he writhed in Sosi's grip. "You can't hold me for ever," he breathed. "Give up. You might be immune to my powers, but I can hurt you in other ways. I know where your mother is, for example."

Smoke curled between Sosi's fingers. The smell of burning flesh filled his mouth, making him wish he didn't have extra senses. The Warrior laughed as he snatched his hands back.

The Eleans moved in swiftly. But before they could seize the Warrior's arms, he gave a wild shriek and flung himself on to their swords. The men swore and dragged their weapons clear, but it was too late. As with the terrorist at Piera, it seemed he preferred death to capture.

Sosi blew on his blistered hands and stared at the dead man. *I*, the Warrior had said. *I*, as if he planned to return. He'd already "died" in Elis, but then his body had disappeared and he claimed he'd poisoned the Sacred Fountain. The Warrior's face at Piera had been covered by his helmet, but it could have been the same man. He thought of what Nike had said. *There's something very odd about these terrorists.* The intruder had not given off any body heat in the dark, and now there was no blood.

"You've got to destroy that body!" he whispered, a horrible suspicion dawning.

The men shook their heads. "Judge Demetrius will want to examine it. We'll put it with the other one, don't worry. You boys try to get some sleep, now. Are any of you hurt?" He eyed Pericles, who was still massaging his calf, but Pericles only grunted and said he thought he'd pulled a muscle.

Sosi watched them carry out the dead Warrior, more scared than he had been since the night his curse had first come upon him. "He was in here already," he whispered. "Down in the storeroom. That's how he got past the guards. No one guards a dead man, do they?"

But the others were discussing the attack in excited voices, and did not hear.

Morning brought Judge Demetrius to the boys' dormitory while they were eating breakfast. The Elean commander and two of his men accompanied him. Shadows under the commander's eyes and stubble on his chin showed that he had been on duty all night. His gaze moved around the room, lingering on each boy in turn, while Judge Demetrius managed to give the impression of frowning at everyone at once.

"I have some bad news," the judge said.

Everyone stopped talking. There had been only one topic of conversation since they woke up, so it was obvious what he was referring to. Sosi's skin prickled. Samos smiled reassuringly at Dion. Pericles tested his weight on his bad leg and tried to appear as if it wasn't bothering him.

"The intruder the guards apprehended in here last night has escaped," Judge Demetrius continued, holding up a hand to silence the outbreak of worried whispers. "It seems he was faking his death. By the time I got down to the storeroom to examine the body, he'd killed two men and vanished. What's more, the body of the Persian infiltrator who was involved in the incident at Piera has also disappeared. This is unfortunate, since I wanted the priests of Olympia to examine it."

A cold shiver went down Sosi's spine. Samos shook his head, as if he didn't believe the judge. Pericles eased his leg and grimaced. Agis growled in his throat. Dion paled.

"That's not all," the judge continued. "The young Persian slave, who joined our convoy against orders the day before yesterday, appears to have stolen a chariot and gone with him. They obviously used the chariot to transport the body." His frown deepened and he cast a dark look around the room. "It now seems certain the boy Rasim is working with these terrorists. When I spoke to him back in Piera, he tried to persuade me not to bring the body of the infiltrator with us to Letrini. Obviously, the schemers are afraid of us examining their dead for some reason. This Rasim has stolen two very valuable colts, to say nothing of an expensive training chariot. Their owner is going to want the boy apprehended and punished." He let this sink in and tightened his lips. "I want a word with Theron. The rest of you, go outside and wait in your chariots. The sooner we get to Olympia, the better. This journey is taking far too long for my liking."

The boys looked sideways at Sosi, obviously wondering what the judge wanted him for.

Judge Demetrius' brows lowered. "What's wrong with you? Move! The sooner we get going, the sooner you'll be safe in the Altis."

Uneasy whispers rippled around the room. "Uh, sir?" Samos said. "We're worried about Judge Lysanias, sir. Is he all right, do you know?"

Judge Demetrius turned to the Elean boy. "He was sick after drinking the poisoned water, but he's being well looked after back in Elis. When I left, he was weak but far from dead. The Fountain of Piera has been temporarily closed while the basin is cleaned. The spring itself has been tested and seems to be pure enough. It's merely a case of cleaning out the channels and letting the water work through. By the time the men and other judges get there for their ceremony it'll be fine, so you needn't worry."

Sosi bit his tongue as the other boys picked up their packs and shuffled past the soldiers at the door. He'd been so worried about the Warrior last night, he had almost forgotten about poor Judge Lysanias.

"What's wrong with you today, Theron?" Judge Demetrius snapped. "I asked what you and Pericles' sister were doing in the hut where Rasim was imprisoned at Piera. Well? I'm waiting. Give me one good reason why I shouldn't disqualify you from the Games."

Sosi thought he'd got used to people calling him Theron, but for a horrible moment his mind went blank and he couldn't remember who he was supposed to be. He didn't know what made him feel worse – that he might be right about the Warriors being dead, or that he had been wrong to trust Rasim.

"We thought it was wrong," he said.

"You thought what was wrong?"

"That Warrior was *torturing* him!" Sosi said more firmly. "It was horrible. If he's helping them, I don't think he's doing it willingly." He explained how Rasim had stopped the runaway chariot, and how he couldn't have had time to go to Piera and poison the fountain.

The judge narrowed his eyes. "I've already spoken to Eretaia. She told me how he stopped the colts and how brave he was. I believe the girl has the facts right despite her romantic embellishments, and her story would seem to back up yours." He sighed. "All right, for the time being I'm willing to believe you were both taken in by Rasim's charm, so you can continue with the training.

But I've got my eye on you, Macedonian. One more act of disobedience, and you're out of the Games."

"I saw that Warrior die last night, sir!" Sosi blurted out, encouraged. "We all did, and I... I think it was the same Warrior who died before. Maybe that was why Rasim didn't want the body transported with us from Piera, because he knew it would come alive and try again."

Judge Demetrius ushered him downstairs to join the others. "Don't push your luck, Theron. The men tell me there was no blood. He obviously faked his death so they wouldn't bother watching him, stole the body of the other Warrior and escaped with Rasim's help. I expect the little spy was only too happy to make himself scarce once he realized I had come to replace Judge Lysanias. Now, let's have an end to this nonsense, shall we? Dead men don't get up and kill people. These Warriors of Ahriman are common terrorists employing standard fear tactics by trying to make us think they're invincible sorcerers. We'll catch them, don't worry, and then you'll see they're as human as we are."

If only you knew, Sosi thought, wondering what the judge's reaction would be if he were to tell him about his curse, right there and then.

Chapter 9

ARRIVAL

IT WASN'T AS far from Letrini to Olympia as they had already travelled from Elis. But when the Sacred Way turned east to follow the River Alpheos inland, the convoy had to compete with traffic bringing spectators from the harbours on the coast, which slowed them down. The rich came in gilded chariots with trains of servants to carry their camping gear, or on horseback. The rest came in humble farm carts, riding mules and donkeys, or simply on foot with only a cloak to keep them warm at night. The river itself was dark with boats, rafts and canoes, rowing against the current until it seemed the Alpheos had reversed its flow.

Sosi tried not to cough as dust stirred up by the horses' hooves blew into his face. Judge Demetrius was recognizable by his wide-brimmed hat, a purple smudge riding at the head of the convoy, shouting at people to get out of the way. The commander had ordered his men to keep the other travellers back from the chariots, but this proved impossible on such a crowded road. After peering into the chariots and not seeing any famous athletes, the crowd jostled them as if they were common spectators. Even Judge Demetrius' threats to exclude people from the stadium did not clear the way. All the boys were tense, and stiffened whenever a stranger came too close.

They passed through two more villages, waited their turn at the bridge to cross the River Kladeos where it surged into the Alpheos, and drew up in a square bordered on two sides by shining white colonnades. The crowds dispersed along the river banks to fight for camping space, and the commander at last managed to organize his men into military formation. Judge Demetrius ordered everyone to dismount, and with huge relief, Sosi climbed out of the chariot and moved away from the horses to join the other boys.

The younger ones stared around, wide-eyed, clutching their packs with sweaty fingers, while the older ones who had been to Olympia before stretched their cramped muscles and tried to look nonchalant. The square was hard packed earth, obviously in regular use, but the rest of the Olympian plain looked lush and green, planted with trees. Between their leaves, Sosi glimpsed marble buildings bright with fresh paint; red-tiled roofs with ornaments glittering gold on top, and hundreds of bronze statues of athletes and horses. A mountain rose to the north of the site, its rocky slopes drawing his gaze. Unaccountably, his palms began to sweat.

"That's the Altis over there," Samos told them, pointing to a collection of temples in an enclosure at the bottom of the slope. "That's sacred ground, so no messing around when you're in there! The Temple of Zeus Olympia is the biggest – you've got to go in and see the statue, it's famous even in Persia, apparently. The stadium's behind that long colonnade – you can't see it from here, squirt!" He smiled as Dion jumped in excitement to see. "You have to go through a tunnel from the corner of the Altis. It's quite dark inside, and then suddenly you're out in the sun surrounded by crowds of spectators up on the bank all screaming for their favourite athlete to win."

Dion must have got a sudden attack of nerves, because he went quiet. Sosi wished the Games were all he had to worry about. He couldn't get over the feeling that he'd been here before and something awful had happened. No one noticed his discomfort, though, because just then an overladen chariot galloped along the river bank, its occupants waving and whistling as they spotted the boys in the square. "May you all dream of victory!" they shouted at the tops of their voices.

"Idiots," Pericles muttered, as the horses in the square shot up their heads and neighed in reply. "Do they think they're at some sort of party?"

"It's a party for them," Samos said with a smile. "You forget what it's like when you're not competing. I bet you were just as excited when your father brought you to watch the Games when you were little."

Pericles mumbled something about the Games being a serious athletic contest and idiots like that ruining it for everyone else, but Sosi didn't pay much attention. As he looked at all the tents pitched on the river banks and the groups of tourists being escorted around the site, his heart sank. The place was huge. How was he supposed to find his mother, or get Nike alone to ask her about his curse?

"Where do the chariot races take place?" asked Dion, interrupting his dark thoughts.

"The starting gates are behind that colonnade." Samos pointed to the far side of the square. "There's quite a good view from the steps."

Dion insisted on dragging them over to see. Groundsmen were working on both sides of the Hippodrome's central barrier, watering the course and raking it smooth in preparation for the races that would take place in ten days' time. Sosi shivered, reminded of when he'd seen the boys raking the stadium back at Elis, the day he'd met Rasim in the wood and first heard of the Warriors of Ahriman.

"They'll be one short in the horse race now," he said without thinking.

"If Rasim turns up, I hope he falls off and breaks his sneaky Persian neck!" Agis said. "If it hadn't been for him, that Warrior would never have got into our dormitory last night."

Eretaia, who had been staring at the Hippodrome with a faraway expression, frowned at Agis.

"It was hardly Rasim's fault," Samos said. "I think Theron's right. I don't think he went with that Warrior willingly."

Agis snorted. "I bet Rasim set up the whole torture thing to make us feel sorry for him. Look at what that creepy Warrior did to Pericles last night! If it'd been *my* leg he messed with, I'd have made sure the judge knew. They're all the same... sneaky Persian scum!" He spat on the polished marble.

There was an awkward silence. Eretaia's back was as rigid as the columns around them.

Pericles frowned at Agis. "You can't cause an injury with magic, don't be stupid. I think I sprained it while I was wrestling him." He rubbed his leg again. "It's a bit numb, that's all."

Kallias touched his friend's shoulder. "Makes sense, Agis. He might even have pulled a muscle in that race at Piera. It would have been easy enough to do on that rough track. My trainer back home says the body can sometimes fool itself in the excitement of a competition, and you don't feel the pain until later. He told me that when he was still competing, one of the men in the wrestling broke an arm but carried on to win three matches before he realized. He must have been in agony later, though," he added.

Agis shrugged him off. "I still say that Warrior did it last night! They'd already tried to injure several of us back in Elis, and poison us all at Piera. It's obvious he came to finish the job. If Theron hadn't woken up when he did, he'd probably have had a go at the rest of us, too." He gave Sosi a suspicious look. "How come you were awake anyway, Macedonian? Bit convenient, wasn't it?"

Sosi couldn't think of an explanation, so he pretended he hadn't heard. He was saved by Judge Demetrius, who mounted the steps of the north colonnade and clapped his hands for attention.

The judge explained how they would be escorted to the baths so they could wash, then to the Council House so that they could take their athletes' vows before the statue of Zeus Horkios, and finally given a tour of the facilities before being taken to their quarters in the Prytaneon. It was here that the goddess Hestia's sacred fire was housed that one of them would have the honour of carrying around the altars on the day of the Great Sacrifice.

"Relax," the judge continued with a smile that was presumably meant to reassure them. "The Altis is sacred ground. Anyone who tries to harm those Zeus has taken under his protection will be blasted to a cinder by his thunderbolts. While you're outside the Altis, the soldiers will act as your bodyguards. You're to stay together and not go wandering off on your own. Trainer Hermon will organize your training schedule exactly as if you were in Elis. There won't be a lot of free time, but if you want to visit the temples while you're here, ask Trainer Hermon or me, and we'll find you a suitable guide. The statue of Zeus

Olympia is worth seeing, but I shouldn't think you'd want to bother with the temples of the goddesses – they're more for the girls, really." He paused, his attention taken by something on the other side of the square.

Sosi followed his gaze, and his skin prickled. Eretaia, who had stayed behind on the other colonnade, had been joined by another girl, whose luminous yellow eyes were fixed on Sosi with the intensity of an eagle watching its prey. For a heartbeat, framed by the columns with the sunlit haze of the Hippodrome beyond, it seemed this second girl was surrounded by a halo of feathers, and he was certain he could see a pair of golden wings glowing from her shoulders.

He blinked, and the wings disappeared. The girl's black hair was bound up in a gold ribbon, and her red chiton was hitched up to expose her thighs, showing off a very unladylike suntan, but it was obviously Priestess Nike. Back in Elis the cloak had hidden her physique, but now he saw she was as muscular as a boy. No wonder she'd had so little trouble carrying off his brother! He knew he was staring, but could not seem to look away. Nike winked at him and put her finger to her lips. She whispered something to Eretaia, who giggled.

Sosi's ears went hot. He nudged Pericles. "That girl over there – Eretaia's priestess friend Nike – has she got... I mean, does she seem strange to you?"

Pericles scowled at the colonnade. "I wondered how long it would take her to show up. What do you mean, strange?"

Sosi sneaked another look at Nike. "For a moment, I thought she had wings."

Pericles laughed and thumped him on the shoulder. "You must be confusing her with the Goddess of Victory you saw in your dream, Theron! There's a statue of her in front of the Temple of Zeus flying on an eagle – that's the Nike I dreamt of. Don't look at me like that! You're not the only one who's allowed to dream of victory, you know. She was a lot prettier in my dream than that ugly friend of Eretaia's, believe me." He sobered and added softly, "That's how I know my leg will be better in time. Look at the way your foot healed – it was a miracle, wasn't it?"

Judge Demetrius was droning on about the rules and regulations of the Games and the special holy rules of the Altis, but Sosi didn't hear a word. The air buzzed. He felt sick and dizzy, like he did when the moon was full. "When?" he whispered. "When did you dream of victory?"

Pericles sighed. "Back in Elis. The night before Eretaia got attacked, as it happens. Goddess Nike told me I'd win the boys' wrestling. Only unlike you, I didn't go round bragging about it. So keep it quiet, huh?"

Sosi clutched Pericles' shoulder. "That's why," he whispered. "That's why the Warrior attacked your sister! He did it to lure you out of the camp so he could try to run you down with his chariot! I was right, they *are* after those Priestess Nike picks to win! It wasn't until you had your dream they were interested in you. And my br— I mean, I was the first to dream of victory, so I was the first to get injured. She must be able to make herself appear in our dreams somehow."

Pericles grunted. "For Zeus' sake, Theron! Will you stop staring at that priestess? You'll make my sister jealous. Careful, Judge Demetrius is looking at us."

Sosi waited until the judge's gaze moved on, his brain still trying to catch up with what Pericles had just said. "But I thought Eretaia... I thought your sister liked Rasim?"

"Don't be soft!" Pericles said.

"But she—"

"You don't understand girls at all, do you, Macedonian?"

Sosi finally managed to take his eyes off Nike. The square steadied, and he felt a bit better. He took deep breaths. The priestess's wings had not reappeared, and she was no longer looking at him. She seemed more interested in talking to Eretaia. Perhaps he was letting his imagination run away with him, and the eagle he'd seen in Elis when Nike had vanished with his brother had been a normal eagle. Could there really be someone else like him in the world, who could shape-change?

The rest of that day was a confusion of new names, places, rules and procedures, leaving Sosi no time to sneak away and ask Nike the questions that were whirling in his head. He was a bit worried about the Olympic Oath, which included a solemn promise that they would not cheat at the Games. But although the priest's gaze lingered on him when he stumbled over the words, Zeus Horkios didn't throw his thunderbolts, no one accused him of cheating, and he was allowed to leave the Council House as "Theron of Macedonian Pella, son of Commander Sarapion and Lady Alcmena, competitor in the boys' sprint and the boys' wrestling at the 113th Olympiad, who has trained diligently for ten months and agrees to abide by all rules, regulations and punishments as decided by the Hellenic judges of the Great Games appointed by the State of Elis and sworn before Zeus Horkios." It made everything seem more official, and he shuddered to think of the judges' anger if they ever found out how he and Theron had deceived them.

By the time the boys were escorted to their dormitory on the top floor of the Prytaneon and allowed some peace, it was almost suppertime and Sosi felt so dizzy, he wondered if he might be coming down with a fever. The others chatted enthusiastically about the facilities they'd seen, but Sosi let their excitement wash over him and lay sweating on top of his blanket. He wanted to get a closer look at the statue of Nike Pericles had told him about, but he was sure Judge Demetrius had mentioned a rule that forbade them to wander about the Altis at night. At least there were no crimson-bearded Warriors in the building with them this time. Their guards, still jumpy after what had happened at Letrini, had made a thorough search before letting anyone inside.

Resolving to get up early and make some enquiries about his mother before breakfast, Sosi turned over and drifted off to sleep staring at the fire that, even on such a warm night, smouldered in the hearth of their dormitory.

"Help me get through this, Goddess Hestia," he whispered. "And I promise I'll never cheat again."

PART 3

OLYMPIA

Then gathering all the host and his rich spoils,
the valiant son of Zeus in Pisa
measured and founded
in his great father's name a holy precinct,
and fenced and marked out on clear ground the Altis...

(Olympian 10)

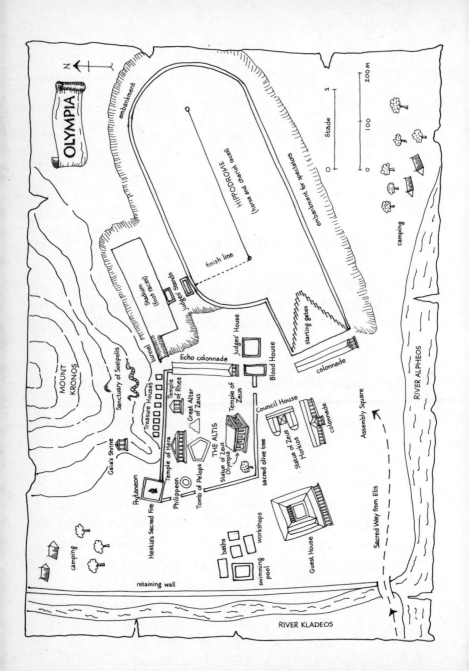

OLYMPIA

N

Stade
0   100   200 m

MOUNT KRONOS

Sanctuary of Sosipolis

embankment

HIPPODROME
(horse and chariot races)

embankment for spectators

finish line

Stadium
(foot races)

Judges' Stands

starting gates

colonnade

camping

RIVER ALPHEOS

tunnel

Echo colonnade

Judges' House

Blood House

Treasure Houses

Temple of Rhea

Great Altar of Zeus

Temple of Zeus

Council House

colonnade

Gaia's Shrine

Temple of Hera

THE ALTIS

Statue of Zeus Olympia

sacred olive tree

Statue of Zeus Horkios

Assembly Square

Prytaneon

Hestia's Sacred Fire

Philippeon

Tomb of Pelops

baths

workshops

swimming pool

Guest House

Sacred Way from Elis

camping

retaining wall

RIVER KLADEOS

Chapter 10

PHILIPPEON

THE ALTIS WAS *full of smoke and armed men. People
screamed and ran into the temples in their panic to claim
sanctuary from the gods. Sosi ran with them, only he was
too slow, and all the temple doors were barred to him.
Alone and frightened, he fled through the tunnel into the
stadium, where he found himself in the middle of a battle.*

*Men spilled blood on sand that had been raked smooth
for the Games, while a vast crowd cheered them on from
the spectators' bank. When Sosi emerged, someone in the
crowd pointed at him and yelled, "Snake-child!" He
stopped, trapped between the two armies, as every sword
and spear swung round and men of both sides glared
through the eye-slits of their helmets. With cries of hatred,
they rushed towards him.*

*Sosi's legs trembled. He tried to run, but the full moon
was in the sky and his curse came over him. Thunder*

crashed around the mountain they called Kronos. Lightning, flashing from the soldiers' shields, blinded him. He fell to the ground, pleading, "Don't hurt me, please don't!" But his body elongated and turned him into a snake before their eyes, taking away his power of speech.

Zeus threw a thunderbolt at him that struck the ground between the armies and burst into flame, distracting the soldiers and stopping the battle. Terrified, Sosi fled, while Nike chased him on the back of an eagle, shouting, "Meet me in the Philippeon! I know you can hear me, Sosipolis! Don't forget, the Philippeon..."

He jerked awake, bathed in sweat, as the echoes of a trumpet blast faded through the dormitory. Still trembling, he counted his fingers and toes. All there. Just another nightmare.

Around him, the other boys threw off their blankets and stretched, grumbling that it was as bad as the training camp at Elis. Sunrise reddened the window. Sosi cursed under his breath. He'd overslept, and now he wouldn't be able to get away until lunch time.

There followed a hard morning of training in the stadium under Trainer Hermon's stern eye, watched by their Elean guards and a few curious spectators whose presence seemed to encourage their trainer to use his whip more often. Only Pericles got off lightly, because his leg went numb during a bout of wrestling and he was sent in early to see the physician. By the time the rest of them were allowed to go to lunch, Sosi had lost two wrestling matches against Kallias, who wasn't even entered in the event, and had a fresh weal on his back for not paying attention, since he'd spent the morning worrying about his mother and wondering if Nike really could shape-change like him. Poor Dion, who had been given a stripe for inattention as well, was in tears.

"Too much excitement," Samos whispered, shaking his head. He waited until they were in the privacy of the tunnel, put an arm around the younger boy and drew him against the wall. "Steady, squirt. Take a moment to pull yourself together. That's right."

A few boys sneered at Dion as they barged past, but left off when Samos glared at them. Despite the fact they were supposed to stick together, Agis and Kallias had gone on ahead with the others. Sosi hesitated. The tunnel was dim and cool after the glare of the stadium. He shivered, reminded of his dream.

"You all right, Theron?" Samos said. "You seemed a bit distracted this morning. You don't have to wait."

Sosi shook his head, wishing for the thousandth time that he could explain about his curse. He glanced at Dion and blurted out, "Have either of you had any strange dreams lately?"

"What sort of dreams?"

"Anything to do with Olympia."

Samos chuckled. "Have I dreamt of victory, you mean? Not yet, though I'm still hoping! You had any victory dreams recently, squirt?"

Dion wriggled out from under Samos' arm. "I don't remember. I'm always too worn out after slave-driver Hermon's finished with us to dream."

Samos laughed again. "There you go! I'm surprised any of us have the energy to dream. You'll be all right now, squirt. Go on in and grab some lunch before the others scoff it all." He smiled as the younger boy ran out of the tunnel, then sobered. "What's all this sudden interest in dreams, Theron? What with your victory dream back in Elis, and you trying to tell us that Warrior at Letrini had risen from the dead, you're turning all mystical on us. If you're not careful, you'll end up as a priest instead of an Olympic champion!"

Sosi wished he hadn't said anything. But Samos had taken his theories seriously before. "You know Priestess Nike's game of picking winners, and how I thought that might be how the Warriors decide who to target next?" he began. Samos nodded, and he took a deep breath. "I think it's connected somehow with our dreams. I found out yesterday that Pericles had a dream of victory the night before that chariot tried to run him down in Elis, and you already know my... I had a similar dream before that javelin went through my foot. It can't just be coincidence."

In the gloom of the tunnel, Samos' eyes glittered. "Pericles dreamt of victory, huh? He kept that quiet!"

Sosi licked his lips and said, "I had a strange dream last night, too. There was a battle in the stadium, and a thunderbolt struck the ground between the armies." *And I changed into a snake, and Nike told me to meet her in the Philippeon.* "What if it was a warning of some kind? What if the Persian army is planning to attack Olympia, and they sent the Warriors here to weaken us with magic? I'm not

150

the only one who thinks the Warriors are sorcerers. Nike thinks there's something odd about them, too."

Samos gave him a gentle thump. "Get real, Theron! The Persians are too busy fighting Macedonians to think about invading us. When did you get a chance to speak to Nike, anyway, you sly thing? Slave-driver Hermon doesn't give us time off to breathe, let alone talk to girls."

He almost told Samos about his curse and how he suspected Nike of having one, too. But he swallowed the words in time. "The Warriors use magic and I'm pretty certain Nike does, too. Maybe they're trying to steal her powers?"

The Elean boy shook his head with a smile. "I told you, the Warriors are human. So is Nike. Sorcery is just tricks and dreams."

"Why has Pericles' leg gone numb, then?" Sosi said, frustrated. "It's the same leg the Warrior touched with his purple flame at Letrini."

"I'm sure there's a perfectly reasonable explanation," Samos said. "Look, Theron, let's forget the Warriors for a bit, huh? They won't get into the Altis, don't worry. There are enough guards crawling round this place to keep out King Alexander's entire army! Are you coming to lunch?"

Sosi shook his head. "I've got to see someone first."

Samos hesitated. "Pericles said we ought to stick together."

"This is the Altis, remember? You just said the Warriors can't get in, so there's nothing to worry about, is there? I won't leave the enclosure on my own. I'm not stupid."

The Elean boy shrugged and headed for the Prytaneon. Sosi watched him go, feeling bad. Samos had only been trying to help.

He eyed the statues and temples. If lunch here followed the same schedule as Elis, he had a bit of time before Trainer Hermon started looking for him. He should make the most of it to search for his mother, but he was unlikely to find her inside the Altis. Telling himself there was a good chance Nike would know where Lady Alcmena was, he headed for the Philippeon.

The circular building, built by King Alexander's father Philip to house the statues of Macedonian champions, seemed deserted. Its yellow columns glowed, and the bronze poppy head on its roof glittered in the sun. A low doorway led into shadows. Yesterday, on their tour, Dion had asked if Theron's statue would be put in there as well if he won the boys' sprint – a comment that had sent Agis into a predictable sulk. Sosi had risked Judge Demetrius' wrath by lingering behind the others to look through the door, but hadn't dared go inside. Now, when there was no one to stop him, he hesitated, his skin prickling. This was the time to make up his mind if he believed in dreams.

A musty smell came from inside. Feeling a bit foolish, he whispered, "Nike? Are you in there?"

"Of course I'm here!" The priestess emerged from behind the statues and regarded him with her hands on her hips. "You took your time, I must say! I've got better things to do than hang around here all day waiting for you, Sosipolis!"

Mixed emotions flooded Sosi... relief, embarrassment, and more than a little fear. Sosipolis. It was the name she'd used in his dream.

Before he could say anything, Nike seized his wrist and dragged him behind one of the statues, where a dark space had been left by the curve of the wall. The musty smell was stronger here. Feathers floated around their feet. Scowling, Nike picked one out of her sandal and fixed him with her yellow stare.

"Listen," she said. "We're in more trouble than I thought! These Warriors of Ahriman aren't just normal terrorists. They're—"

"Dead," Sosi said.

He'd surprised her. She stiffened, and the feathers stirred in a draught. "Dead? How do you know?"

"I can't see their body heat. And it's the only thing that explains why the bodies keep disappearing, and how that Warrior got into our dormitory at Letrini."

Nike let out her breath. "Of course! You have the snake's heat-sense." She paused, thinking. "I was going to say they're sorcerers, but if you're right it would explain a few things that have been puzzling me. Oh, Zeus, we are in trouble! I didn't realize at Elis how powerful they were, but my senses always sharpen as the Games approach. I expect you find the same with the full moon?" She rushed on without giving him a chance to answer. "I still don't know what the Warriors want, but if they're using magic your brother's foot won't get better with any kind of herbs, and nor will Pericles' leg. The victims will only recover if we break the enchantment at its source. It won't be easy, especially if you're right about them having risen from the dead, because we can't just kill them."

"Hold on!" Sosi said, sensing that the conversation was in danger of leaving him more confused than ever. "Is my brother all right? Do you know where my mother's hiding? Because I need to see her. And what have you got to do with our dreams? Last night, I dreamt of a battle, and you were in it too..."

Nike shook her head impatiently. "Of course you did! It's part of your old memories, and of course I was in it. How else was I supposed to get a message to you? Those Elean soldiers have you boys watched more closely than criminals. Stop wasting time asking idiotic questions, and let's concentrate on the problem at hand, shall we? I've told you already, this could be *serious* for me!"

"It could be *serious* for me, *too*!" Sosi shouted back. He didn't know what scared him the most – that Nike believed him about the Warriors of Ahriman being dead, or her telling him things about himself that he didn't remember.

"Shh!" Nike said, slamming her hand over his mouth and pulling him down behind the statue. Sosi froze as feet crunched the gravel outside. A head darkened the doorway, then withdrew. After a moment, the feet crunched away again.

"Only old Priest Rhexibius," Nike said with a sigh. "It's all right, you can relax. I don't think he saw us."

Sosi stayed in a crouch, staring at her. Like when he'd seen her with Eretaia on the steps of the Hippodrome

Colonnade, ghostly wings surrounded her. The feathers formed a golden cloak that floated down to enclose them both. The musty smell increased, and he broke into a sweat.

"Oh, stop staring!" Nike said, pushing the wings aside. "I only do it when something upsets me. It's a reflex, all right? I can't help it."

Her wings were fading. Sosi blinked, shuddered, and picked up a feather. It felt real enough. He wet his lips, remembering the way she'd vanished in the barley field at Elis. "You *are* like me, aren't you? It's not just in our dreams. You really *can* change your shape. Oh, this is so strange..."

"I'm not a bit like you." Nike scowled. "I'm part eagle, not part snake. You know very well it's different for me. Do get up. And stop poking those feathers around! I bet you don't like people messing with your old skin after you've shed it."

Sosi's head spun. "Do you...? Do we...?" All his questions flooded out. The things he'd wanted to ask his mother about his curse, but never dared to. Everything that had made him sick with anxiety and fear throughout the long, lonely years of his childhood.

Nike's expression passed from irritation through surprise and impatience to something approaching sympathy. "Are you telling me you don't remember anything? I thought you were acting strange in Elis! Oh, Zeus, that's all we need."

Sosi bit his lip. He couldn't seem to stop shivering. "Remind me," he said.

He listened in a mixture of disbelief and terror as Nike

calmly told him how he'd lived many times before, and was the immortal snake-child Sosipolis, whose name meant "saviour". It was worse than Sosi had ever suspected. According to Nike, he wasn't merely a boy with a strange, snaky curse, but some kind of ancient demon. When he was needed in the world, he had the power to reincarnate himself in the body of an unborn child so that he could protect the Olympic Games. The last time had been thirty-six years ago when, exactly as in his dream, he had stopped a battle between the Eleans and the Arcadians in the Olympic Stadium.

Nike was clearly annoyed that she'd had to explain everything. Sosi stared at her, dumbfounded. He couldn't take it in. He wanted to scream that he wasn't half snake, he wasn't immortal, he was just a normal Macedonian boy… but, deep down where his nightmares came from, something dark stirred in response to her words.

"I still don't remember," he whispered.

Nike grimaced. "I can see that. What on earth did you think when you first shed your skin?"

"I thought I was cursed," Sosi said, shivering. "I was only four when it first happened. Mother used to beat me for it."

"Your mother beat you so you wouldn't shape-change?"
He nodded.

"But that's awful!" Nike shook her head. "I hope the Judges do discover her here during the Games! It'd serve her right. Perhaps I'll tell them where to look."

"No!" Sosi grabbed her arm, forgetting the wings. A

few feathers came off in his hand. "Please, Nike! Don't."

"Oh, don't panic, I won't. It'd only put the other women in danger. But you must hate her. Fancy beating you for trying to be yourself! No doubt it's her fault you lost your memory in the first place. At least my mother tried to help me when I started changing shape. If you learn how to control it early on, things are much easier."

"I think she was scared," Sosi said, his fear receding as he realized knowing the truth changed nothing. "Father got so angry when I changed shape. Theron didn't like it much, either. I kept copying his body when I was little."

"Huh!" Nike snorted. "Seems to me he liked it well enough to let you take his shape and train in his place at Elis! Didn't you ever try anything else? An animal? Or a girl?"

Sosi shook his head, feeling stupid and scared at the same time. Did she really think he'd have wanted to be a girl? "I was too afraid to experiment much, and all I really wanted to be was like Theron. He was so handsome and athletic, and he was older than me and allowed to stay up longer, and everybody loved him."

Nike pulled a face. "It's not surprising, I suppose. If no one ever told you how special you were or what you could do, how were you supposed to know what was possible? Perhaps it's just as well. If your family didn't like you changing into your big brother, I hate to imagine the panic you'd have caused if you'd become a snake! You learnt your mother's lessons too well. You're so good at hiding your snake half, I thought you were twins when I first saw you together."

"Pain's a good incentive," Sosi said, touching the weal on his back. Was it really possible to change himself into a snake?

Nike eyed him warily, then laughed and punched him on the shoulder with as much force as Samos would have. "You'll be all right, Sosipolis! I expect your memory will start to come back now you're here. I don't suppose growing up in the wilds of Macedonia helped much."

Sosi shivered. "What happened to the last Sosipolis... I mean, me... last time?"

Nike waved a hand. "Oh, after he changed into a snake to stop the battle, he couldn't change back again. He used to hole up in the old sanctuary where the married women hide while they're here. Makes sense, I suppose. Best place to see if one of them was pregnant so you could reincarnate yourself."

Sosi turned even colder. "What old sanctuary? It wasn't on our tour."

"Of course not. It never was included in the modern ceremonies. The old earth-spirits aren't popular these days. The judges ordered temples built for the goddesses Hera and Rhea, and they keep Hestia's fire burning in the Prytaneon, but everything else in Olympia is to do with men and their glory. All these statues, everywhere! And all their stupid rules. They'd cancel the girls' games if they could – though if these Persian terrorists get their way, they might have to cancel the men's and boys' games too." Her wings glimmered around her. "I wouldn't mind so much if I could work out what the Warriors are up to. It's playing havoc with my Olympic duties. I have to pick at least some of the winners correctly or I lose my shape-changing powers for the whole Olympiad. And if you boys that I have chosen don't win, I'll be too weak to open the channel to the gods at the Great Sacrifice."

It took Sosi a moment to work out that she was referring to their victory dreams. "Have you chosen anyone for the boys' boxing yet?" he asked, relieved to get back to something he could understand.

Nike smiled. "Not yet, but I know who I'm going to choose. I'm just leaving it a bit longer to make sure the warriors don't get to him."

"Samos?"

She pulled a face. "Of course Samos. Who else? But don't you go telling anyone!"

"I'm not that stupid," Sosi said.

"Good." Nike fixed him once more with her yellow gaze. "Because unless we find a way to defeat the warriors' magic, I've already lost power from Theron in the sprint, Pericles in the wrestling, and Rasim in the horse race. That's more than enough to stop me flying, so if there is trouble at the Games, I'm afraid I won't be much help."

"Can you really fly?" Sosi asked, curiosity overcoming his fear.

Nike laughed. "How do you think I got back from Elis so quickly?"

"Then I... What can I do?" Sosi said, dry-mouthed. "Can I fly, too?"

"Snakes can't fly, silly!" laughed Nike. "But you can see living bodies in the dark and you can change your skin at the full moon and take any shape you believe you can become. Isn't that enough?"

Sosi coloured. Nike was just an ugly girl again as she peered out of the door and hissed, "Your trainer's coming. Looks like the others have finished lunch. I'd better go. I've still got to decide who's going to win the men's events – not that I'll be sending them any victory dreams until we know more about what these Warriors are up to, but I need to get back to Elis and watch them train. Don't do anything stupid while I'm away, Sosipolis, will you? Look after the other boys. When I get back, we'll make a plan for the festival. Enjoy your afternoon!" She ducked out of the Philippeon.

"Wait!" Sosi called after her. "You forgot to tell me where the old sanctuary is...!"

But Nike had vanished, exactly as she had in the field at Elis.

Trainer Hermon marched into the Philippeon and dragged Sosi out by one arm. "Thought I'd find you in here, Macedonian!" he said. "Getting delusions of grandeur, are we? At the rate you're going, you'll be last in the sprint and knocked out in the first round of the wrestling. Some of you boys seem to be using the threat of these Warriors as an excuse for not training properly. No terrorist is going to get within a hundred stades of Olympia, so snap out of it and get back to the stadium before I report you to Judge Demetrius."

Chapter 11

SANCTUARY

THE ENCOUNTER WITH Nike left Sosi feeling more anxious than ever; being told half of something was worse than not knowing at all. *I've been here before. I changed into a snake. I couldn't change back.* He needed more answers, but his enquiries about the old sanctuary turned up only myth and rumour, and there was no one he could talk to until Nike returned from Elis. He wished he had wings like her, instead of his silly shape-changing ability that was dependent on the moon. Then he could fly far away from Olympia and whatever terrible fate awaited him. Except he couldn't flee, because he had sworn the Olympic oath as Theron, and either he or his brother had to run the boys' sprint well enough to persuade their father to let Theron become a professional athlete, or all their efforts would be for nothing.

The boys settled into a routine similar to the one at Elis. They were fit now, which meant the training was easier. Sosi felt tired by the end of the day, but pleasantly so, his muscles stretched and his body was more relaxed than usual at this time of the month when his curse approached. Despite the terrifying, half-glimpsed dreams that returned nightly, no crimson-bearded men showed themselves at Olympia, and there were no more "accidents". Their discussions about the terrorists changed to arguments about fitness and tactics as the boys became more and more excited about the coming events. Only Pericles, with his leg that some days was fine and other days suddenly went numb, and Eretaia, who had the job of massaging it with herbal remedies, shared Sosi's anxiety.

Every day yet more people arrived at the camp sites, crowded the embankments around the stadium and the Hippodrome, and came on guided tours of the Altis. But there was still no sign of Nike. Two days before the opening ceremony, when the men would be setting out from Elis, Sosi decided he couldn't wait any longer. He had to find his mother and talk to her about the truth behind his curse.

He lingered in the stadium after training had finished for the day, watching the groundsmen rake the course in a cloud of amber dust. The other boys straggled back to the Altis to fetch their strigils and oils for the baths, chatting quietly to one another. Since there had been no trouble so far at Olympia, the guards were not as nervous as they had been on the first day, and no one called for Sosi to keep up. The sun, setting over the River Kladeos, turned the ornaments on the roofs of the Altis to fire. A three-quarter moon hung low in the sky over the slopes of Mount Kronos, reminding him how little time he had before his curse came over him again.

He closed his eyes and tried to think like a snake.

There were several versions of the story about the boy who had changed into a snake to stop the Eleans and Arcadians fighting, but opinion was divided as to where he had gone after the battle. Sosi's nightmares ended with him fleeing in panic when the thunderbolt fell, but the direction was frustratingly unclear. The snake wouldn't have gone south to the Hippodrome, though. It was always full of horses, and he'd have wanted to avoid them. Through the tunnel to the Altis? Maybe, since it was dark and cool, but that was where he'd run from originally. That left north up the slopes of Mount Kronos, or east across the plain. The armies would have used the flat eastern route – which left the mountainside with its rocks and caves. Sosi's stomach fluttered as he remembered how the mountain had drawn his gaze on his first day at Olympia. A sanctuary didn't have to be a building. A cave would make a good hiding place for the married women.

He remembered getting to his feet and climbing the spectators' bank to reach the rocky slope beyond, thinking maybe he'd have time to look for the sanctuary before the boys got back from the baths. Then his head began to itch... and the next thing he knew, he was underground with no memory of how he'd got there.

A stone rolled nearby, and Sosi flattened himself to the rock in confusion and terror. Light flickered ahead, casting a deformed shadow around the tunnel walls. An old woman, bent under the weight of a basket and carrying a clay lantern, emerged from a side tunnel barely five paces in front of him and disappeared into another opening further along. The light disappeared with her. Pure, human panic sent Sosi racing after it.

The woman wasn't hard to follow. She grumbled under her breath, and her body heat glowed in the gloom. Still trying to remember how he'd got into the caves, Sosi followed her down some rough steps. He kept touching his face to check he was human. Then he heard voices up ahead and a burst of girlish laughter, and remembered why he'd come.

His guide hurried into a well-lit cavern, to be greeted by excited questions. There came the sound of things being unloaded from the basket, and the smell of fresh bread and cheese. Sosi listened for his mother's voice, but couldn't recognize it among the others. While he was trying to decide what to do, the old woman came back out again carrying an amphora. She bustled up another side tunnel, stopped at an alcove where red gauze shimmered across the entrance, and said, "Lady Alcmena? I've brought your medicine."

Sosi's triumph at having found the women's sanctuary was replaced by tension. *Her* medicine? Was his mother sick?

He crept closer. The woman he'd followed was doing most of the talking. His mother whispered a question he couldn't hear, and the other woman said, "He's just fine, dearie, so don't you worry. He's training well. Drink this, and I promise you'll be better in time to see him crowned. Try to rest. Worrying won't help you recover."

The old woman emerged without the amphora. Sosi counted to a hundred to make sure she wasn't coming back, and hurried into the alcove. "Mother?" he whispered. "It's me."

His eyes watered in a cloud of herbal smoke coming from a brazier. His mother lay on a couch, her hair loose and her forehead beaded with sweat. Her eyes glittered with fever.

For a moment he didn't think she recognized him. Then her face lit up. "Theron!" she cried, and tried to sit up. "Are you really here? I must be dreaming again."

Sosi knelt by the couch and gripped her hand. He did wonder if he might be dreaming, too, but her touch was hot and sticky, and the cave had a bad smell under the scent of the herbs. "Mother, you're not dreaming. It's me – Sosi. I took Theron's shape, remember?"

She frowned a little. Then she looked down at his foot, and her face twisted in disappointment. "What are *you* doing here?"

"I followed that woman who brought your medicine. How long have you been like this, Mother? You need to see a physician—"

"Never mind me!" She struggled into a sitting position, refusing Sosi's help. "Where's your brother? What are you doing at Olympia? You're not supposed to be seen together!"

"There's... been some trouble. We had to come to Olympia early." How much did she know about the Warriors of Ahriman? He drew a deep breath. "That javelin hitting Theron wasn't an accident. We think it was thrown by a Persian terrorist, and that they're going to try to stop the Games. Theron's still in Elis. He's too ill to travel, so it looks like I'm going to have to compete in his place."

His mother broke into a fit of coughing. She took a gulp from the amphora and shook her head. "Don't be stupid, Sosi. He's here. His foot's better. I've had reports."

Sosi bit his tongue. He seized his mother's arm and snatched away the medicine. "Don't you understand? The reports were of me. Theron's wound was poisoned by enchantment! It won't get better until we defeat the Warrior of Ahriman who threw that javelin. I met a girl who is like me, except she changes into an eagle. She's gone to Elis to pick the men's winners, because she gets her power by sending victory dreams to the athletes – but it only works if they win. She's already in trouble because the Warrior is targeting the boys she picked to win their events. She knows all about me and Theron, and she told me all sorts of stuff about my curse. I've started to remember things... I've been here before. I had a dream about a battle I stopped. When you came here twelve years ago, you were pregnant, weren't you? I took the shape of your unborn child."

Lady Alcmena glared at him. She tried to free her wrist, but Olympic training had hardened Sosi's muscles and he held her easily.

"Let go of me!" she hissed. "Or I'll take the whip to you! You're not too old yet."

Sosi tightened his grip. "Did you see the snake-boy last time you were here? Do you know what happened to him? Tell me about my powers!"

"You haven't got any powers! You're cursed, you've ruined my life..." But her eyes slid away from his, and she blinked at the gauze. The women's laughter could still be heard faintly along the tunnel. "Wait until you change back to your own shape," she whispered. "I'll teach you a lesson you won't forget."

"I might not change back," Sosi said, also softly. "I might change into a snake and never be a boy again."

His mother paled. "Oh, Sosi... I knew it was a mistake to let you come to the Games with us. Please don't make me angry. I don't feel well..." She closed her eyes and slumped against the cushions.

Alarmed, Sosi cradled her head and tried to get her to drink some more of the medicine, but it dribbled out of her slack mouth. While he hesitated, not knowing what to do, the gauze was snatched back. The old woman he'd followed through the tunnels stared in at him. "Who are you?" she demanded. "How did you get in here? Leave Lady Alcmena alone!"

"She's my mother," Sosi said. "She's sick. You can't keep her down here like this."

The old woman frowned. "How did you find us? No one would have told a boy about our sanctuary! The women's lips are sealed."

Sosi stayed silent. He couldn't tell her if he didn't know himself.

Lady Alcmena moaned, and the woman pushed Sosi out of the way and rushed to her side. "You boys!" she tutted. "You've no idea how to treat the sick! Get out of here. Go and wait for me in the cave with the others. I expect they'll have masses of questions for you, but it serves you right for sneaking down here. Go on, out!"

Sosi had little choice. His mother seemed to have slipped back into her fever. He hesitated outside the alcove, watching the two women – old and young – through the red gauze, his stomach doing strange things. Their mother must be really ill if she hadn't been able to get back to Elis to help her favourite son. He wanted to rush back in and apologize for upsetting her, except she wouldn't be able to hear him now.

He eyed the cavern mouth where the women's laughter spilled out. He meant to creep past and try to find his own way out of the tunnels. But suddenly he was furious with the mothers for being here, when the law said they could be thrown over the cliff if they were discovered, and their husbands and sons could be disqualified from competing in the Circuit Games for life.

He burst into the cave. "You're all selfish!" he shouted into the sudden silence. "Don't you care about getting your sons disqualified? How did my mother get ill? Tell me!"

Seven women stared at him, frozen in shock. He had time to see their cavern was decorated with rugs, cushions, jewelled perfume bottles, spare chitons, cloaks and bangles, all strewn around in a homely mess. Then one of the women said, "It's Theron, isn't it? Alcmena's Theron?" And they all started asking questions at once. How their sons were getting on with their training, if they were eating properly, if they'd been whipped much by their trainer...

Sosi put his hands over his ears. "Tell me how my mother got sick!" he demanded. "Tell me!"

The cavern quietened as the woman who had recognized him raised a hand. She smiled at Sosi, and his fury subsided a little when he saw it was Pericles' mother.

"We're sorry your mother's ill, Theron," she said gently. "She was sick when we got here. Priestess Eileithyia found her wandering in the tunnels in the dark, raving about purple fire. She's been down here before, I gather, some years ago, but she didn't seem to know where she was. Eileithyia thinks she must have dropped her lamp and fallen and hit her head in the dark. She'll get better, Theron, don't worry. Old Eileithyia's good with herbs. How's your foot holding up? And how's Pericles? Eretaia tells me he had some trouble with his leg. Won't stop him for long, though, knowing my boy!"

Sosi hardly heard anything past "purple fire". A chill went down his spine as he recalled the Warrior's words back in Letrini. *I can hurt you in other ways. I know where your mother is.*

"You've got to leave this place!" he said. "It's dangerous for you here!"

Pericles' mother smiled. "Don't you worry about us. We know how to hide if anyone comes."

The others nodded, and a shy young woman at the back of the cave asked, "How's my Dion? He was so excited about coming here. You're competing against him in the boys' sprint, aren't you? How's he holding up against the older boys?"

Sosi blinked at her, distracted. "Dion's fine."

"And Glaukos?" ... "And Milo?" They fired names at him.

He shook his head. "You've got to listen to me. Please! It's not just that the judges might find you here. You remember that Persian terrorist they caught in Elis? Well, at least one of the terrorists is still at large, and I think he knows about this place. You've got to go back to Elis and take my mother with you, right now!"

The women smiled at one another. Clearly, they still thought him a child.

"Priestess Eileithyia says there's been no sign of the terrorists at Olympia," Pericles' mother said. "Maybe they've given up?"

"They haven't given up!" Sosi said, unable to believe

grown women could be so stupid. "You have to believe me! That purple fire my mother saw—"

"Was a fever dream," the old priestess Eileithyia said firmly, bustling into the cavern. "She's sleeping now. She'll be a lot better when she wakes. But if you don't get back to the Prytaneon before the guards make their rounds, my boy, you'll be disqualified from the Games, and that'll upset her all right. Come on. Out."

Sosi followed the priestess through the maze of tunnels, his skin prickling at the thought of dead Warriors watching them, unseen, from the darkness. He was so busy looking over his shoulder that, when Eileithyia stopped and swung her lantern into his face, he jerked back in surprise. They were in another cave, surrounded by shadowy heaps that smelled musty and strangely familiar. A boulder near the entrance looked as if it could be rolled across to seal it. He experienced a flicker of unease.

"Right!" Eileithyia said, setting down the lantern. "How did you get in here? I know you didn't follow me from the Altis. I'm cleverer than that, after all my years caring for this place! So who told you where to come?"

Sosi swallowed. "I worked it out by myself." The smell of the cave was making him feel faint. He touched one of the heaps and broke into a sweat. *Snakeskins*. "This is the place, isn't it?" he whispered. "This is where the boy who changed into a snake fled after the battle."

Eileithyia chuckled. "Quite so. No one else knows the way to this cave. I'm not moving another step until you tell me the truth. You can try to find your own way out if you like, but the oil's almost gone. It gets very dark down here, and there are shafts that will kill you if you fall down them." She eyed his trembling in amusement. "Not so brave now are you, dearie? Well? I'm waiting."

Sosi sank into the skins and hugged himself. "He died in here." The trembling wouldn't stop.

Eileithyia huffed impatiently and shook her head. "Your mother told you that, I suppose. Oh, stop it. I thought you were tougher than that... a boy your age! I'm not showing you the way out until you tell me how you found this place. Better be quick. The lantern's about to go out."

Sosi attempted to pull himself together, but it was like a waking nightmare. The walls of the cave closed in on him. He picked up one of the skins and clutched it to his chest, staring around at the heaps. So many of them. Thirty-six years since the battle, Nike had said, and it had been twelve years ago when his mother came here, pregnant. How long did that leave? "He tried to change back into a boy, didn't he?" he whispered. "What happened? Why couldn't he? Twenty-four years of shedding his skin down here."

Eileithyia sucked in her breath. "How do you know how long it was?"

"Because..." Sosi closed his mouth. He dared not tell her about his curse.

The old priestess shook her head. "Stop trying to change the subject. How did you find us?"

Sosi closed his eyes. "I don't remember." *I don't remember dying, either.*

Eileithyia let him sweat a bit longer, then grunted. "I reckon it was that girl Eretaia who told you how to find this place. I'll have words with her later. I should never have let so many of the women come, but they're worried sick about their boys this year with these Persian terrorists about." She picked up the lantern with a sigh. "All right, let's get you out of here before you faint on me. Never seen a boy so scared of a few old snakeskins! Maybe I should seal you in here for bit, like I used to do to my son – might teach you not to go poking your nose where you shouldn't next time. Remember! You breathe a word to anyone about this place, and your mother will be thrown over the cliff with the rest of them. The other boys can't know their mothers are down here. It has to be that way. Understand?"

The rest of the journey was a blur. Sosi followed the old priestess on numb legs, the snakeskin clasped to his breast. *My son?* Had he been Priestess Eileithyia's son in his past life? It was too strange to think about.

His fear did not ease until moonlight showed ahead and they emerged on the mountainside in the night air. Eileithyia urged him up the slope rather than down, puffing and wheezing, taking a twisty route that brought them over the ridge and down to the plain beside the Kladeos campsite. "You're on your own from here," she said. "If you get caught creeping back in, you can always make up some excuse about seeing a sweetheart. If it gets you whipped, that's your own lookout. Give me that thing. I'll get rid of it."

Before she could touch it, Sosi stuffed the snakeskin inside his tunic and broke into a run. The air and the exercise cleared his thoughts. He raised his face to the moon and took deep breaths that, although tainted with smells of burnt meat and sewage from the camp, seemed gloriously sweet after the snake cave.

"That won't happen to me," he chanted fiercely as he ran. "It won't, it *won't!*"

Chapter 12

TEMPLE OF ZEUS

SOMEONE WAS SHAKING him.

Sosi opened one eye, saw it was not yet properly light, and rolled over with a groan. He thought he'd got used to the dreams, but last night's had beaten them all. He could still smell the dark tunnels, his mother's fever-sweat smothered by herbs, and the cave of snakeskins.

The hand shaking his shoulder grew more insistent and a voice hissed, "Theron? Wake up, for Zeus' sake!"

He opened his other eye to see a large shadow bending over him, jerked upright with his heart pounding, and focused on Samos' concerned face.

"Steady! It's me. I have to talk to you before the others wake up. What's *that*?" Samos stared at the snakeskin that had been exposed when Sosi threw off his blanket. In the dawn, it was smoke-black.

"Nothing." Sosi stuffed the skin under his blanket and

glanced around the dormitory. All seemed normal. The other boys were stirring in anticipation of the trumpet call, their bodies trained to wake at sunrise as surely as they had been trained to run, punch and wrestle. "What's wrong?"

"What's *wrong*, he says!" Samos perched on the edge of his pallet and shook his head. "Where were you last night? I bundled your clothes under your blanket for you, like I used to do for Pericles back in Elis, so the guards wouldn't get suspicious. But I thought we agreed, no creeping off on our own? The others said you'd probably gone to the Blood House for a checkup on your foot. They didn't seem worried, but I stayed awake half the night afraid you'd been kidnapped by Warriors. I was going to alert the guards if you didn't come back, only I fell asleep..." He leant closer, his face tight with excitement. "I had a dream," he breathed.

Sosi stared at him in confusion. Had Samos dreamt of the snake cave, too? "What sort of dream?" he said.

The Elean boy pulled a face. "You know. Victory. She flew in through the window, and she had eagle's wings, just like you said! She told me I would win the boys' boxing, simple as that." He looked pleased, but a little worried, too. He glanced over his shoulder. "I'm not boasting, Theron. I just wanted to warn you, in case anything happens to me." He grinned and added quickly, "Not that it will, not here at Olympia. I reckon those Warriors of Ahriman are too scared of Zeus' thunderbolts!"

Sosi gripped the snakeskin tightly under his blanket. "Priestess Nike's back? Are you sure?"

Samos frowned. "I didn't see *that* Nike, silly. The Victory I saw in my dream was beautiful, a goddess." He grinned again. "I'll show you exactly what she looked like today. That's the other thing I wanted to warn you about. You weren't at supper last night, so you didn't hear. We've got the day off training! Most of the Eleans are being sent back along the Sacred Way to meet the other athletes and judges, and Judge Demetrius has decided we'll be safer if we stay inside the Altis until they get back. We're to have an official tour of the temples instead. Wait until you see the statue of Victory in the hand of Zeus Olympia! You'll soon forget that big-nosed priestess, believe me."

Sosi's brain was catching up. Last night hadn't been a dream. He had one of his old skins from his previous life to prove it. And Nike must be back from Elis, or Samos wouldn't have dreamt of victory.

"Which temple does Nike work in?" he asked urgently. "I have to talk to her."

Samos smiled. "Still interested in her, Theron? Don't worry, she's not likely to miss the Games. I expect she's travelling with the procession from Elis."

"*Which temple?*" he insisted.

"How would I know?" Samos frowned. "Ask Eretaia. She's coming on the tour today."

There was no time for further talk because the Prytaneon vibrated with the morning trumpet blast blown in the Echo Colonnade. Boys threw off their blankets and rummaged for the stained loincloths they wore for exercise. There was a pause as they remembered today was different. Then an excited murmur broke out as everyone dropped their oils and strigils, hunting instead for their sandals and best tunics.

Their tour guide turned out to be the large-bellied Priest Rhexibius, who had witnessed their Olympic oaths on the first day. As a senior priest of the Altis, he was very knowledgeable, but he spoke in a monotone that quickly became boring. Only Dion, still wide-eyed about being at Olympia, pushed to the front and listened to every word.

Sosi trailed behind the others, thinking about the old priestess who had taken him to the snake cave, and looking in vain for Nike. He'd asked Eretaia where she was, but the girl hadn't even known her friend was back, and as the tour wore on he began to have doubts himself. They visited the temples of the goddesses Hera and Rhea and admired the carvings at the tops of the columns. They were told the sponsor of every single treasury and were allowed to handle the offerings inside, which was quite interesting the first few times but soon lost its appeal. They gazed up at the Great Altar of Zeus, a huge hill of ashes three times the height of a man, while the priest told them how it had been sited on the spot where a thunderbolt, thrown by the King of the Gods from distant Mount Olympus, had struck the ground. They heard how the legendary strongman, Hercules, had founded the Games at Olympia to celebrate men's glory and strength. They stood under the sacred olive tree, while their guide told them how the prize at the Games used to be an apple, but an oracle had told the King of Elis to crown victors with a wreath from this very tree. And they sneered at the Tomb of Pelops, a disappointing mound of earth where a hero was supposed to be buried.

By the time they reached the statue of the goddess Nike on its tall pillar in front of the Temple of Zeus, everyone was hot and sticky under their tunics and impatient for lunch. Sosi did his best to pay attention to what their guide was saying, but it was boring stuff about how long the statue had taken the sculptor to complete, how high the pillar was, and how much marble and gold leaf had been used in its construction. His neck ached with looking up, and the sun glinting off Nike's gold-plated wings gave him a headache. He decided the sculptor must have been an idiot, anyway, because no one with wings of her own would have much reason to ride an eagle.

Finally, Priest Rhexibius beckoned them to follow him up the steps of the great temple itself, and paused dramatically in front of the doors. "I've kept the best to last," he announced, opening one of the doors a crack. "How many of you have been inside here before?"

Only Pericles, Samos, Eretaia and one or two of the older boys raised their hands. The rest of them quietened. The Temple of Zeus was nearly always closed when they passed it, and they were curious enough to crane their necks in an attempt to see inside.

Priest Rhexibius smiled. "When you first go in, it's a good idea to stop for a moment to let your eyes adjust. It's quite dark in there. I won't spoil the surprise for you. Visitors can never quite believe what they're seeing the first time. Go on in and wait for me by the pool. You men can relax. There are no enemies inside the Temple of Zeus Olympia."

The small detachment of Elean soldiers accompanying them on the tour did not look convinced. Two of them insisted on going in ahead of the boys to check out the interior. The others spaced themselves around the steps to keep watch.

Sosi's skin prickled, but Eretaia tugged her brother's hand. "Come on," she said. "I want to see everyone's reactions!"

Pericles, whose temper had been slowly deteriorating throughout the tour, grunted and rubbed his leg. "We're not tourists," he muttered. "This whole day's a stupid waste of time, if you ask me. I need to sit down. I've already seen the Zeus." He sat on the temple steps in the shade around the side and stretched out his legs with a sigh.

At once, Eretaia knelt beside him. "Is your leg giving you trouble again?"

"It's fine." Pericles pushed her concerned hands away. "I expect it's all the standing around listening to that priest! If he talks much more, his tongue'll drop off. I'll be all right, sis, don't worry. You go on in."

Samos hesitated. "I'm not sure you should stay out here on your own. I've seen the Zeus, too. I'll wait with you."

"Don't be stupid," Pericles said. "I don't need a nursemaid!"

"You're the one who said we should stick together until we find out what the Warriors are up to," Samos said. "And you shouldn't sit there. Those waterspouts are always falling off the roof. One of them might hit you."

"Oh, this is ridiculous!" Pericles clambered to his feet again. "All right, fine, we'll go in together. You're acting as if there are Warriors in every shadow."

Which there might well be, Sosi thought with another shiver. *And I wouldn't see them.*

Because of this, they were the last to go inside. The doors swung shut behind them, cutting out the sunlight with a thud. Priest Rhexibius had not been exaggerating. The Temple of Zeus had no windows and was gloomily lit. Sosi was very aware of Eretaia's hand gripping his in the shadows, and of Samos and Pericles breathing behind him.

His snake senses took over. The boys' heat pulses moved slowly around the interior, vanishing and reappearing from behind the huge columns. They were whispering, as if afraid to raise their voices in the presence of the god. When his eyes adjusted, Sosi realized the columns were in two tiers, the lower ones supporting a gallery that ran the length of the temple, the upper ones reaching to a vaulted roof. Directly ahead of them, glittering darkly on an enormous throne that filled the central nave, sat the famous statue of Zeus Olympia. A second, distorted Zeus glimmered upside down at his feet, reflected in a pool of black marble.

Sosi caught his breath and stepped backwards, making Eretaia giggle. "Don't worry, it's too shallow to drown in." She let go of his hand to scoop up some of the pool's contents. She smeared slimy fingers against his arm and giggled again as he stiffened. "It's only oil, silly! What's wrong with you and Samos today? Pericles is right, you're both acting scared of your own shadows. Getting worried about how hard my brother's going to throw you in the wrestling, is that it?"

Sosi grimaced. "I'll beat him in the sprint," he said, only realizing after he'd spoken that this was exactly what Theron would have said.

He thrust his brother to the back of his mind and blinked up at the massive statue. Zeus' throne had been carved with animals and battle scenes inlaid with ebony and jewels. His golden sandals were each big enough for a man to lie down in, and the cloak that draped his huge ivory body was of gold cloth decorated with glass lilies that sparkled in the light of the torches set around his feet. In his left hand he held a sceptre crowned with an eagle, and on the palm of his right hand stood a small statue of Nike. Zeus' head, crowned with an olive wreath, touched the rafters. Their guide was on the other side of the pool in a cloud of incense, explaining the scenes carved into the throne to Dion and a few other interested boys. Red-robed priests moved quietly around the Zeus, polishing his ivory skin with cloths soaked in oil from the pool. Sosi eyed them suspiciously, but their bodies all glowed faintly to his heat-sense in the gloom.

"Alive," he whispered.

"Good job Zeus isn't alive!" Samos said, mis-understanding. "If he stood up, he'd knock the roof off."

Eretaia huffed. "You boys are so silly sometimes. Come on, let's go up to the top floor!"

She led the way up a spiral staircase that emerged on the upper-gallery level with Zeus' head. There was no rail at the edge. Sosi felt dizzy as he peered over and saw the whole enormous statue reflected in the pool of oil. He lifted his gaze quickly to the winged Nike in Zeus' hand and realized that, although she'd looked tiny from below compared to the huge statue of the god, she was actually life-sized. She looked even less like the Nike he knew than the statue on the pillar outside.

Samos and Pericles, bored with the statue, went to look over the edge of the gallery. Sosi's skin prickled again. "Eretaia..." he began, meaning to ask the girl if she knew her priestess friend could shape-change. Before he had a chance, Eretaia's eyes widened. She gripped his arm, staring at the shadows behind him.

Sosi whirled in time to see a cloaked figure emerge from behind one of the columns further along the gallery and walk slowly towards them. *Warrior*, he thought in panic. But the figure was too small.

"It's Rasim!" Eretaia whispered.

The Persian boy was thinner than when they'd last seen him at Letrini, and had dark circles around his eyes. When Eretaia spoke his name, he hesitated but did not look their way. His eyes stared past them to where Samos and Pericles were still standing at the edge of the gallery, chuckling over something they could see below.

Sosi pulled Eretaia back, wary.

"How did you get in here?" he demanded. "Why did you steal that chariot at Letrini? Are you working for the Warriors of Ahriman? What did they do to you? How did you escape?"

Rasim continued walking. He didn't seem to hear Sosi's questions. He was barefoot, and around his ankles were black blisters. Burns. The hairs on the back of Sosi's neck rose as he passed them.

"Did they force you to go with them?" Eretaia said. "We were worried about you. Rasim? Can you hear us?"

Rasim entered a shadow and disappeared. When he emerged, he was running straight for Samos and Pericles with the same vacant look in his eyes as before.

A scream swelled inside Sosi, but no sound came out. Everything seemed to slow down. Eretaia's hands rose to her mouth as she realized what Rasim intended. *"Pericles!"* she shrieked. *"Look out!"*

Pericles looked round in surprise. His expression darkened when he saw Rasim. Samos began to turn. As he did so, Rasim launched himself through the air in the same way he had leapt from his horse's back to stop the runaway chariot, and wrapped his arms around Samos' knees. The Elean boy grunted with surprise and overbalanced, flailing in space. Pericles reacted quickly and grabbed Samos' arm, legs braced and muscles bulging. For a moment it looked as if he might drag the big boxer back to safety, but Rasim's momentum had carried Samos over the edge and their combined weight proved too much. Pericles swore as his bad leg buckled, and he staggered dangerously close to the drop.

"No!" Eretaia screamed. "Samos! *Pericles!*"

Sosi broke free of his trance. Yelling for the guards, he flung himself on his belly and grabbed a handful of Samos' tunic. It was no use. Even as two of the Eleans pounded up the spiral stair, the linen in Sosi's hand tore. Pericles valiantly tried to keep his hold, down on one knee, his face twisted in pain. But the linked bodies of Samos and Rasim slipped from his grasp and fell, twisting and kicking, towards the pool at the feet of Zeus. They splashed through the oil and struck the marble beneath with a sickening crack. Samos' heavy body bounced up again and lay still, oil and blood lapping his dark curls. Rasim was thrown aside by the impact and flung to the edge of the pool, his neck twisted at an unnatural angle against Zeus' toes.

Sosi heaved Pericles back from the edge and lay on the gallery floor, gasping with effort and shock. There was a moment of stunned silence. Then Eretaia started screaming, and boys and priests ran towards the pool. Someone opened both doors of the temple to call the guards. Soldiers surrounded Rasim's body with drawn swords, while others helped the priests pull Samos out of the pool.

Eretaia's screams turned to wild sobs as she clung to Pericles. "I thought you were going to fall as well!" she sobbed. "Poor Samos! It's all my fault! I made you come in... you would have both stayed outside, you'd have been *safe.*"

Pericles was white. He couldn't put his weight on his leg, but he fended her off. "Stop it," he said in a peculiar tone. "It wasn't your fault. It was Rasim. He deliberately dragged Samos over. No question he was working for those Warriors, now." He stared down at the limp body of the Persian boy, which was being lifted by the guards. They had put away their swords and were shaking their heads.

The priests shook their heads over Samos in much the same way. They laid him on the black marble beside the pool. One of them sponged blood from the boxer's scalp with his burnishing cloth. The boys hovered nearby, silent with disbelief.

"Samos..." Pericles whispered. He clenched his fists and blinked hard, struggling for words. When they emerged, his voice was cracked like an old man's. "Why did he have to pick on Samos? If it'd been me, I could understand. But Samos stood up for him... all the way." A tear trickled from his eye.

Sosi stared at the scrap of tunic in his hand. He said with a sick feeling, "Samos had a dream of victory last night. That's why."

Brother and sister glanced at each other. Not even Pericles said anything about dreams being nonsense.

Eretaia whispered, "I don't think Samos is dead, Pericles. Look – Nike's back, she'll know what to do."

It was not the reunion Sosi had hoped for. He watched helplessly as the yellow-eyed priestess squeezed past the doors of the temple and pushed through the group around Samos. She fell to her knees beside the boy and put an ear to his lips. She straightened with a grimace, snatched the cloth from the priest, and started giving orders. To everyone's relief, Samos was lifted on to a stretcher and carried towards the doors. Priest Rhexibius clapped his hands and told the boys to stay together. He looked up at the gallery and called for Sosi and his friends to come down.

Between them, Sosi and Eretaia managed to get Pericles down the staircase. A stricken Dion rushed across, closely followed by Agis and Kallias. Everyone started asking questions at once, wanting to know how Samos and Rasim had fallen. Pericles stared at the doors where the Elean boy had been carried out, leaving Eretaia to explain. A chill crept over Sosi as he eyed Rasim's body. Besides the burns on his feet and ankles, the boy had a Warrior's cord knotted around his throat in a strange fashion. The guards had given up trying to get it off.

"Broke his stupid neck," he heard one say. "Other boy's lucky to be alive, but his boxing career's over, poor lad..."

Judge Demetrius crashed through the doors, took one look at Rasim's body, and ordered them all out of the temple and back to the Prytaneon. "Not a word about this to anyone!" he warned as they filed out. "It's over.

The Persian's body will remain in the temple until we've investigated this matter. If anyone asks, Samos fell and it was an accident. If I hear any of you have been shooting your mouths off about him being pushed, I'll disqualify you from the Games. I don't want the spectators and other athletes alarmed unnecessarily. Understand?" He signalled to Priest Rhexibius, who lifted a panel around the back of Zeus' throne so the guards could carry Rasim's body inside.

There were a few uneasy mutters, but the boys were too shocked and upset to argue. It was only when they were out in the sunlight and air that Sosi realized what had been bothering him about Rasim's sudden appearance in the gallery.

He looked back at the Temple of Zeus. The doors were closed. Judge Demetrius, half the guards, and Priest Rhexibius were still inside. "Rasim's a Warrior," he whispered, knowing it was the only thing to explain what the boy had done. "They made him into one of them."

Pericles clutched his injured leg and said in a fierce tone, "They've gone too far this time. I don't care if I get disqualified from the Games, not any more. My leg's had it now, anyway. I'm going to find those Warriors of Ahriman, and I'm going to make them pay."

Chapter 13

TRUTH

THE SHOCK WAS almost physical. The boys clustered around the hearth in the banqueting hall of the Prytaneon as if winter had come early and they needed the fire to keep warm. Sosi couldn't stop shivering. He kept seeing Rasim with his blank gaze walking through the shadows of the temple gallery. He should have realized something was wrong. Why hadn't he stopped Rasim before it was too late?

Pericles was arguing with his sister, who wanted him to go to the Blood House and see the physician about his leg. It was a measure of how upset they all were when he heaved himself off the edge of the table and shouted at Eretaia, "The physician's busy! Don't you understand? Think I care about my stupid leg when Samos might never wake up again?"

Agis scowled, his arms folded. Kallias hovered at his

friend's shoulder, biting his lip. Dion knelt, stared wet-eyed into the flames and whispered, "Goddess Hestia, please don't let Samos die, please don't let him die," over and over. The other boys cast sideways glances at him, but no one made fun of his prayers.

"Oh, stop it!" Agis snapped, grabbing the younger boy's arm and giving him a shake. "Praying won't help Samos now, and the judges obviously aren't going to do anything. Pericles is right. We've got to find these Warriors ourselves, before they finish the lot of us off. The boys' events are tomorrow afternoon, so we've got to find them fast."

Dion blinked. "We've got to help Samos first."

"Get real! Samos is finished. You saw the blood. Never mind his boxing career, his head was smashed open like an egg." Agis let go roughly, and Dion burst into tears.

"You're attracting attention, Agis," Kallias muttered.

Two of the guards who had escorted them back from the temple were keeping watch at the door, swords drawn. They glared across the hall, but didn't interfere. Maybe they sensed this wasn't the time for petty discipline.

Pericles limped to the other side of the hearth out of earshot of the guards and motioned they should follow. "I agree," he said. "Whatever happens to Samos now, we have to find out where the Warriors are hiding. They must have sent Rasim to the Temple of Zeus to do their dirty work for them because they couldn't get into the

Altis themselves. I don't expect he was meant to fall as well. He was probably supposed to go after me or Theron next." His lips tightened and he lowered his voice. "This is what I think. If the Warriors sent Rasim in here, then they'll be nearby, maybe watching to see if he succeeded. They might have seen Samos being taken out of the temple, but they won't know yet that Rasim is dead, and if Judge Demetrius keeps the body under wraps like he said he would, they won't find out for a while. It's my guess they arranged to meet up somewhere afterwards. They don't seem to send out more than one Warrior at once, so one of us can wear a cloak and pretend to be Rasim. The rest of us can wait nearby and jump the Warrior when he comes. We'll have to watch he doesn't kill himself like the others did, and we'll need to make him tell us where the other terrorists are hiding. Then we'll hand him over to the guards and tell the judges what we've discovered. Agreed?"

Sosi turned cold. The others glanced at one another.

"Who's going to pretend to be Rasim? Most of us are too tall," queried Kallias.

Everyone eyed Dion. The younger boy paled and shook his head.

"It'll have to be you, squirt!" Agis said. "Don't be such a coward. Don't you want to help catch Samos' killer?"

"Samos isn't dead," Dion whispered.

Eretaia sighed. "Leave him alone, Agis. I think it's a stupid plan! How do you think you're going to make one of those Warriors of Ahriman talk when the Eleans haven't managed to?"

"The Eleans didn't even try!" Pericles scowled at his sister, glanced at the guards and lowered his voice again. "They're too worried about protecting their Games. You heard Judge Demetrius. He doesn't want anyone to know the terrorists are here at Olympia, because he doesn't want to cause a panic. The judges didn't take the Warriors seriously enough; we'll be more careful. We won't carry weapons the Warrior can use to kill himself. We'll use our muscles and Olympic training to overpower him. Tonight would probably be best. Theron, are you up for it? You'll have to do most of the wrestling because my leg's too weak to be much use. Anyone else want to help? It might get you disqualified from the Games, so you've got to be prepared for that."

There was a pause while the others digested this. They actually seemed to be considering Pericles' plan.

"Wouldn't it be better to wait until the procession arrives from Elis?" Kallias asked. "Then everyone will be watching the opening ceremony, and we'll be able to get out of the Altis easier."

"That's the morning of our events!" Agis said. "Don't be stupid. We've got to do it before the Warriors find out Rasim's dead. That's the whole point!"

"They're unlikely to find out before tomorrow," Kallias said. "Priest Rhexibius seemed pretty interested in those burns on Rasim's body, didn't he? I bet he'll keep it in the temple as long as possible so he can examine it."

Agis scowled. "I'm not doing anything on the day we compete. I haven't trained for ten months to ruin my chances now! We do it tonight, or I'm not helping."

Pericles gave him a disgusted look. "Theron?" he said again. "You in?"

Sosi shook his head, knowing it was time to tell the truth. "It won't fool the Warriors," he said. "They'll know it isn't Rasim in the cloak. You see, he's not dead... I mean, he *is* dead, but he's like the Warriors, enchanted so he can come back to life again. I think that's why he didn't care about killing himself when he pushed Samos off the gallery. He might already have risen from the dead and got out of the Temple."

The other boys looked at him sideways and made crazy signs with their fingers against their heads.

Pericles sighed. "Not that nonsense again! Face facts, Macedonian. Rasim was a sneaky Persian spy, and that's all there is to it. I was right about him all along."

Sosi closed his eyes. "It's the truth. Please believe me. I *know* the Warriors and Rasim are dead, and the reason I know is..." He looked at the ring of curious faces and shook his head. He couldn't betray his brother in front of everyone. "It's complicated. I need to talk to Pericles and Eretaia in private."

The others smirked and pulled "I told you so" faces. Pericles frowned at Sosi. But he indicated the others should wait, heaved himself up from the hearth and grabbed Eretaia's arm. Leaning on his sister, he limped towards the stairs.

In the dormitory, surrounded by clothing and blankets cast aside by the guards' frantic search for terrorists, they eyed one another warily.

"Well?" Pericles said. "This had better be good, because climbing those stairs just about finished my leg."

Sosi gazed out of the window at the slopes of Mount Kronos, bathed in the afternoon sunshine. From this side, he couldn't see the fissure that led to the tunnel system and the snake cave. He went to his pallet and rummaged under his blanket, afraid the guards might have confiscated the snakeskin. But it was still there, a crackly mass of dark scales. He pulled it out, and Eretaia stiffened.

"Where did you find that?"

Pericles frowned at the skin. "What's this all about? Sis, do you know something I don't?"

"I found it last night," Sosi said. "Up in a cave on the mountain."

Eretaia bit her lip. "Theron, I don't think you should..."

"You don't think he should *what*?" Pericles demanded. "No more secrets, remember! This is too serious now."

Sosi took a deep breath. "It's one of my... ancestor's... old skins. He was a boy who could change his shape. His name was Sosipolis, like mine, and he died in that cave after a battle in the stadium when he changed into a snake to save the Games."

He told them about his extra senses and the Warriors not giving off body heat because they were dead; how he could shed his skin and change his shape; how he had dreams about past Olympic Games; and how, after his mother's "fever dream", he suspected the Warriors were hiding in the caves under Mount Kronos – though he didn't mention his mother and the other women.

When he had finished, there was a long silence.

"Snake senses?" Eretaia repeated.

"Your name's Sosipolis?" Pericles said, frowning. "But you swore the Olympic oath as Theron of Macedon!"

Sosi grimaced. "That's because I'm acting as Theron to keep him in the Games. He's my brother. You didn't really think his foot healed up so well in a single day, did you? I took his shape. I've done it before, when we were little, but it was a joke then and this isn't."

Eretaia stared at the dark scales in his hands. "You... you really shed your *skin*?" she whispered with a shudder. "Ugh!"

Pericles shook his head. "You expect us to believe you're some kind of creature from Olympic legend? That's just an old snakeskin. It proves nothing. I've wrestled with you, Macedonian. You're human enough!"

"You said I was acting strangely after Theron got injured. That's when I took his shape."

"That's true," Eretaia said, still staring at Sosi. "You told me Theron was different after he recovered, remember? Not so arrogant, you said. More human..." Her voice trailed off. "When your brother told me you had a curse, I never imagined he meant this!"

A flicker of doubt crossed Pericles' face. His expression darkened. "I can't believe the pair of you are still talking about magic at a time like this!" he said. "Theron, if you're too scared to help, or too selfish like Agis, then for Zeus' sake say so! But don't make up stupid lies about snakes and curses as an excuse, because I'm not an idiot."

"I'm taking a risk telling you!" Sosi shouted, frustrated by Pericles' stubborn refusal to believe. "If the judges find out what we've done, Theron will be disqualified from competing in the Circuit Games for good, and Zeus only knows what they'll do to me! But you're right. The Games aren't important any more, and I've had beatings before. I agree we've got to stop the Warriors, but you can't just go up there and wrestle them! It's too dangerous. Ask Nike if you don't believe me. She knows they're sorcerers, and she knows about me and Theron. Ask her about your victory dreams. That's why Samos was targeted in the temple. You know it was."

"Oh, I see!" Pericles gave a harsh laugh. "You and that ugly lump of a priestess have got together, and now you're having a joke at our expense. I'm sorry, but we've got more important things to think about right now. Come on, sis. I've heard enough." He grasped Eretaia's arm.

Eretaia hesitated, forcing her brother to stop, too. "I think he's telling the truth, Pericles."

Pericles scowled at her. He stared Sosi in the eye. "All right, prove it! If you really are half snake, shed your skin and change your shape right here and now. Why not take mine? You can wrestle in my place at the Games, since I'm not going to win anything with this leg. On second thoughts, change yourself into Rasim. I don't see why poor Dion should be the decoy to lure out the Warriors. You can do it."

Sosi shivered. "I can't."

"Ha! See, sis? What did I tell you?"

"It only happens at the full moon," Sosi said.

"How convenient," Pericles muttered, grasping the stair rail. "I thought better of you, Macedonian. But now I see you're just as selfish and arrogant as the rest of your countrymen. If there were any justice in this world, Rasim would have pushed *you* off that gallery, not Samos! Don't bother helping, then. I don't want someone I can't trust watching my back when there's a Warrior around. I'm going to the Blood House to see how Samos is."

Eretaia stared after him, her face stricken. "I'm sorry," she whispered. "My brother's upset about Samos. They've been friends and rivals on the circuit for a long time."

"Eretaia!" Pericles called up the stairs.

She glanced round. "He needs me to help him with his leg. I'll try to get Nike alone and ask her about the Warriors. Is it true, what you said? She's not human, either?"

Sosi nodded. He felt numb. The last thing he'd expected was that they wouldn't believe him.

Eretaia gave him a little smile. "I think I knew you weren't Theron. He was... well... you're younger than him, aren't you?"

Sosi nodded. At least he seemed to have convinced Eretaia. In spite of everything that had happened today, he smiled back.

"ERETAIA!" Pericles yelled again.

The girl jumped and gave Sosi another stricken look. "I've got to go. If you're right about the Warriors, the sanctuary's not safe. I'll try to persuade the women to go back to Elis. What are you going to do?"

Sosi gripped the snakeskin. That was a good question. Somehow, he had to think of a way to convince Pericles he was telling the truth before the boy got himself and the others killed. There was only one thing he could think of.

"I'm going to see Rasim," he said.

He waited until after supper, knowing that the priests would be busy then with their evening rites. The guards at the door of the Prytaneon were reluctant to let him outside alone. But he claimed he felt queasy and needed a potion to settle his stomach, and one look at his sweat-beaded face persuaded them. "Poor lad," he heard one of them mutter. "Sick with nerves! How are any of them supposed to be at their best tomorrow afternoon, after what happened to the Elean boy?"

Sosi walked slowly across the Altis, taking deep

breaths. The sun had gone down, and in the dusk everything seemed cool and peaceful, as if nothing terrible ever happened in the world. He hid behind the statue of a racehorse until the last of the red-robed priests had emerged from the Temple of Zeus, then slipped inside.

It was eerily quiet. A shiver went down his spine as he looked up at the gallery where Samos had fallen. He fought an urge to turn and run. The braziers and torches still glowed around the magnificent statue, making Zeus' robe glitter. He hurried round the back of the throne, found the place where he'd seen Priest Rhexibius lift the panel, and squeezed through into a musty, cobwebby space. He stifled a cough, every sense alert, afraid Rasim might try to jump him. But the boy's body lay where the priests had left it, on a bed of mouse droppings, shadowy and still.

Sosi dropped to his knees and ran his hands over the cold flesh, stifling a shudder. "Rasim? Can you hear me?"

The boy had been stripped down to his loincloth, but the Warrior's cord was still knotted tightly about his neck. Sosi's fingers recoiled from it.

"Rasim!" he hissed, shaking the limp body.

No response.

He sat back on his heels and tried to think. How did the Warriors resurrect themselves? He touched the knot again. It was faintly warm and difficult to untie, but he managed to loosen it.

As he pulled the horrible thing off the boy, a draught stirred the cobwebs and dust under the throne. The torches flickered, and the hairs on the back of his neck stood on end. Rasim's body jerked. At the same time, there was an echoing thud at the far end of the temple as the bar fell into place across the huge doors.

Sosi's knees weakened. He should have realized they'd lock the temple at night. But there was no time to worry about that now. He overcame his disgust at the thought of touching dead flesh, and secured Rasim in a wrestler's hold with one hand over the boy's mouth. "Don't be afraid," he hissed. "You're not with the Warriors any more. It's me, Sosi— I mean, Theron."

Rasim struggled, making terrified noises behind his hand. At least he'd snapped out of his trance. He stared wildly around the dusty space under the throne, then focused on Sosi's face. He stopped struggling and panted through his nose.

Sosi couldn't think how to begin. What did you say to someone who was dead? "They made you into one of them," he said. "Didn't they?"

Rasim's whole body trembled.

"You broke your neck when you fell. Do you know what you did?"

The boy's eyes flickered.

"Do you know where you are?"

Rasim shook his head.

Sosi glanced at the ebony panels that surrounded them. All was quiet outside. They seemed to be alone in the temple.

"If I let you go, will you promise not to run?" he said.

"This is the Temple of Zeus. I think we're locked in for the night, but there are guards all over the Altis. If they hear us, they might come to investigate. Priest Rhexibius wants to take your body apart to examine it. That won't be much fun if you can't die properly."

Rasim cast a terrified look at the open panel and gave a small nod.

Sosi removed his hand and backed off, ready to seize the boy again the moment he tried anything. Rasim eyed the cord and swallowed. He seemed to have difficulty speaking. "How did you get that thing off me? I remember he tied it around my neck. I couldn't breathe... it was like a bad dream... What did I do?"

"Never mind that now," Sosi said. "We need to know exactly how many Warriors are here at Olympia, and what their plans are for the Games."

Rasim closed his eyes. "I can't tell you that."

"You've got to tell!" Sosi gentled his tone. "Please, Rasim. If you help us, I promise I'll do my best to help you."

The Persian boy rubbed the back of his neck and gave a bitter laugh. "No one can help me now – especially not you, Macedonian! You don't understand the darkness your King Iskander has woken in the hearts of my people."

Sosi pressed his lips together. "I understand darkness, believe me."

Rasim shook his head. "No, you don't. You might think you do, but you can't really know. Not until you've died."

"I *have* died!" Sosi hadn't meant to tell him, but it came out in a rush. He paced around the interior of the throne, brushing cobwebs out of his way. "You want to know why I scare horses? I'll tell you why! I'm only half human. My other half is a snake, and I've lived before – probably many times before, only thank Zeus I don't remember. My real name is Sosipolis. I reincarnate myself, just like your Warriors, but in an unborn child rather than my old body. So I do understand, all right? I know you're scared because I'm scared, too. But you've got to help us, because if you don't lots of innocent people are going to get hurt, and I'm not going to let that happen. We're going to be in here all night. If I have to, I'll use my powers to make you tell, so you might as well make it easy for yourself."

He didn't know if his bluff would work, but it got a reaction from Rasim. "So *that*'s what Father meant! Now I see why he's so wary of you, and how you managed to untie that cord from my neck." He hugged his knees in the gloom. "It's no good, snake-boy. He'll find me again. I can't escape him."

Sosi blinked, caught off guard. "You mean to say the Warrior who took you from Letrini is your *father*?"

"He was my father, before he became one of Ahriman's walking dead." Rasim sighed. "He's changed, but even though he hurt me, I can't betray him."

Sosi stared at the boy in horror and sympathy. "Why did you come here? Is it because the Macedonians burnt Persepolis? I can understand you're angry, but how is injuring the ephebes going to help your people? Do you want revenge?"

"Revenge?" Rasim sighed again. "The Warriors of Ahriman want a lot more than revenge, snake-boy. They want to destroy your gods and your King Iskander, once and for all."

"So what are they doing *here*? Why are they at the Olympic Games, when King Alexander's in Persia? How is injuring the ephebes going to help your people? It makes no sense!"

Rasim smiled. "Maybe you should ask your friend Victory."

"Nike," Sosi breathed, remembering her game and how she'd told him her power relied on those to whom she had sent victory dreams winning their events. "What are they going to do to her?"

Rasim folded his arms and refused to answer.

"I know where they're hiding," Sosi said, getting angry. "They're in the caves under Mount Kronos, aren't they? Pericles and the others are going after them."

"That's a mistake," said Rasim, worried. "They'll get hurt. Father's gone too far to let anyone stop him now."

"Enough of us have got hurt already. Come on, Rasim! Tell me. Maybe we'll be in time to stop Pericles. We helped you at Piera, and you owe us after what you did this afternoon. Don't you remember anything?"

Rasim wrinkled his brow. "I remember that girl, Eretaia, calling to me..." He shuddered. "Whatever I did, I'm sorry, but I didn't have any choice. No one can fight Ahriman."

"You pushed Samos over the edge of the temple gallery," Sosi said harshly. "He cracked his head open on the marble and broke both his arms. His boxing career's over. I hope you're proud of yourself."

Rasim closed his eyes. "Samos? The gentle Elean boxer?"

Sosi nodded, and Rasim's expression twisted in anguish. When he opened his eyes, he seemed to have come to a decision.

"My father's the only Warrior here," he said with another sigh. "He's working on his own, but soon he won't be. He plans to use your fire-altar as a gateway to bring the dead from the House of the Lie through to the world of the living. The followers of Ahriman have managed this before in a small way in Persia, but King Iskander destroyed many of our fire-altars, and the priests of Zarathustra guard the others against such use. By sacrificing your Priestess Nike to Ahriman at the great fire-altar of Zeus, Father thinks he can bring a great army of Warriors through to Olympia. That's why he's been after you boys, to weaken Nike so that she can't escape him or interfere by opening a channel to your gods. Then he'll march his army of the dead north to Macedonia and destroy King Iskander's land and people, even as he is destroying ours. Iskander will have to bring his army back from Persia to save them – but he'll be too late."

Sosi's heart beat faster at the thought of the Warriors of Ahriman burning his home. "Our fire-altar? You mean the Great altar of Zeus, don't you? Then we were right in the first place – they'll strike at the Great Sacrifice!"

He thought furiously. They still had time. The Great Sacrifice wasn't until the third day of the festival. He could tell the judges, and the Eleans could take a force up to the caves under Mount Kronos and arrest the Warrior. Except if he did that, they'd find the women and Lady Alcmena, and then the judges would sentence his mother to be thrown over the cliff and disqualify his brother from the Games.

He clenched his fists and pressed his forehead against one of the ebony panels.

Rasim touched his shoulder. "I know. It's horrible, isn't it? But maybe…" He lowered his voice, as if afraid someone would overhear. "Maybe you can stop him."

Sosi stiffened. "How?"

"I don't know. But Father's scared of you. It must be something to do with your powers."

Sosi sighed. His powers – powers that he couldn't remember and no one would tell him about. "Let's try the door," he said, not wanting to think about it just then.

They scrambled out from under the throne, but the temple doors were firmly barred, and there was no other way out. Sosi did consider banging on them to attract the attention of the guards, but that would only get Rasim arrested and probably himself as well, and any chance he had of stopping the Warrior would be gone. He sank to the floor and rested his back against one of the columns.

Rasim eyed him. "I've told you all I can. If you let me

go in the morning, I promise I'll try to stop Father. Maybe I can persuade him to go back to Persia and find another fire-altar powerful enough for his purposes."

Sosi hardened his heart. "As soon as that door opens, we're going to find Pericles. I want you to tell him what you told me. And if you try to run back to your Warrior father, I swear before Zeus that I'll tie this cord back around your neck and hand you straight over to Priest Rhexibius." He showed Rasim the Warrior's cord with the black hair threaded into it, and the boy turned pale.

Chapter 14

NIKE'S PLAN

BY THE TIME the bar on the door was lifted the next morning, Sosi had heard Rasim's side of the story. He still didn't understand quite how anyone could cold-bloodedly throw a javelin through his brother's foot or push Samos off the gallery, but he thought he understood the Warriors' hatred. Rasim's father used to lead a group of devout followers of Zarathustra, who fled to the hills and took up arms to defend their homeland against the Macedonians. King Alexander attacked their camp, killed all the men and women, and sent the children across the Aegean Sea to be sold as slaves. Rasim was seven, old enough to remember his father fighting like a crazed man to save his family, and the way he'd called on Ahriman, the Dark One, as he died. The night of shared confessions helped calm Rasim. When Zeus' priests hurried in to replenish the braziers, the boys slipped out of the temple unobserved and hurried to the Prytaneon.

Hestia's fire crackled fiercely in the hearth, but there were no guards, which was strange. The dormitory was empty. Bedding and clothes lay in a tumbled mess. Most of the strigils and oils had gone, which meant the other boys were at the baths. Sosi relaxed slightly, then stiffened when he looked out of the window and saw a small group heading up the slopes of Mount Kronos, hustling a cloaked figure in their midst.

"It's Pericles," he said, pushing Rasim back down the stairs. "Hurry!"

They raced back into the carnival atmosphere of the Altis and ran smack into a boy with unnaturally black hair, limping towards the Prytaneon with the aid of an olive branch, his bandaged foot stuck out in front of him and a furious look in his eye.

As Rasim stared in amazement at their identical faces, Theron frowned at Sosi and said, "You'd better have a good explanation for all this, little brother."

Even as Sosi's head spun, trying to catch up with the fact his brother was at Olympia, he managed to keep them all moving. They left the crowds behind and headed up the slopes of Mount Kronos, exchanging news on the way.

It turned out that Theron had travelled with the procession from Elis, keeping well shrouded by his hood and hiding at the back of the convoy among the many hangers-on, his limp unremarked among all the old and crippled athletes who haunted the Games Circuit. He'd hung about outside the Prytaneon, waiting for Sosi to emerge with the other boys going to the baths, and caught Pericles and the others on their way up the mountain. Pericles had recognized him at once, despite the black hair. Apparently, he'd stared at Theron's bandaged foot and spat something about him being truly cursed before pushing past him.

"He probably thought you were me," Sosi said. "I mean, me pretending to change my appearance by dying my hair and bandaging my foot to make him believe in my curse. He's as stubborn as a mule! He just refuses to believe in magic. I'm glad you're here. When he sees us together, he'll have to believe."

He itched to run. But Theron couldn't move very fast with his injured foot. Sosi consoled himself that Pericles couldn't move very fast with his bad leg, either, and having a reluctant Dion along would slow them down, too. He kept an eye on Rasim, expecting him to make a break for freedom now they were out of the Altis, and led them straight up the spur of the mountain by the steepest route, aiming for the ridge over which old Eileithyia had guided him in the opposite direction two nights ago. As they climbed, a winged shadow passed over them. Sosi glanced at the sky, and his heart gave an extra thud as a golden feather floated out of the sun.

Rasim blinked at the feather and looked at the Kladeos campsite spread along the riverbank below them. "The race," he whispered, breaking his silence for the first time since they'd left the Temple of Zeus. "I'd forgotten... Where's my horse? I should be with Lightning! I need to give him a last gallop."

Sosi grabbed the boy's arm before he could escape back down the hill. "Your horse is fine," he said, watching the eagle as it swooped low over the ridge and landed on the other side, out of sight. "The others must be up there. Hurry!"

He scrambled up the rocks and peered over. The first thing he saw was Nike in her red chiton, blocking the path with her hands on her hips, her muscular legs planted apart like a man's. Pericles, Kallias and three boys Sosi didn't know very well, faced her. They held Dion between them, muffled in his cloak. "Don't let the Warrior get me," the younger boy pleaded when he saw Nike. "Please make them let me go. I've got to be back in time for my race."

At the bottom of the hill, looking very small and distant, the stadium was packed with spectators fighting for space on the banks to watch the boys' events. Sosi felt a pang of regret for Dion and the others. The Olympic Games, the events for which they'd trained a whole ten months, were about to start, and here they were up on the ridge chasing a terrorist they could not hope to defeat because he was already dead.

Theron gazed down at the stadium as well, the look in his eyes twisting Sosi's heart. Rasim stared blankly as if nothing could touch him any more. The boys on the path hadn't noticed the newcomers yet. They were all looking at Priestess Nike.

"Stop!" she commanded. "Where do you think you're going? You're supposed to be in the stadium!"

"Get out of our way, Nike," Pericles said through gritted teeth. "We're going to find ourselves a Warrior."

The other boys nodded and muttered. They had armed themselves with sticks and stones, Sosi noticed. He wondered if they had seen the priestess flying, or just thought she'd jumped out from behind the rocks. He could see her wings glimmering in the sunlight, but the others didn't seem amazed by her appearance, only annoyed.

"There's no time," Nike snapped. "You've got to go back down and compete! If you don't win like you're supposed to, I won't be strong enough to stop the Warrior disrupting the Games."

"Compete?" Pericles said bitterly. "Look at my leg! I'm not going to win anything, am I? We're going to stop the Warrior before he gets as far as the Games. Get out of our way before we throw you out of it."

The other boys exchanged awkward glances. Nike's yellow eyes flashed dangerously.

Sosi seized Rasim's wrist in one hand and Theron's in the other and dragged them over the ridge. "Priestess Nike's right! You've got to go back. You can't fight the Warrior. He's not human. Nike and I are the only ones who can stop him now."

There was a hush as the boys stared at him and Theron. Then Pericles' gaze fell on Rasim, and he launched himself at the Persian boy with a growl of fury. "I might have known you weren't really dead!" he hissed. "You ruined Samos' life... come back here!" Rasim danced back out of range, and Pericles' leg collapsed as he tried to grab the boy.

Sosi darted between them and caught hold of the wrestler's shoulders. "No, Pericles! Listen to him. He knows about the Warrior's plans. Tell him what you told me, Rasim!"

Pericles was so angry, Sosi thought he'd be thrown despite the boy's bad leg. But Theron limped over to help, and Pericles' fury faded as he gaped at their identical faces.

"Oh Zeus... you weren't making it up, were you?" he whispered, turning pale.

Sosi shook his head.

Pericles closed his eyes. His whole body shuddered. He took a deep breath and supported himself on Theron's crutch, his lips twisting in bitter humour as he eyed the other boy's bandaged foot. "We're a right pair, aren't we, Macedonian?" His light tone betrayed him when it cracked. He took another breath and straightened his shoulders. "All right, what does the Persian know? It'd better be worth sparing his life for, because I'll never forget what you did, Persian! You won't escape justice, if I have to carry it out myself."

Rasim seemed unconcerned by this threat. After further prompting, he repeated what he'd told Sosi in the Temple of Zeus. He spoke in an emotionless tone, and the other boys listened in confusion that quickly turned to horror. When Sosi explained about his curse and the trick he and Theron had played on them all, they edged away from him. Kallias gave Dion's shoulder a squeeze and whispered, "It's all right. Rasim's here now. You won't have to be the decoy any more."

Finally, Sosi told them how the Warrior planned to bring through his army of the dead, and Nike sucked in her breath. "Don't worry," he said, realizing the priestess must be terrified. "We won't let him touch you."

Nike gave him a contemptuous look and dragged Rasim aside. She asked him some urgent questions, to which Rasim replied without emotion as before. Sosi couldn't hear what they were saying, but Nike's expression changed to one of determination. Letting Rasim go, she faced them with a glint in her eye.

"I've got an idea."

The other boys, who had been glancing down the hill at the stadium, perhaps wishing they had stayed with Agis and the rest, looked at her in sudden hope. Sosi glanced at Rasim, surprised to see him smiling.

"When the Great Altar gets its power from the sacrifice, I'm the one who opens the channel to the gods," Nike continued. "As Rasim just told us, the Warrior's plans rely on him making me too weak to open the channel or change my shape to escape from him, and he's doing this using the magical link I have with those I've sent victory dreams. Most of the men's events are after the Great Sacrifice, which is obviously why he's been concentrating on injuring you boys."

"Sending his son to do his dirty work, you mean," Pericles muttered, glaring at Rasim.

Nike scowled at him. "Shut up and listen, or Samos' pain will be for nothing! This Warrior thinks he's clever. He thinks he's fixed me good and proper by injuring Theron, Pericles and Samos, and taking Rasim out of the horse race. But if we all work together to make sure at least some of my choices still win, I should be able to help Sosipolis fight him when the time comes. Together, we might just be strong enough to send the Warrior back where he came from. I need you boys to get back down to the stadium and compete as normal. I'm going to arrange for Pericles to have a bye through to the final in the boys' wrestling. It won't be questioned, since he was champion last time. Whoever meets him in the final must let him win." She fixed them with her luminous gaze. "Understand?"

It took a moment to sink in. Dion and Kallias, neither of whom was entered in the wrestling, smiled at the cleverness of her plan. Theron glanced at Sosi. The other three looked uncertain. "Let him win?" said one of Pericles' opponents. "But that's cheating. We swore an oath to do our best."

"Absolutely not!" Pericles growled as he realized what she was suggesting. "I won't take an Olympic wreath dishonestly."

"This isn't for your sake!" Nike snapped. "It's not for mine, either, or even for the Macedonian King – he's just one man, and someone's bound to kill him eventually if he carries on like he is, then the wars in Persia will stop whether the Warriors attack Macedonia or not. It's for the future of the Olympic Games and the freedom of our people here in the West. What do you think will happen if this Warrior succeeds in bringing his army of living dead through to Olympia? What'll happen to you and your friend Samos, the rest of the athletes, your families back home, and everyone else? These dead cannot be killed, but they can kill us and make us into them. Believe me, you don't want that. Look at the Persian, and then tell me no."

Pericles stared at Rasim. "But he's alive."

"Oh, don't go all stubbornly blind on me now!" Nike sighed. "Don't you understand a word Sosipolis has been trying to tell you all this time? Rasim was *already* dead when he fell off that gallery with Samos. He died when his father took him from Letrini and made him Ahriman's. He would be a full Warrior by now if he hadn't tried to help you. Fortunately, he's been brave enough to resist them and, thanks to Sosipolis removing that cord from his neck, he still remembers what it was like to be alive, which means there's still hope for us."

She looked round at their pale faces and drew a breath. "If you let Pericles win as I said, that takes care of the wrestling. Obviously, Pericles can't run with his bad leg, so in the boys' sprint that leaves Kallias, Agis, Dion and Theron... Theron's foot is still infected, so Sosipolis will have to run in his place just as they planned. I'm not sure if it'll work, because as far as I know it's never been tried before, but I'm hoping Sosipolis absorbed some of the victory link from me when he took Theron's shape, maybe enough to make a difference. It's worth a try, anyway. So you boys need to make sure Sosipolis wins the sprint, right?"

Dion nodded solemnly. Kallias pulled a face and said, "I don't really mind. I'll probably mess up my start, anyway. But Agis will never agree. And he's in the wrestling, too."

"Then Sosipolis will just have to run fast enough to beat Agis," Nike said impatiently. "And surely one of you can knock Agis out of the wrestling before he meets Pericles? He's as skinny as a spear."

Theron made a disgusted sound in his throat at all this talk of cheating, but didn't say a word. It was, after all, no worse than what he and Sosi had done.

Nike continued, "We can't do anything about the boys' boxing now. But I'm going to arrange for Rasim to ride his colt Lightning in the horse race tomorrow. He's certain the colt will win, despite its interrupted training. When the judges see Rasim, of course, they'll try to arrest him, so he'll have to stay in hiding until then, and none of you must mention that you've seen him. Once he's out on the track, they'll have to let the race finish before they make their move, otherwise they'll risk spreading panic through the crowd. Afterwards, we can try to think of something to help him. The important thing is that he wins. You sure about this, Rasim?"

The Persian boy gave a quiet nod, which twisted Sosi's heart because he didn't see that there was any way they could help Rasim now.

"Good!" Nike clapped her hands. "Then everyone get down to the stadium and do what you're trained for. We might save these Games yet!"

PART 4

THE GREAT GAMES

And the great fame
of the Olympiad Games shines far afield,
in the course known of Pelops, where are matched
rivals in speed of foot
and in brave feats
of bodily strength.

(Olympian 1)

THE GREAT GAMES OLYMPIAD 11

		Morning
DAY ONE	ALTIS COUNCIL – HOUSE	Public prayers and opening ceremony.
		Public prayers and opening ceremony. Swearing-in ceremony for competitors, trainers and judges. (The boys and Judge Demetrius do this early, on arrival at Olympia
	ECHO – COLONNADE	Contest for heralds and trumpeters.
DAY TWO	HIPPODROME	Procession (starts Assembly Square), chariot races, horse race.
DAY THREE	ALTIS	Lighting of altar fires by winner of boys' sprint, followed by sacrifice of 100 oxen t Zeus Olympia at the Great Altar.
DAY FOUR	STADIUM	Men's wrestling, men's boxing, men's pankration.
DAY FIVE	TEMPLE OF – ZEUS OLYMPIA	Prize-giving ceremony.

FESTIVAL PROGRAMME

Afternoon		Evening	
TADIUM	Boys' events (sprint, boxing, wrestling).	ASSEMBLY-SQUARE	Public readings by poets and philosophers.
		PRYTANEON	Victory party, for boys.
TADIUM	Men's pentathlon (discus, javelin, long jump, sprint, wrestling).	ALTIS	Funeral rites of Pelops and sacrifice of a black ram, followed by parade of victors. *FULL MOON TONIGHT.*
TADIUM	Men's foot-races (dolichos, sprint, double-sprint).	PRYTANEON	Public banquet.
TADIUM	Race-in-armour.	Private parties	
LTIS	Public thanksgiving service and closing prayers.	PRYTANEON	Victors' banquet, invitation only.

Chapter 15

GAMES

SOSI, KALLIAS AND Dion ran down the slope of Mount Kronos dangerously fast, leaping boulders and risking their ankles on the rough terrain, while Pericles followed more slowly with the other three competitors. Theron had stayed behind on the mountain, demanding Sosi show him the entrance to the caves before they'd parted. There had been no time to argue. The boys' sprint was the first event of the afternoon. If they didn't hurry, they would miss it altogether.

By the time they reached the terraces at the bottom of the hill, they were breathing hard and thankful for Trainer Hermon's strict training regime that had hardened their muscles and strengthened their ligaments to bring them down the mountain unscathed. Sosi pushed his anxiety for his family to the back of his mind and darted between the Treasure Houses, looking for

Agis. If he didn't get a chance to talk to the boy before the events started, Nike's plan would fail.

A herald spotted them. "Oi, you boys! You're late! Your trainer's looking for you. The others have already gone to the stadium. You're in a lot of trouble."

They didn't need telling. There was no time to oil and change. They pounded through the tunnel, their sandals spraying damp gravel against the walls, and almost collided with Trainer Hermon and two Elean guards at the other end. The men lowered their spears. "Halt!" one commanded, in danger of stabbing Dion in the gloom.

But Trainer Hermon knocked aside the guards' weapons. "Where have you three *been*?" he bellowed. "Just look at the state of you! Where's Pericles? You're meant to be lining up for the sprint! So far, Agis is the only competitor out there. The judges are about to award him the victory without even running the race. The crowd deserves a better show than that."

Kallias was too breathless to reply, bent over a stitch with his hands on his knees. He looked as if he'd run his race already. Dion slumped against the wall – a reaction to the mad race down the mountain, followed by the shock of the spear that had nicked his throat.

"I'm sorry we're late, sir," Sosi said, knowing that they needed the old trainer on their side. "It's my fault. Pericles is coming – he'll be here in time for the wrestling, but his leg's too bad to do the sprint so he sent us on ahead. Please let us run."

Their trainer pressed his lips together. "I might have

known this would have something to do with you, Macedonian. All right, I'll listen to your excuses afterwards. You're late enough already – hold on a moment." He pulled a cloth from his belt and wiped the blood off Dion's throat. "Catch your breath, boy," he muttered. "Can't run an Olympic sprint in that state. Stay here and prepare yourselves. You men – wait with them, and keep alert! The terrorists might still try something. I'll go and explain to the judges. Don't worry, I'll make sure you have a chance to run – but don't you dare disgrace me!"

They smiled at one another in relief as they removed their sandals and tunics, bundled them together and passed them to the guards. At least they didn't need to warm up. They watched Trainer Hermon work his way round to the judges' stand. Six judges sat inside the enclosure; another three stood in a huddle near the gate, arguing. There was no sign of Judge Lysanias. Agis, stripped ready to run, limbered up on the course in glorious isolation, practising his start. The crowd didn't seem to realize anything was wrong. Some of them whistled and called out, "Victory to Agis the Athenian!" Sosi gestured frantically, trying to catch the boy's eye. But Agis was showing off to his supporters and didn't notice.

Trainer Hermon spoke quietly to the judges, and Judge Demetrius turned and scowled at the tunnel before straightening his hat and nodding to the herald. A trumpet blast rang round the stadium. The crowd quietened. Dion gave Sosi a nervous grin, and Kallias said, "Don't worry, Sosi, you're going to win."

A thunderous cheer greeted them as they emerged from the tunnel.

"Victory to young Dion!" someone cried, recognizing the youngster. "Champion of the Isthmian Games!"

"Victory to Kallias of Ephesos!"

"Victory to Theron of Macedonian Pella!"

Agis stopped in mid-stretch to glower at them.

The walk past the thousands of cheering people to the other end of the stadium seemed twice as far as the journey from Elis to Olympia. Sosi's skin prickled, sunlight flashed from the trumpets, and the course blurred. Sweat broke out all over his body as the ghostly soldiers of his dream shimmered around him, and for a horrible moment he couldn't remember what shape he had.

"What's wrong?" Kallias hissed, gripping his arm. "Don't faint on us! You've got to win, remember?"

The ghostly memory disappeared. Sosi shuddered and pulled himself together. He was strong and fit. He had Theron's body. A winged shadow passed overhead, and he felt a bit better when he glimpsed Nike, her black hair in tangles, elbowing her way through the crowd towards the judges' stand. He took deep breaths as he lined up next to Agis. Under pretence of cleaning out the starting grooves with his finger, he whispered, "We've got to talk."

Agis scowled, but crouched beside him. "Where's Pericles? Did he find the Warrior?"

"No, he didn't. Listen, Agis, you've got to trust me!

This wasn't my idea, and it's not for me, or any sort of personal glory. There isn't time to explain everything now, but you've got to let me win the sprint and you've got to let Pericles win the wrestling if you meet him in the final. Otherwise the terrorists will destroy the Games."

He hadn't explained it well enough. Agis' scowl deepened. Kallias and Dion were delaying, pretending to stretch their already warm muscles, while Trainer Hermon tapped his whip against his leg. "On your marks, boys!" he said. "We're running late enough."

"You've got to let me win, Agis!" Sosi hissed as the skinny boy straightened and wriggled his toe into the groove in preparation for the start.

Agis scowled. "No way, Macedonian. I beat you in Piera, and I'll beat you again here at Olympia. If you're stupid enough to wear yourself out racing all over the mountain before your event, that's your lookout. I swore an Olympic oath. I'm not cheating."

"You don't understand! It's not cheating—"

"No talking, you two!" Trainer Hermon moved behind them to check they were in the starting position. "Or you'll feel my whip, Olympia or not. Now remember. If anyone dares jump the start, they'll be publicly flogged." He tapped Kallias on the shoulder. "Understand?"

Kallias swallowed and nodded. "Yes, sir." He winked at Sosi.

"Right, then. Make it a good race, boys. May the best win."

Trainer Hermon walked back to the side of the course and nodded to the herald, who announced, "The boys' sprint! Four runners: Agis of Athens, Theron of Macedonian Pella, Kallias of Ephesos and Dion of Corinth. Two non-runners due to injury: Pericles of Rhodes and Samos of Elis."

The starter raised his trumpet and a hush descended over the stadium. A ripple of unexpected excitement went through Sosi. He leant forward, bare toes gripping the starting groove, trying to remember everything he'd been taught about getting a good start.

Such a short distance. Six hundred paces. One stade.

An Olympic olive crown, glory and honour for the winner. Nothing for the losers. And the stakes were so much higher today.

Theron should be doing this, not me.

Time slowed.

The trumpet blared and the four of them burst from the start, locked together. As he'd been taught, Sosi focused his gaze on the finish line at the other end of the stadium and tried to empty his mind of everything else. Out of the corner of his eye he could see the others racing, their tanned legs a blur, their arms pumping wildly. Kallias had got one of his best starts ever, and Dion was racing flat out – he must have forgotten in all the excitement that he was supposed to let Sosi win. Agis' teeth were clenched with determination.

Forget them. Concentrate on the line, only the line.

Sosi felt, rather than saw, first Kallias and then Dion

drop behind slightly. Only Agis was a danger now, and the line was rushing closer. He clenched his fists. A dead heat wasn't good enough. He had to win. He made a supreme effort and drew ahead slightly. Then his calf muscle cramped, and he remembered his mother's words when he'd taken his brother's shape.

You haven't a hope against the other boys.

He shook his head, fighting the cramp, only to hear his brother's voice.

If you run in my place, you'll lose.

All at once, he remembered who he was. Slow, cursed Sosi, who had never won a race in his life. His stride faltered, and Agis shot him a look of triumph as he drew abreast. It was no good, the pain was stopping him, the line was too close.

Three strides...

Two...

"Don't you dare give up, Sosipolis," Nike whispered in his head. *"You're the snake-child who can stop battles. The others can't do that."*

One...

Ancient pride filled him. Teeth gritted against the pain, he threw himself forwards across the line.

Sosi's legs gave way. He rolled over and lay on his back, sobbing for breath and clutching his calf in agony. There was such a long pause, he wondered if it had been a draw despite his efforts. But after consultation with the judges, the trumpet sounded a long, triumphant note, and the herald announced, "Winner of the boys' sprint! Theron, son of Commander Sarapion of Macedonian Pella! Theron will have the honour of carrying the torch to light the fires for the Great Sacrifice on the third day of the festival. Victory to Theron of Macedonian Pella!"

Hands pulled him to his feet, and suddenly everyone was cheering and shouting his name. Flowers showered into the stadium as Nike brought him the winner's red ribbon, petals settling in her dark hair like snow. Pride and strength filled Sosi like a second sun, and at that moment he understood exactly why his brother wanted to be a champion athlete. Nothing to do with not wanting to fight, and certainly not because he was a coward. But for this wonderful, painful, sweet, hard-won breath of glory.

But the crowd was chanting his brother's name, not his. And Nike was walking slowly and carefully, like an old woman. Sosi's triumph turned to a sick feeling in the pit of his stomach as he remembered why he'd won. "It didn't work, did it?" he whispered as Nike tied the woollen ribbon around his arm with trembling hands.

She shook her head. "I don't think I'll be able to fly for a few days."

Her whisper was very unlike her usual bravado, and hopelessness flooded Sosi. "I'm sorry, Nike! I heard you, I really did. But my curse—"

She knotted the wool, scowled, and said in her more usual voice, "Shh! Act like a winner! I'll be fine if Pericles wins the wrestling. Don't let everyone know. I'm good at hiding it."

She walked away, slowly and steadily, and no one noticed how weak she was because everyone was looking at Sosi, clapping and calling for him to run a victory lap. Kallias and Dion rushed up to congratulate him. "I'm sorry I forgot to hold back," Dion whispered. And Kallias said, "Hush, he won anyway. That was brilliant, Sosi! Theron himself couldn't have done better."

"Your start was good," Sosi mumbled, not knowing what else to say, and Kallias beamed.

But Agis, who had been sulking nearby, pushed closer and said, "What do you mean, 'Sosi'? You mean to say he's not Theron?"

"Shh!" Kallias grabbed the Athenian's arm. "You're up against Glaukos in the first round of the wrestling. Let me help you with your oil. The boxing's next, so you've got time to visit the baths..." Between them, he and Dion managed to hustle a bewildered Agis out of the stadium.

Sosi hardly noticed. After his victory lap, which he managed to limp round while his cramp eased, he had to report to the judges' stand, where Theron's name was entered in the official list of winners, and the judges gave him a palm branch to go with his winner's wool. To his relief, he discovered that because he'd missed the draw for the wrestling he had been given a bye through to the second round. Only after the judges had dismissed him and the Eleans were escorting him through the cheering crowds to the tunnel, did he realize what this meant.

If Glaukos didn't manage to take out Agis in the wrestling, he'd meet the Athenian in the second round. And after his defeat in the sprint, Agis would be out for blood.

His escort took him to the oiling room of the baths, where the others entered in the boys' wrestling were getting ready for their event. More soldiers guarded the door, still on high alert for a terrorist attack. Kallias and Dion had trapped Agis in the corner. To Sosi's relief, Pericles was there as well, his bad leg propped on a bench while Kallias massaged it with foul-smelling unguent from a jar. It seemed the three of them were trying to talk Agis round, but Sosi could tell by the expression on the Athenian's face that they weren't getting very far.

As he went across to join his friends, several boys he didn't know clapped his shoulder and congratulated him on his win. He mumbled thanks, feeling like a traitor. The red ribbon trailed uncomfortably from his bicep, reminding him every time he looked at it of how he and Theron had cheated. He wanted to rip it off, but athletes did not remove their victory ribbons until they were crowned at the end of the festival. To do so would offend Zeus, and Sosi suspected he had offended the god quite enough already.

Agis' gaze fastened on his arm. "Think you're clever, don't you, Macedonian?" he hissed. "Distracting me with all your stupid talk so I lost the race!"

"Sosi won because he ran faster than us, Agis," Kallias said. "You can't deny that."

"He cheated. He raced under the wrong name. The boys' sprint should have been mine."

"You wouldn't have beaten Theron."

"Who says? If this crazy story you told me is true, the real Theron's still got a poisoned foot. Even Kallias could beat him!"

"Keep your voices down," Pericles growled, glancing at the guards. "Everyone else entered in the wrestling knows they're supposed to let me win if they make the final, so all I'm asking that if you get through, you do the same."

Agis scowled. "I'll think about it."

"Thinking isn't enough. You've got to promise! Otherwise, Glaukos will do what he can to take you out in the first round. He knows some tricks, don't you Glaukos? Things to make sure you won't compete again." Glaukos, who had been with them on the mountain, nodded and folded his oiled arms.

Agis licked his lips and swallowed. "If you cripple me on purpose, you'll be disqualified from the Circuit for life," he said.

"Glaukos is prepared for that," Pericles said. "But obviously he'd prefer to keep his name clean. All we need is your promise. Come on, Agis! I thought you were as keen as anyone to stop these Warriors from disrupting the Games? Now's your big chance. Think I like it any more than you do? Believe me, the last thing I want is an Olympic crown because someone let me win! But Nike's right, it's not about us any more. It's about the future of the Games and the whole of the Hellas. Even if you don't care about that, at least have some thought for the athletes. Everyone she sent dreams will be affected."

"Nike didn't send *me* a dream," Agis said with a bitter twist of his lips. "I can't see why you're all panicking, anyway. The Warrior hasn't managed to stop the boys' events—"

Pericles staggered off the bench and grasped him by the throat, making the guards at the door stiffen. "Was that the only reason you were worried? Don't you care about *anyone* else? I never realized quite how selfish you were! I'm not surprised Nike's never sent you a dream of victory! Right then, have it your own way." He let go of the boy and nodded to Glaukos. "Try not to injure him too badly. If he gets as far as me, I'll finish him off."

Agis staggered back against the wall, his eyes swivelling from side to side. "I'll go to the judges," he threatened. "I'll tell them about Theron and this... cheating brother of his." He spat at Sosi. "Do you honestly believe he can change his shape? Isn't it obvious he's lying? They're just twins, pulling a stupid trick on us all."

"We're not twins," Sosi said, feeling a bit sorry for the Athenian boy. He knew what it was like to be one against many, and Agis was the only one of them who hadn't broken his Olympic oath.

"Stop trying to change the subject," Pericles growled, rubbing his leg. "If you do go to the judges, it'll be worse for you afterwards. Everyone else is with us."

The other boys gathered round and nodded. The guards must have decided Agis could stick up for himself, because they didn't interfere.

Agis gave them another trapped look. "I didn't say I wouldn't do it," he muttered. "I'm just pointing out that it's cheating."

Glaukos looked a bit relieved. So did Pericles. "Then you agree?" Pericles asked. "And you won't tell the judges?"

Agis avoided their eyes. "I won't go to the judges yet. But if this stuff about curses and dead Warriors turns out to be a trick, I'll tell them how you all cheated, and then they'll award the boys' sprint to me." He glared again at the ribbon on Sosi's arm and pushed past them.

By the time the rest of them got back to the stadium, they'd missed most of the boxing. Sosi was glad because seeing the boys with their fists bound in leather thongs reminded him of Samos and the way he'd never box again. One of the finalists had a cut above his eye. He kept shaking his head to get rid of the flies feasting on the blood that ran down his face. The crowd was noisy, cheering on both boys. Meanwhile, the first rounds of the wrestling were taking place at the quieter ends of the stadium, where Agis had just thrown Glaukos for the third time to win his heat.

"Damn," Pericles muttered. "He's a tricky one. Watch him, Sosi."

After that, the afternoon went from bad to worse.

Sosi lost the second round of the wrestling to Agis, distracted at the crucial moment by a roar from the crowd as the boxer with blood on his face crumpled to his knees. "Got you, Macedonian!" Agis puffed, looking down at Sosi in satisfaction. "Doesn't feel so good when you lose, does it?"

Sosi climbed painfully to his feet, worried about Nike, who was holding on to the enclosure rail with another priestess fussing over her. When the winner of the boys' boxing went to receive his wool at the gate, the other priestess had to help Nike tie it on. Then Nike sat down and put her head between her knees. Sosi desperately wanted to talk to her, but she was surrounded by judges. He brushed himself off and staggered over to join Kallias and Dion, who had been watching the fight from the athletes' section of the bank.

"Did Agis cheat?" Kallias wanted to know. "Why did Nike collapse like that?"

"It's because Samos didn't win the boxing." Sosi eased his bruised back and shivered with foreboding. His sweat had broken out again, mixing with the oil and sand on his skin to form a gritty layer. The fierce afternoon sun turned the crowded stadium into a dust bowl. He couldn't seem to get his breath. "Don't worry, Agis wanted revenge for me beating him in the sprint. It'll be different with Pericles. He knows how important this is."

"He'd better keep his promise," Kallias muttered, scowling at his friend.

"Poor Nike!" Dion said. "She looks awful. Will that happen to you, Sosi?"

Sosi shook himself. "It's not the same. I don't have Nike's link to humans. I get the power every full moon. Nothing can stop me changing." He hoped. *I changed into a snake. I couldn't change back.*

Dion bit his lip. "What about tomorrow night? Whose shape will you take?"

"I don't know," Sosi said with another shiver. The full moon was rushing towards him as quickly as the finish line had in the sprint, and he wasn't ready. "It would be best if I kept Theron's shape, I suppose. Everyone will be expecting him to carry the torch for the Great Sacrifice, and his foot's still bad so he can't do it himself. Also, he'll be expected to attend the prize-giving ceremony on the last day. I'll probably have to do that for him as well."

Assuming there was a prize-giving ceremony after the Warrior had made his move. Assuming any of them were still alive.

"I hope he gets better soon so you can take your own shape," Dion said. "It'd be good to see what you really look like."

"Shh!" Kallias hissed. "They're starting."

The centre of the stadium had been raked clean of blood and levelled for the final of the boys' wrestling. Pericles and Agis sanded themselves under the stern gazes of Judge Demetrius and the physician. Pericles' leg seemed worse, and it was obvious the judges were only letting him compete for the crowd's sake, perhaps to make up for their earlier disappointing announcement that Samos of Elis had been too ill to compete in the boys' boxing. Agis looked tired, but smiled as he stepped into the prepared area. The crowd fell silent when Pericles limped to join him, sensing at last that something was not right. Sosi could hardly bear to watch.

When Agis scored the first throw, they knew at once he was not going to let Pericles win. Only Pericles' greater bulk and skill kept the contest from being a walkover. Somehow, with a massive effort, he managed to throw Agis once. But it finished his leg, and the skinny Athenian scored two more throws to win the contest. By this time, the crowd was wincing whenever Pericles hit the ground, and urged him up with shouts of encouragement. Agis' final throw resulted in silence as Pericles lay motionless with his eyes closed.

The physician rushed to attend him. There was an embarrassing pause before the trumpet blared and the herald proclaimed Agis of Athens as winner of the boys' wrestling.

"The little *snake*," Kallias said, then glanced at Sosi. "Sorry... but he promised! What does he think he's playing at? Just wait till I get him alone!"

"What about Pericles?" Dion cried. "Why won't he get up?"

Sosi clenched his fists. Sweat drenched him, and he felt as weak as if he had lost the wrestling final himself. "Nike," he whispered. "It's her link to the athletes, it works both ways. Her weakness affects all those she's sent dreams. Pericles, Rasim, Samos, *Theron...*" He looked at the slope of Mount Kronos and turned cold.

Nike had fainted in the judges' stand, so the other priestess had to tie on Agis' wool. Pericles was lifted on a stretcher and carried out through the tunnel, while another stretcher was brought at the run for Nike. The crowd overran the stadium, demanding to know why an injured boy had been allowed to compete. Frantic relatives mobbed the judges' stand, wanting to know if their sons were all right, why the athletes and priestesses were collapsing, and was there a plague? The Elean guards gave up trying to keep control and hustled the ephebes back towards the Altis.

In the gloom of the tunnel, the boys closed around Agis with ugly looks and snatched the palm branch from his hand. Sosi felt dizzy. He didn't know if it was the approach of his curse, reaction to winning the sprint, the bruising he'd received from Agis in the wrestling, or what was happening in the tunnel.

Just as he thought the day could get no worse, one of the priestesses from the Blood House ran past with the news that Samos of Elis was dead.

Chapter 16

SNAKE

AFTER SAMOS' DEATH and Nike's collapse, the traditional party in the Prytaneon to celebrate the victors of the boys' events was a miserable occasion. Winners and losers alike hung about the edges of the hall in muttering groups; no one could face the feast. Even Agis, after his lucky escape in the tunnel, sensed that this was not the right time to flaunt his victory ribbon and left the party early.

Sosi felt too sick to eat. Kallias had gone to the Blood House to see Pericles, and Dion slept in a corner, having gulped down three cups of specially watered wine before anyone could stop him – the poor squirt had been so shaken up by Samos' death, it seemed cruel to wake him. Worried about Theron, Sosi took one of the torches from the supply used to light the altar fires and slipped out of the Prytaneon. No one noticed him leave.

He risked the shortest, steepest route to the sanctuary. The moon was bright, and he found the fissure easily enough. But it was not as easy to force himself inside. He broke into a sweat as he remembered the cave of snakeskins where he'd died in his past life.

"I don't have to go down there," he told himself. "Theron will be with the women. It's not the full moon until tomorrow night. We'll be out of the caves long before then."

At least, he hoped so. Thoughts of his brother collapsing like Pericles had done, and lying helpless in the dark, gave him the strength to go on. His torch sent shadows dancing round the tunnel walls. Everything seemed unfamiliar. He closed his eyes, trying to remember the way he'd come last time when his snake instinct had been guiding him, but it was no good. He wished Priestess Eileithyia would appear with her lantern.

Each time he stopped to get his bearings, it was harder to go on. He imagined Warriors watching him from every dark opening. But eventually, a whiff of perfume reached him over the musty smell of the rock, and he recognized the tunnels that led to the women's cavern. No light showed ahead and hope flickered. Maybe Eretaia had persuaded the women to leave, and they were all safely back in Elis? He hurried around the final bend – and stopped in confusion.

The way ahead was blocked.

He stared in dismay at the pile of rubble that filled the tunnel. "Mother?" he shouted, propping his torch against the wall and digging with his bare hands. "Theron? Eretaia? Are you in there? Can anyone hear me?"

There was a soft chuckle behind him, and an accented voice said, "I can hear you, snake-boy."

Sosi whirled in alarm and grabbed for the torch. A foot kicked it out of his hand. The torch hit the rock in an explosion of sparks and went out, leaving him and his assailant in absolute blackness. He crouched against the rockfall, sweating in terror. His eyes could still see ghosts of the light, but he ignored them and used his heat-sense to search desperately for the glow of a body in the dark.

Nothing, of course. His assailant chuckled again, and purple flared around the tunnel walls. The crimson-bearded Warrior who had been in the dormitory at Letrini stood between him and freedom, his eyes glittering in the light of the flame he held in his bare hands. "I knew you would come, snake-boy," he said.

"You've got it wrong." Sosi's voice cracked in fear. "I'm Theron."

The Warrior laughed. "Is that so? You might look amazingly like your brother, but I think we both know that's a lie. You're not as good an athlete as he is, and you never will be, no matter what shape you take. You're a failure, Sosipolis. You failed last time you were here, and you're about to fail again. Oh, yes, I know your name. After a little persuasion, the old woman told me everything about you. How you changed into a snake to save the Games but couldn't change back again, and how you died down here. Your only way out was to reincarnate yourself in the body of a Macedonian – I can only think you must have been desperate, but there won't even be a Macedonian available next time. You've interfered for the last time. Congratulations on your victory in the sprint, by the way. Shame it didn't work out. How's the proud Priestess Nike? Is she ready to submit to me yet?"

Sosi clenched his fists. The purple flame held his gaze, flickering and dancing in the darkness. He could not look away. "What have you done to my brother?" he whispered. "Where's my mother? If you've hurt them, I'll—"

The Warrior raised an eyebrow. "You'll what? You can't fight me down here, snake-boy. I'm stronger than you while you're in your human shape. And, thanks to old Eileithyia's fascinating tale, I think I know how to keep you from changing it."

Sosi licked his dry lips. "Rasim told me what you're planning! If you bring Ahriman's army to Olympia, everyone will die. Don't you even care about your own son?"

The Warrior frowned. "Ah yes, you foolishly untied the cord I knotted around his neck, didn't you? I suppose he has some misguided idea he can escape Ahriman by helping you. Not to worry, the Dark One will reclaim him soon enough, and many more of you besides. Shame about your brother's foot. He'd have made a good Warrior with his athletic abilities."

Sosi shuddered. "Where is he?"

"Can't you guess?"

Sosi looked at the rubble in despair. "You... you've killed them..."

The Warrior laughed, stepped up close behind him and whispered in his ear, "Now, snake-boy, be sensible. Would I kill my hostages? Your mother and brother are alive for the time being, and they'll stay that way as long as you behave. They're in a safe place, and you'll be joining them shortly. It seems I don't have the power to send you to Ahriman just yet, but I need to make sure you don't interfere with my plans. The old woman told me that without moonlight your shape-changing ability will not work. Where better to imprison you than in the same cave where you so tragically 'died' twelve years ago?"

Fear flooded Sosi, but his brain still worked. He might be able to get past the Warrior if he were to knock the flame out of his hands as he had done at Letrini. He'd find the way out eventually in the dark, using his snake senses... But there was his mother and brother and the other women to consider.

"Eileithyia!" he shouted at the rock pile. "Eretaia! Can anyone hear me?"

The Warrior sighed in his ear. "There's no point shouting. The other women were of no further use to me."

Sosi spun in sudden fury, his foot hooking behind the Warrior's heel and his hands gripping the dead man's arms through the thick cloak. He heaved, trying to throw him as he had been taught. But the Warrior twisted in his grip and touched his flame to the end of Sosi's victory ribbon. Purple fire flared along the wool, and Sosi was forced to abandon his wrestler's hold to tug at the ribbon. His heart beat wildly. Nike's knot was a good one, and before he could get it undone the fire licked his skin.

He gasped, expecting the flame to be hot, only to find it was ice-cold. His arm tingled. Before he had a chance to recover, the Warrior kicked his legs out from under him, produced one of his enchanted cords from beneath his cloak, and wound it tightly about Sosi's wrists. He finished by wrenching out a handful of Sosi's hair and threading it through his bonds. Sosi struggled, but it was no good. He ended up on his knees, staring at the final scraps of burning ribbon as they floated to the ground.

Theron's victory. Gone. Useless.

"I have you now, snake-boy," the Warrior said, jerking on the end of the cord to demonstrate. His limbs heavy with enchantment, Sosi overbalanced and bloodied his nose on the rock. The Warrior kindled another purple flame and let it lick the flesh under Sosi's chin – another touch of ice. "Up! Or your mother and brother will suffer."

Sosi rose on wobbly legs. They went the way Eileithyia had taken him, his captor jerking on the leash to keep him moving. The cord around his wrists was tight, and his hands went numb as he stumbled after the Warrior deeper into the mountain. "Please," he whispered. "Please don't put me in there."

They came to the cave of snakeskins. As Sosi had feared, the huge boulder had been rolled across the entrance to seal it. He tensed, looking for something to use as a weapon. The Warrior would have to let him go to move the boulder. He might be able to get the cord off, fetch help... But he'd forgotten his captor was a sorcerer. Keeping a firm hold of Sosi's leash and watching him all the time, he touched the purple flame to the boulder and called on Ahriman.

Sosi cringed as fire filled the tunnel and the boulder rolled aside, revealing the piles of snakeskins beyond. They sparkled dark violet in the unnatural light.

"Welcome to your tomb, snake-boy," the Warrior said with a chuckle.

Every part of Sosi screamed against going into that place. He braced his legs in the entrance. Then he heard something move in the skins and saw Lady Alcmena's dark hair. "Mother!" he cried.

Her wrists and ankles had been bound with the Warrior's enchanted cords and her eyes were closed, but as the Warrior dragged Sosi inside, stirring up the dust, she coughed in her drugged sleep.

"She's not well!" Sosi cried, forgetting his own fear. "Let her go!" Then he saw his brother, similarly tied and unconscious on the other side of the cave, his bandaged leg bloody and swollen. "Theron's hurt! It's not fair to tie them up like that!"

The Warrior jerked on his leash and threw him face down in the skins. He knelt astride him, knees pressing into his ribs, and touched his cheek with the flame. "Shut up and stop struggling," he hissed. "Or I'll kill them both and leave you in here alone."

Sosi closed his eyes and lay still.

The Warrior tied Sosi's wrists to his ankles until he could barely move, gave the bonds a final tug and climbed off him. "Now, snake-boy, I want you to listen very carefully, because I've a few things to do before the Great Sacrifice, and I don't want you getting free and sticking your nose in. Let me explain about the magic in the cords. Ahriman's fire seals the ends and your hair completes the link. If you try to escape by loosening the knots or cutting them, I will know. Every time I feel you struggle, I will kill one of your friends down in the Altis. Understand?"

Sosi managed a nod. A chill went through him as he realized the Warrior must have known the moment he'd untied that cord from Rasim's neck.

"Victory will be mine very soon. You shouldn't starve or die of thirst before then. Afterwards, I'll have more time to deal with you. You can no doubt be controlled by the proper rituals. Failing that, I can simply keep you in here and make sure you don't get the chance to reincarnate yourself."

"It's different this time," Sosi whispered, trying to convince himself as much as the Warrior. "I'm not a snake."

"No, I can see that." The Warrior's lips twisted into a cruel smile. "Couldn't even take the one shape that might have saved your friends, could you? And now you never will. You'll never see the full moon again."

He rekindled his flame and pushed Sosi over

sideways. The boulder rumbled back across the entrance, cutting off the last flicker of light.

Half-glimpsed terrors surrounded Sosi, like his nightmares only more frightening because this time he wasn't asleep. He wasn't sure how long he lay sweating in the dark, cursing himself for being so stupid, before a voice whispered, "Is that you, little brother? Did he catch you, too? Are you all right?"

Sosi twisted his head and saw his brother's body heat move. He closed his eyes, relief and hopelessness mixed together.

"Theron! I'm sorry... I tried to help, but the Warrior was too strong."

Theron sighed. "It doesn't matter, little brother. I know you tried your best. I don't really mind about the sprint. I didn't expect you to win, anyway."

"But I did win!" Sosi struggled to roll over, realizing his brother must think he'd been captured *before* the events. He heard skins rustle as Theron moved as well. "I won the boys' sprint for you, just like we planned! Only it didn't help Nike..." Quickly, he explained everything his brother had missed, sparing him nothing. Theron listened in silence, even to the part about Samos' death. But when Sosi told him about the avalanche blocking off the women's cavern, his brother made a choked sound.

"Mother?" he whispered. "And Eretaia? Please tell me they got out."

Sosi bit his lip. "Mother's in here with us. She coughed when the Warrior brought me in, and I can see her body heat so she's alive, though I think she's very sick." He hesitated. "Eretaia didn't turn up to watch Pericles compete. She must have been in the cave with the other women..." He paused, imagining Eretaia's bright hair buried under the rubble. "I'm really sorry, Theron. At least he didn't make her Ahriman's."

There was a muffled sound in the dark. Sosi didn't say anything, knowing his brother was crying and trying to hide it. After a suitable pause, he eased his wrists and said, "Can you reach Mother? She's over to your left. I can't move much."

There was more skin rustling. Sosi tried to wriggle towards her as well, but it was impossible. The Warrior had tied him too tightly.

Theron made a frustrated sound, clearly having the same problem. "Mother?" he called. "Mother? You've got to wake up!"

No answer.

"We have to get out of here somehow," Theron continued. "I wish I had a knife."

"We can't cut the cords!" Sosi told him what the Warrior had said.

"Do you believe that? He might just have said it to stop us from trying to escape."

"We can't take the risk."

His brother grunted. "I haven't got a knife, anyway, and these knots are horribly tight. My hands are numb."

"Mine, too."

"Do you think he'll really be able to bring an army of dead Persians into the Altis?"

"I don't know. But Priestess Nike seems to think he can."

There was another pause as they both thought of the fate planned for Nike and the panic an army of Persian Warriors would cause at the Olympic Games. "I wish Father were here," Theron whispered. "I want to tell him I don't hate him for making me join the army... before I die."

"Don't talk like that!" Sosi said, alarmed. "There's still plenty of time to stop the Warrior. The Great Sacrifice isn't until the day after tomorrow, and it's the full moon tomorrow night. If we can get out of here before then, I can change."

"Big deal," Theron said with a flash of his old bitterness. "Who'll you change into? Ahriman himself, maybe?"

Sosi took a deep breath. "A snake," he whispered. "It's obvious. It's what I did before to save the Games, and the Warrior more or less told me it's the only shape that can stop him. I *am* supposed to be half snake."

Theron was silent a while, digesting this. Then he said gruffly, "I'm sorry, little brother. I'm sorry for getting you into this mess and for calling you useless all the time. You're not, you know. Coming up here on your own, knowing the Warrior was here, that was really brave. And who'd have guessed you would win the boys' sprint after only a month's training? That's an achievement for anyone."

Sosi felt like crying again. "I wasn't brave. I was stupid! I should have brought the others with me."

"The Warrior would only have killed them. You did the right thing. It's not your fault the terrorist came to Olympia. Can you really change into a snake?"

"I don't know. Nike seems to think I can. But I have to get out of here first, or I won't be able to change at all."

They discussed various plans for getting out of the cave, each one more fantastic than the last. But it soon became obvious their position was hopeless. Unless someone rescued them before tomorrow night, the Warrior had won. The only other person who knew the location of the snake cave was Priestess Eileithyia, who was trapped under the rockfall, if not already dead. They lapsed into silence. Sosi's brain had gone numb. Was this what Rasim had felt like when his father had knotted that cord on him and sent him to Ahriman?

"You can still change, Sosi."

The words were so quiet, Sosi barely heard. He stiffened. He didn't realize their mother had been awake and listening.

Lady Alcmena coughed and whispered, "If you want to try it, I won't stop you. Maybe it won't be the same for you as it was for Eileithyia's son."

At first, he couldn't work out what she was telling him. But Theron said sharply, "What do you mean? I thought Sosi couldn't shape-change if he was sealed away from moonlight?"

Lady Alcmena made a choked sound that was almost a laugh. "Maybe that's what the Warrior thought Eileithyia told him, but it's not true. I know very well Sosi can change without moonlight. That was the first thing I tried, locking him in a dark room to stop him doing it, only it never did. I expect Eileithyia told the Warrior what she told me, that her son Sosipolis couldn't change back into a boy and was sealed in this cave. She used to seal him in *because* he couldn't change back, not to stop him changing. She wanted to keep him away from curious eyes. There's a slight difference. Poor woman... I hope that Warrior didn't hurt her too much."

Sosi's skin prickled, but Theron let out a harsh laugh. "I'd love to see the expression on that Warrior's face when he realizes Sosi changed into a snake, after all!"

"I'll still have to get out of here." Sosi's heart was beating very fast.

"If you make yourself small enough, you should be all right," their mother said. "There must have been several earthquakes since Eileithyia's son was sealed in here. That boulder doesn't fit exactly. There's a gap at one corner. I noticed it when the Warrior brought me in here. It's about finger-sized, so don't make yourself too big. We'll have to stay here, of course, but I'm sure you'll think of a way to let people know where we are."

"As long as I don't forget I was ever a boy," Sosi said, the fear talking.

"You won't forget," Theron said firmly. "Whenever you think you're becoming too much like a snake, just remember what it was like to win that sprint!"

The waiting was terrible. In the dark there was no way of telling the time, or even if it was night or day. Sosi drifted in and out of nightmares, sweating. He dared not struggle against his bonds in case the Warrior had spoken the truth about being able to sense the knots, and killed one of his friends. He developed a terrible cramp. Sometimes Theron spoke to him, and sometimes their mother, but it was like people speaking in a dream and he couldn't remember what they said. He kept wondering if it would hurt to change into a snake. Then he was afraid in case he couldn't do it, after all.

In the end, though, it was easy, almost as if his body had been waiting for him to give it permission to take his snake form. The curse settled over him like a dark blanket, and his bonds loosened as his limbs shrank away and his body became thinner and smaller. He slipped out of the Warrior's knotted cords and wriggled through the snakeskins towards the boy who had called him brother. He wanted to touch him, but he no longer had hands. He pushed his head close to his brother's cheek and flickered his long, forked tongue.

Theron.

No word came out. But the boy stirred and whispered, "Little brother?"

He tasted fear in his brother's sweat.

"Well done, little brother! Don't forget us, will you? Remember you're human! Don't forget that race!"

Sosi wriggled over to his mother and flickered his tongue at her, too. She made no response. He found the gap under the boulder and squeezed through.

The tunnel floor was rough, and he kept wanting to get to his feet. But as he got the hang of slithering, he found he could move surprisingly fast. The air in the tunnels was thick with fascinating smell-tastes. He couldn't stop his tongue from flickering out to sample them.

He passed the place where the avalanche blocked the tunnel and paused. Something sad here. He flickered his tongue at the rubble, but could only taste traces of burnt wool. There was an inviting hole where someone had dug into the rubble. Changing his skin always exhausted him, and this last change had been the greatest yet. He slipped inside, curled up and slept.

A slight warming of the air woke the little snake. He crawled out of the hole and paused, chasing a strange dream where he'd been running upright on two feet like a human, cheered on by a great crowd. He headed for the warmth, slithering faster as light showed ahead. He'd been in the cave too long. He needed to sunbathe and dry his new skin.

The entrance to the tunnels had been blocked by another avalanche, but he was a very small snake and wriggled out between the rocks. He warmed himself in the first rays of the sun, keeping a lookout for predators from the sky. Activity raged below – many humans and animals, rushing about. Their voices carried up the mountain on the motionless air, which was charged with an excitement he could almost taste. There was something he was supposed to do, only he couldn't remember what.

A trumpet blast startled him, echoing across the plain. His snake body jerked in response as it remembered countless mornings waking in a dormitory surrounded by human boys, and his memory came back in a rush.

My name is Sosipolis. These are the Olympic Games. I am the Saviour.

Chapter 17

SACRIFICE

CLOUDS WERE BUILDING into towers on the horizon as Sosi slithered up one of the columns of the Philippeon and coiled himself around the poppy head on its roof. From this vantage point, he could see the judges' purple hats holding back the crowd surrounding the Great Altar, while on its summit a priest poured oil over kindling in preparation for the sacrificial fire.

A procession of red-robed priests and priestesses led a hundred white bulls with garlands of scarlet flowers around their necks through the Altis gate, while Elean soldiers gripped their spears and kept watch. The noise was incredible. Singing and flute music accompanied the bellowing of the oxen, competing with the neighing of horses from the riverbanks and the laughter and shouts of the crowd, until he longed to flee back to the caves.

An argument started outside the Prytaneon, where the

athletes were emerging in their dazzling white robes to attend the ceremony. The men hurried to take their places at the Great Altar, but the ephebes remained in a knot around the door. A tall, skinny boy thrust his way through the others, holding a torch. He wore a pristine white loincloth, his skin had been freshly oiled, and a red victory ribbon trailed from his arm.

"Sosi should carry the torch!" said one of the boys, his voice carrying on the still air. "Wait a bit longer, Agis. Please."

"Don't be stupid," the skinny boy said. "He's been gone more than a day! It's obvious the lying little brat's done a runner. I don't blame him. He'll be in a lot of trouble when the judges find out what he and his brother did. Judge Demetrius said if he wasn't back in time, I could carry the torch. I don't see anyone here who looks like Theron, do you?"

"I still say we should have looked harder for those caves," the first boy said, glancing up the mountain. "The entrance can't just have disappeared. Theron got inside somehow, didn't he?"

"Ha!" the skinny one sneered. "That hillside's out of bounds for a good reason. Those tunnels are dangerous. Theron and his sneaky brother probably got themselves buried in there, and it serves them right for pulling such a dirty trick on us all! Out of my way. I've a lot of altars to get round before this thing goes out."

"I'm going to have another look," the other boy said. "I'm worried about Sosi. He wouldn't have just left without saying goodbye. I don't mind about missing the Great Sacrifice. Anyone else coming?"

Several boys nodded, and the skinny one scowled. "Go ahead! All you'll find when you get up there is empty caves, see if I'm not right."

A great cheer went up from the crowd as he jogged towards the Temple of Hera, the torch held high so that its flame trailed behind him like a banner. People formed a corridor for the torch-bearer, and whistled and clapped as he ran past. Sosi stared after the torch, knowing he should feel something, yet unable to think what.

Don't forget the race.

Of course, the boys' sprint. That should be him carrying the Olympic Torch. No, it should be his brother...

Too confusing. Human stuff. Don't think about it.

Another trumpet blared, and for a horrible moment he forgot what shape he had. He grabbed at the poppy with non-existent hands and slipped off the roof. It didn't hurt much because he was so small and light. Some of the boys left the Altis and headed up Mount Kronos. The skinny one with the victory ribbon emerged from the Temple of Hera, still carrying the flaming torch, and ran on through the cheering crowds to the Temple of Rhea. Sosi flickered his tongue; the smoke had a strange taste.

A threatening rumble came from the thunderclouds as he slithered unnoticed between people's feet and along the edges of paths, using what cover he could find. It was difficult to get his bearings so close to the ground, and he looked for something else to climb.

Then two priests strode over him carrying a stretcher. On the stretcher lay a girl dressed in ceremonial red. Her black hair, bound into a long braid threaded with gold ribbon, had flopped over the edge of the stretcher and trailed along the ground. He slithered after it, spooking the oxen at the front of the procession, which bellowed when they caught his snake-scent and pushed against the rest of the herd. The priestesses in charge of the animals shouted a warning, and the crowd surged back in alarm, fearing a stampede. The priests carrying the stretcher stopped, their way blocked by white rumps and dung-splattered tails. In the confusion, Sosi wriggled up the girl's braid and hid in a fold of her robes.

Nike! Wake up! I'm here!

She was barely conscious. He flickered his tongue at her cheek in an effort to wake her, but had to slip quickly back under her hair as the priests set down their burden at the foot of the Great Altar. The steps cut into the side of the ash mound were too steep to negotiate with the stretcher, so one of them draped Nike over his shoulder and climbed with her, puffing under her weight. Sosi curled up in a fold of her chiton and stayed very still.

They reached the top, and the priest set down his burden with a jolt that almost dislodged Sosi from his hiding place. "Phew!" the priest grumbled. "I swear she's heavier than a grown man! Don't know why we bothered bringing her up here this year, Priest Rhexibius sir. She's too sick to be much use."

The big-bellied priest sighed. "Don't worry, I'll do her part of the ceremony. She'll be better after the Sacrifice, she always is. She has to be here, you know that."

"I know she's Zeus' chosen one. But people are asking what's wrong with her. And it's not gone unnoticed that the judges are one short this year. Rumours are still spreading about a plague."

"Then we'll show them everything's fine when Priestess Nike miraculously recovers, won't we? There's been no leak about the Elean boy being pushed, has there?"

"None, sir."

"Thank Zeus for small mercies. And the Persian boy is under guard?"

"He's not going anywhere with those injuries, sir. But the other priests don't like keeping him in the Blood House. They're saying he ought to be dead, and several of them swear his neck was already broken when he fell from the gallery with the Elean boy. It's unnatural the way he turned up in the Hippodrome yesterday, and his horse went crazy – did you see?"

Another flicker of memory tugged at Sosi, but it was more human stuff. He had to concentrate, or he'd forget what he had come to do.

The young priest lowered his voice. "Sir, *is* there something unnatural going on? It looks as if it's going to thunder before we're done. It'll be seen as a bad omen during the Great Sacrifice. Are the terrorists going to try something today? The ephebes seem to think they will."

Priest Rhexibius fixed him with a stern eye. "Judge Demetrius knows what he's doing. Terrorists cannot be allowed to stop the Olympic Games. I know some bad things have happened, but we'll sort out the mess after everyone's gone home. The important thing is that the festival goes as smoothly as possible from now on. Go down and tell the others to start slaughtering the oxen, quick as you can. Where's that damned boy got to with the torch? Let's see if we can't get the sacrifice finished before this storm breaks. We need a good show this year. The people are nervous. They need the reassurance of their Zeus."

Feet crunched away down the ash steps, and Sosi's hiding place moved again as Nike was propped against the fire pit. A slap jolted her. "Come on, Nike! It's time for you to do your stuff. Snap out of it."

The clapping and whistling below rose in volume as the torch bearer reached the Great Altar. Sosi risked a peep. From the time it took for the torch to appear at the summit, he decided Agis must have prolonged the climb. But finally, the sacred flame glowed against the threatening sky. A trumpet blared, and there was a hush below as the torch touched the kindling in a rush of heat and flame. The cheer that went up from the Altis must have been loud enough to be heard in Elis.

The priestesses started singing, and the oxen bellowed as the priests moved in with their knives. The smell of blood mixed with the smoke as a steady procession of priests climbed the steps of the Great

Altar, bringing legs carved off the slaughtered oxen. Priest Rhexibius supervised the throwing of the offerings into the fire. Nike, propped against the side of the fire pit, was ignored. Sosi flickered his tongue at her eyelids, desperately trying to wake her, but with no more success than the priest had earlier. As the sacrifices went into the fire, the horrible smell of burning hoof surrounded them. Since four hundred legs had to be carried to the top, and each priest could carry only two at a time, this took a while. Sosi began to dream of cool, dark caves.

"I'll take over now," said a quiet voice, jolting him back.

Priest Rhexibius frowned at the final "priest", who was dressed in red and clean-shaven like the others but had a fanatical glitter in his eye. "Who are you?" he said. "I don't remember you—"

Beware!

Sosi's warning came out as a hiss, as the disguised Warrior swung the ox legs he was carrying at Priest Rhexibius' head. The priest crumpled to his knees. The Warrior hit him with the hooves again and kicked his unconscious body over the edge. Screams sounded below as it bounced down the steep side of the Great Altar into the crowd.

The Warrior raised his arms against the brooding sky, purple flames flaring from his hands, and cried in a terrible voice: "DEATH TO THE WORSHIPPERS OF ZEUS AND THE FOLLOWERS OF ISKANDER!"

A terrified hush descended over the Altis. People seemed frozen with shock. Then someone shouted out, "It's a Persian terrorist!" and panic broke out as everyone tried to push their way out of the enclosure. The crowds were so thick that blockages formed at the gates, and those who climbed the walls found themselves trapped by yet more crowds outside.

The Warrior thrust his arms into the sacrificial fire and chanted:

"Immortal Ahriman, I call on your power!
Send your faithful Warriors into this world to
destroy the enemies of Persia!
Immortal Ahriman, I call on your power..."

There was a crackle, and the smoke of the sacrificial fire turned purple. A wall of rippling flame joined the summit of the Great Altar of Zeus to the sky. Sosi coiled himself tightly around Nike's braid in horror. Through the flames, as if through water, he could see the ghostly forms of men with fierce eyes and dark Persian skins and curled crimson beards, ranks upon ranks of them stretching away into the shadows of another world. At the same time, the fires that had been lit that morning on the other altars of the Altis exploded, shooting purple sparks high into the sky. Priests and priestesses ran out of the temples, screaming.

A few brave Elean soldiers elbowed their way through the crowds and leapt up the steps of the Great Altar with drawn swords. The Warrior laughed and cast down balls of purple flame that clung to their clothes and hair. They fell back, yelling and beating at the unnatural fire, blocking the way of their comrades trying to get up from below. People fell over one another in their rush to escape, slipping and sliding in the blood and entrails of those oxen that had been slaughtered. The surviving animals stampeded, trampling the visiting dignitaries, who grabbed the arms of the soldiers and yelled, "Arrest the Persian scum! There's only one of him! Go up there and get him down!" But with only two narrow flights of steps, the frantic crush of beasts and people, and the fiery missiles falling on their heads, the Eleans' numbers were useless against the Warrior. Some of the athletes valiantly threw themselves upon the stampeding oxen's horns and wrestled the animals to the ground, while others launched themselves at the steep sides of the altar, but even their Olympic-trained muscles could not carry them through the purple fireballs to the Warrior who laughed at them all from the summit.

Above the chaos, the Warrior produced one of his enchanted cords and cupped Nike's chin in his smoking hand. "Victory," he whispered, tugging out one of her long, black hairs to wind about the cord. "At last, you are mine."

His touch did what Sosi and the priest had failed to do. Nike stiffened and opened her eyes. She stared numbly at the Warrior as he bound her wrists together.

"No..." she breathed, struggling weakly. "Zeus won't let this happen. Sosipolis will stop you."

The Warrior laughed. "Oh, I don't think so. I've got the snake-boy in a safe place. He won't be bothering us, don't worry." He waved a hand at the rippling wall of flame. "See Ahriman's power? See his eager Warriors waiting? When I sacrifice you to the Dark One, they'll be able to come through into this world and live again. A fair exchange, don't you think? Your life for theirs?"

Sosi's scales were dark, so the Warrior had not yet noticed him clinging to Nike's braid, but it was only a matter of moments before he did.

He flickered his tongue at the girl's cheek.

Nike! I'm here, in my snake form. What do I do? How do I stop him?

"Sosi...?" Nike rolled her eyes sideways to see him.

Thunder rumbled overhead, setting off more screams below. Distracted, the Warrior glanced up as the sun disappeared behind the cloud.

What do I do, Nike?

"Do what you did before. Hurry, Sosipolis!"

But I don't remember!

"You must remember. You have dreams, don't you?"

His dreams! Sosi's new skin tightened as he tried to recall the details of the battle in the stadium. There had been a thunderstorm that day as well. Zeus was always angry when he changed into a snake. Maybe he didn't need powers of his own? He was cursed. Maybe he had only to expose himself in this sacred place in his snake form and let Zeus do the rest.

At last, the Warrior noticed the little snake clinging to Nike's braid. "*Snake-boy!*" he hissed. For the first time, his face showed a flicker of doubt. "I don't know how you got out of that cave, snake-boy, but you won't stop me now!" He rekindled purple fire in his hand and seized Nike's braid, at the same time grasping Sosi and cutting off his light and air.

Overhead, the sky cracked with an enormous thunderclap, making the Warrior cringe. But he did not let go. Sosi wriggled desperately. His small snake body was smothered by the Warrior's hand. He could not see, could not breathe. Nike struggled too, but could not escape the grip on her hair as the Warrior dragged her closer to the wall of flame and Ahriman's waiting army.

Great Zeus! Sosi screamed. *I cheated in the Olympic Games! I swore a false oath! Zeus, I'm here, I'm cursed! Strike me!*

There was a second tremendous crack overhead, and the holy ground of the Altis vibrated. The Warrior's grip slackened, and Sosi squeezed his head between his fingers to see a ball of orange flame drop out of the clouds towards where he and Nike and the Warrior struggled, growing larger and larger until it filled the sky.

He closed his eyes. There was a pause, as if all the people below were holding their breath. Then Sosi's world turned upside down as the thunderbolt landed in the sacrificial fire, spraying ash, purple flames, and blackened ox hooves high into the air.

The Warrior screamed, his hair and clothes on fire. He let go of Nike's braid and fell headfirst through his own rippling gateway. The wall of purple flame fell apart in flares. The ghostly Warriors disappeared, and the Great Altar of Zeus began to crumble.

Sosi fell amidst glowing embers and a hissing downpour of rain. He twisted his snake body in the air; saw people running below to avoid the debris, and others at a safer distance stopping to point at the sky. As he braced himself for the landing that would have broken his boy's body, a flap of large wings snatched him out of the air.

"Victory to Zeus Olympia!" one of the priests below cried in a powerful voice, and the crowd's panic turned to celebration as they realized the thunderbolt had struck the terrorist. People began to sing praises to the gods. Others pointed at the eagle as it carried a small, dark snake high into the air above the steaming Altis.

"Nike!" they cried. "Isn't that Goddess Nike? Zeus has saved our Games! Victory flies again!"

The little snake wriggled in the grip of Nike's powerful talons, soaked and buffeted by the rain. He was prey to an eagle. He must escape.

Nike gripped him harder and hissed, "Stop it, Sosipolis! You're slippery enough with all this rain. We haven't much time if you're going to be a boy again. You'll be in trouble if I drop you and lose you... Ah, there are your friends! Trying to move the mountain on their own. Just like boys."

Nike glided down smoothly and landed behind the boys who had gone up the mountain earlier to look for the caves. They were scraping at the cliff face, but in the wrong place. She transformed back into a girl and kept a tight grip on Sosi as the boys whirled to stare at him with expressions that ranged from revulsion to horror.

"Sosi...?" breathed the smallest boy, breaking the silence and taking a step closer. "Is that you?"

"Of course it's Sosipolis, you dimwit!" Nike snapped. "Do you think I make a habit of carrying around live snakes? He's almost forgotten he's human. We're running out of time. I have to get him to his mother. Can one of you run down and get Pericles and the others? We'll need as much muscle power as we can get. The Warrior used Ahriman's power to move the rock, but we're going to have to do it the hard way. You go, Dion. You're the fastest."

"Will he change back again?" the small boy whispered, still staring at Sosi.

"Is Pericles better, then?" said one of the others with the beginnings of a grin. "That was quick."

"Everyone the Warrior enchanted will be fine now," Nike said. "Zeus destroyed Ahriman's House of the Lie. But we've still got to get Sosi's brother and the women out of those caves before they collapse completely." She pointed to the blocked fissure. "Well, don't just stand there! Dig – that's the way in."

Sosi struggled some more when he saw the entrance enlarged by the boys' efforts, but Nike refused to let go of him.

Eventually, Pericles arrived, hoisted two head-sized boulders out of the way with his bare hands, and squeezed through the opening shouting for Eretaia. The others scrambled in after him. More boys puffed up the slope, led by a breathless Dion, and plunged into the caves. They had brought lanterns with them, and the glow showed deep in the hillside.

Dion hesitated. "Agis wouldn't come," he said, glancing at Sosi. "I'm sorry. I tried to tell him, but he wouldn't believe Sosi had really changed into a snake."

"We don't need Agis," Nike said. "How are they getting on in there?"

"I'll go and see."

Dion vanished after the others. Noises echoed from the depths of the mountain – the rattle of rock, shouts, sharp orders from Pericles as he directed the excavations. Nike tried to interest Sosi in the trumpet blasts and cheers from the stadium, where the men's foot races were in progress, but all he could think of were the cool, dark tunnels, and escape.

At last, a lantern reappeared and a string of women and boys came stumbling out of the hillside, shading their eyes and blinking in the afternoon sunshine. They were dirty, blood-streaked, and had dust in their hair, but they were smiling and hugging one another in relief. Pericles came out with Eretaia in his arms. Finally, Theron emerged, no longer limping, supporting a woman who moved stiffly but seemed recovered from her fever.

Sosi's skin rippled in recognition, and Theron rushed across. "Let my brother go! You're hurting him!"

Nike glared. "I do, and you'll lose him. Where's his mother?"

Lady Alcmena stepped forward, a little shaky. "Here."

The yellow-eyed priestess and the Macedonian woman faced each other, watched by the boys and other mothers, some of whom clutched their sons to them in relief, while others rested their hands on their boys' shoulders. A purple-clad judge could be seen marching up the mountainside at the head of a troop of Elean soldiers, but no one attempted to run. It was far too late for that.

"You have to bring your son back to his human shape," Nike said, holding out the wriggling Sosi. "Only you can do it."

Lady Alcmena stared at the snake and bit her lip. "How?"

"I don't know, or I'd have done it already! Hold him. Tell him you love him, or something. That's what mothers are supposed to do."

Their mother reached out a trembling hand to touch Sosi's scales, and withdrew it with a shudder. "I... I'm sorry! I know what he did for us, but I can't—"

"Mother!" Theron exclaimed. "Do what Nike said, for Zeus' sake!"

Lady Alcmena stared helplessly at Sosi. "But he's not my son any more. He's a *snake*." She wrapped her arms around herself and began to cry.

"Pull yourself together, woman!" The old priestess Eileithyia limped forwards, shaking rubble from her cloak. "Of course he's your son! He's just saved you from the terrorists. He saved us all. Nike's right. Tell him you love him. Don't make the same mistake I made with my son, please. You have to do it before the moon rises again. When it's no longer full, it'll be too late. Hurry, Alcmena! Time's running out."

The other mothers stared at Lady Alcmena in horror. Even the boys, who had shuffled their feet in embarrassment at all the talk of love, stopped smirking and clenched their fists, willing her to do it. Eretaia roused herself from her brother's arms to shout, "Tell him!" And suddenly they were all shouting at Lady Alcmena. "Say it! Tell him you love him! Tell him!"

Sosi stopped struggling, sensing freedom. She wouldn't do it, he knew. She'd see this as the perfect opportunity to get rid of the son who had always been such an embarrassment to her family.

"He's a snake every full moon," Nike explained gently. "Otherwise he couldn't shed his skin and change his shape. Usually it's so quick, you don't notice. But the longer we stay in our animal shape, the harder it is for us to remember what we are. Don't let that happen to Sosipolis. He doesn't deserve it. Quick, Lady Alcmena – Judge Demetrius is nearly here."

Their mother glanced down the slope at the soldiers. Her face twisted. Tears rolled down her cheeks. She closed trembling fingers about Sosi's tail. "Please be a boy again, Sosi," she whispered. "I promise I won't punish you for changing shape, ever again. What you did was very brave, and—"

Nike smiled and let go. But it was not enough. It was too painful to hear his mother say she couldn't love him. Sosi convulsed out of Lady Alcmena's weak grip and fled for the caves.

"No!" A boy landed on top of him. Strong hands gripped him, and tears wet his scales. "No, Sosi! Little brother! *I* love you, and I don't care who knows it. Just change back, will you? Please? I need someone to wrestle with, and someone to beat at running practice... though no doubt I'll have to try a bit harder now you're an Olympic victor. I'm so proud of you, little brother, really I am."

A great shudder went through Sosi. His skin prickled, and the darkness fell away. He found himself naked on the ground with his brother's arms around him and his brother's tears wetting his hair, and everyone staring at them. He twisted in embarrassment and threw Theron off with a trick Pericles had taught him at Elis. The boys cheered, and several of the women wept with joy.

Chapter 18

JUDGEMENT

JUDGE DEMETRIUS REFUSED to listen to their explanations and placed them all under arrest. The women were escorted to the Judges' House to await trial, and the boys were sent back to the Prytaneon where the public banquet was already under way, with a strict warning not to leave the Altis until the matter had been investigated.

"I know about the trick you two pulled," he said, giving Sosi and Theron a dark look, his gaze lingering on Sosi. "Cheating at the Olympic Games is a serious offence. I'd lock you up, too, if it wouldn't cause more questions than we need right now. For the time being, consider yourselves under house arrest and don't talk to anyone."

It turned out that Agis had told the judge everything, even where to find them on the mountainside. Perhaps he'd expected the other boys to side with him once they realized Sosi and his brother were in trouble. He was out of luck. When he saw Pericles striding towards him, he paled and ducked into a corner of the hall, trying to hide behind the banqueting tables. Pericles seized one arm and Glaukos took the other. Between them, they marched the Athenian to an ivy-covered shrine in a quiet corner of the Altis. Sosi and the others followed.

Agis must have realized the futility of fighting them, for he didn't try to escape. He still wore his victory ribbon, though it was singed and tattered after the events earlier that day. As the boys gathered round, he cowered at the back of the shrine. "If you hurt me, Judge Demetrius will know you did it!" he said in a quavering voice.

The others muttered. Pericles motioned them back, seized Agis' wrist and threw him full length into the ivy. He sat astride the skinny boy, his knees pressing into his ribs, and hissed into his ear, "If you'd let me win the wrestling like you promised, Samos might still be alive."

"It wasn't my fault he died!" Agis squealed. "It was Rasim who pushed him over the gallery... Let me go, or I'll scream!"

Pericles did not let go, so Agis screamed. No one came to his rescue.

"Punch the telltale, Pericles!" one of the boys growled.

Theron took a step forward, ready to do the punching if Pericles didn't. But Sosi laid a hand on his brother's arm. "Don't," he said, thinking of the wrestling match. "This is between Agis and Pericles."

Pericles applied an arm-lock, lifted Agis to his feet, braced his legs and tossed the Athenian on to his back. It was a clean throw and couldn't have hurt much with the soft landing, but Agis just lay there, shaking.

"Get up and fight me," Pericles said, tugging the boy's victory ribbon until Agis got to his feet. Pericles threw him again, and this time the Athenian started to sob in fear.

Pericles shook his head. "That's three," he said. "You're not worth more." He tore the ribbon from Agis' arm, leaving the tattered end knotted around his bicep like a scar. With a disgusted look at the boy, he dusted himself off and strode back to the Prytaneon. The others cast similar looks at Agis and followed.

Sosi watched awkwardly as Agis knelt in the ivy, snivelling and fingering his torn ribbon. "Are you hurt?" he asked, feeling sorry for the boy, even though Agis had been responsible for the women's arrest and betrayed them all.

Seeing Pericles had gone, Agis clambered stiffly to his feet and wiped his eyes. He blinked at Kallias. "I thought you were my friend."

"I thought you were ours," Kallias replied. "You deserved that, Agis! Admit it."

"I kept my Olympic oath..."

"Zeus take your Olympic oath!" Kallias shouted. "Don't try to hide behind that now."

Agis said in a small voice, "You cheated. All of you cheated. You can't blame me for that."

Theron pulled a face. "You could have helped when Sosi asked you to. It wouldn't have been hard. Instead you chose to use everyone else's misfortune to steal yourself some glory. So, now you've got to live with it. Pull yourself together and try to act like a winner! You're still going to get an Olympic wreath for the boys' wrestling. You'll probably get one for the boys' sprint as well, after the judges have punished Sosi and me. It'll be better if you do, actually, because I certainly don't want it. I just hope you realize how little you deserve either of them. When Nike recovered, my foot healed and so did Pericles' leg, and Lady Alcmena recovered from her fever. Samos might have got better, too, if you'd only been a bit less selfish. Think about it."

The Athenian boy eyed Theron's foot. "I never meant for Samos to die," he said in a small voice. "I didn't believe Sosi and Nike had magic powers. I even carried the Warrior's fire around the altars. He must have tampered with the torch, only I didn't realize. I'm sorry. I know it won't bring Samos back, but I'm sorry anyway." He raised his chin a little. "It wasn't all my fault, though. How was I to know Sosi was telling the truth about being able to change his shape? Is that really him? I thought Dion said he was a snake..."

"He was until just now!" Dion said. "And you wouldn't even come to help him change back into a boy! I hope Sosi gets to keep the sprint crown, because he deserves it a lot more than you do. If I was him, I'd change back into a snake and bite you."

Sosi met the Athenian's gaze, amused to see the uncertainty on his face. He was aware of being taller than usual, and he felt stronger. His Olympic-trained muscles had not vanished when he changed shape. For the first time in his life, he hadn't been worrying what shape to take when his skin had come off. It had just happened. Curious, he pulled a lock of hair forward and saw it was glossy black in the torchlight. He wondered about his eyes.

Whatever colour they were, they must have showed his new confidence, because Agis looked away first.

The trial was scheduled for lunch time the following day, slotted between the men's heavy events and the race-in-armour, which was put back to the end of the afternoon to allow the judges time to make their decision. After the scare the terrorist had given everyone, the men's events went smoothly. But no one had forgotten the way their Games had nearly been ruined, and the Eleans wore grave expressions as they escorted Sosi and Theron to the Council House.

Standing with their mother before the statue of Zeus Horkios, Sosi's stomach churned with nerves. He had barely slept, and didn't feel ready to explain his curse before a formal session of the Hellenic judges of Olympia. Even the fact Judge Lysanias had recovered from his poisoning and travelled from Elis to join the other nine in time for the trial didn't lift his spirits.

Theron reached for his hand and gave it a squeeze. "Don't worry, little brother. You saved their Games. They can't deal too harshly with us."

Sosi wasn't so sure. The judges had a lot of power, and they'd dealt harshly enough with Rasim. It seemed Lightning had arrived at the last moment for the horse race as planned, galloping into the Hippodrome with the Persian boy clinging to his back to startle the other colts processing around the track. But that was where Nike's plan had started to go wrong. The grey colt went wild, no doubt sensing its jockey was one of Ahriman's dead, and the other jockeys must have found out what he'd done to Samos in the temple, for they worked together to bring his horse down at the final turn. There was a pile-up worthy of a chariot race, and Rasim got trampled. Terribly injured, but unable to die because of Ahriman's enchantment, he'd lain in agony in the Blood House until Sosi defeated the Warrior at the Great Sacrifice. Later, during the funeral rites of Pelops, an unidentified body had been quietly burnt on the sacrificial fire.

Sosi had been thinking about it all morning, and every time he felt sick. What if the judges decided to burn him, too? Considering the unusual circumstances, the other women had been let off the traditional punishment of being thrown over the cliff and had been sent back to Elis under guard, but it was different for Lady Alcmena because this wasn't her first offence. At the very least, Theron would lose his Olympic victory.

Judge Demetrius banged his staff on the tiles to call the court to session and gave the three of them a stern look. "I suppose you realize the seriousness of the charge. Whose idea was it to cheat at the Games?"

Theron straightened his shoulders. "Sir, it was my idea. I wanted to win so badly that I made Sosi take my place when I got injured in Elis."

"That's not true!" Sosi protested. "Theron didn't *make* me. I wanted to get to Olympia to find out more about my curse. I'm the one who swore the Olympic oath falsely. If anyone should be punished, it's me."

Lady Alcmena stepped forward. "They're both lying to protect me. It was my idea originally, and I'm the one who should be punished for it. My sons are still minors. Under the law, they're not responsible for their own actions."

This was technically true. The judges muttered amongst themselves.

Judge Demetrius sighed in exasperation. "Usually the guilty party can't pass the blame quickly enough! Perhaps you don't appreciate quite how much trouble you're in. For breaking an Olympic oath, the punishment is public flogging in the stadium before all the athletes and spectators. Theron will, of course, be stripped of his Olympic victory that was won dishonestly. And for such a serious deception as yours, banishment from the Circuit Games for life would not be out of order. In your case, Lady Alcmena, if you are found guilty of cheating on their behalf, then your sons and your husband and any other male relations, living or unborn, can be banished from competing."

Their mother's stricken expression told them she hadn't realized this.

Sosi bit his lip. "It was me," he said again, though his legs trembled at the thought of a public whipping. "My mother only helped us, and Theron had nothing to do with it. He was feverish with his wound. He didn't realize what he was agreeing to. I'm the cursed one."

"No, little brother!" Theron gripped his hand. "I knew very well what I was asking you to do, and you're not cursed. You just have a strange gift that I took advantage of, and I refuse to let you take the punishment for my stupid pride!"

Judge Demetrius gave them a baffled look. For once, he didn't seem to know what to do.

Judge Lysanias stood up, and the court quietened.

"As you all know," he said, "I've had direct experience of the terrorist's magic. They tell me I almost died. When I recovered yesterday, it was like a miracle, and I understand I've Sosi to thank for that. He defeated the Warrior with his own special powers, even though he knew he would get into trouble for revealing himself in such a way. It seems to me we should not be talking about punishments here. Rather, we should be talking about a reward."

The other judges raised their eyebrows. Lady Alcmena put her arms around both her sons.

Judge Demetrius spoke. "Everyone believes Zeus destroyed the terrorist and saved the Games. If we tell them that Sosi called down the thunderbolt while he was in his snake form, we'll have half the priests of Olympia clamouring for our blood, and the other half for the boy's! The time of the old earth spirits and demons who used to haunt this place is over. I know we have our legend of the snake-child saving the Games by stopping the battle between the Eleans and the Arcadians, but that was then and this is now. People just aren't willing to believe in such nonsense these days."

"I'm not suggesting a *public* reward," Judge Lysanias said in his quiet voice. "But how about a private one, so those who know the truth can see we've honoured Sosi for his part? I suggest a small temple, dedicated to the snake-child Sosipolis. We don't have to include it in the Altis ceremonies. We can say it's in memory of the battle nine Olympiads ago, maybe even keep a live snake there."

The other judges nodded thoughtfully. After further discussion, it was decided to build the temple up on Mount Kronos near the old caves and charge Priestess Eileithyia with looking after the snake.

Judge Demetrius banged his staff again, and the court quietened. "I also propose we should strip Theron of his victory in the boys' sprint and award the crown to the Athenian boy, Agis. Since he came second in the race and has already carried the torch around the altars, it would not be seen as a strange decision."

"No!" called a shaky voice from the gate, and everyone looked round. Agis gripped the bars, held back by two Eleans with crossed spears. "Please, sir, I don't want the sprint crown! Sosi won it fair and square. He should keep it."

Theron scowled, but Sosi looked at Agis with new respect. It must have taken a lot of guts for him to come to the Council House and say that.

"Get that boy out of here!" Judge Demetrius ordered. "One thing we can *not* do is award the crown to Sosi. He doesn't even look like his brother any more. But I agree giving it to the Athenian might be awkward if he refuses to accept it. Any suggestions?"

Judge Lysanias spoke up again. "I understand Sosi ran his best to win the boys' sprint. He was Theron when he won, and Theron's foot is now healed. No one need know about the substitution. Why not let Theron accept the crown at the ceremony?"

"But I didn't even run!" Theron protested. "I don't want—"

Judge Lysanias cut him short. "Think of it as a private punishment, to go with the private nature of your brother's reward."

His expression was solemn as he addressed the court. "Every day Theron sees his Olympic wreath, he'll remember the shame of cheating at the Great Games. So will his mother and brother. We don't need to flog anyone. I am of the opinion that both boys are conscientious young citizens of the Hellas, and will therefore feel a punishment of this nature more deeply than the whip. The scars will last longer – definitely longer in the case of the snake-child, who I understand sheds his skin every month and therefore heals physical scars quickly."

Sosi's skin prickled. Lady Alcmena flushed. Theron stared at his feet, while the judges whispered among themselves and studied the family to see if Judge Lysanias might be right.

"Of course," Judge Lysanias continued after a suitable pause. "If we decide to punish the family in this private way, then we can't flog either boy in public, or banish them or any of their relations from competing at future Games."

Theron stiffened, and Sosi held his breath in sudden hope. Agis clung to the gate, waiting to hear the verdict. At the side of the courtyard, Nike appeared in the shadow of a column, her golden wings glimmering around her. She winked at Sosi.

Judge Demetrius glared at them for what seemed like an age. Finally, he sighed. "Very well, it shall be as Judge Lysanias says. A clever way out for us, and one that will cause the least disruption to the Games. The Olympic crown for the boys' sprint will be awarded to Theron of Macedonian Pella. Lady Alcmena can return to Elis with the other women. Sosipolis can stay to watch his brother accept the crown. Someone get the boy a ribbon... Nike?"

Sosi thought his nerves could not stand any more. But as Nike stepped forward to tie a red victory ribbon around Theron's arm, there was a commotion outside the gate and an Elean soldier rushed into the courtyard.

"What now?" Judge Demetrius said in a resigned tone.

"Messenger, sir! Claims he's come all the way from Persia. He's demanding to speak to the judges. Says it can't wait."

Judge Demetrius nodded. "All right, let him in. We've finished here."

Before the Eleans could open the gate, there was a clatter of hooves and a foam-covered horse sailed over the barrier, scattering guards and judges alike. The rider, sweating in dusty Macedonian armour, dragged his mount to a halt and bellowed as if he were on a battlefield, "You have to stop the Games at once! We've uncovered a terrorist plot that could destroy Olympia! You're all in great danger. Thank Zeus I arrived in time! I've a company of men with me. We'll root the devils out for you, if you give us permission to search the camps. One of my sons is supposed to be competing this year – is he all right...?"

His voice trailed off as he realized none of the men in the courtyard were reacting the way he expected. He pulled off his helmet to reveal sun-bleached curls dripping with sweat and looked around in confusion.

Lady Alcmena's hands flew to her mouth, and Theron stiffened. Sosi's heart jumped as he recognized the dusty soldier he'd last seen six years ago, riding off to Persia with King Alexander's army.

"Father!" he cried, a choke in his voice. "It's Father!"

Chapter 19

VICTORY

THE GAMES CLOSED with a prize-giving ceremony in the Temple of Zeus. Races and contests of strength had been won or lost. Hopes and dreams had been realized or shattered for the next four years. Now was the time for serious celebration, which had already started in the camps. All in all, it seemed the judges had done an excellent job of covering up the real horror of the Warriors of Ahriman and the magical nature of their defeat, as well as the true extent of the danger everyone had been in.

There were some things even the Hellenic judges could not cover up, though. All through the ceremony, the memory of Samos and Rasim falling towards the black marble pool, their bodies twisted together in death, haunted Sosi. But there were no ghosts in the temple. Wherever Samos and Rasim had gone, it could not be

Ahriman's House of the Lie. Samos' statue was going to be erected in the Altis in memory of his tragic fall, and although no such memorial would be erected for Rasim, the priests said he had a better reward. Freedom, the only way possible.

Commander Sarapion, stiff and proud in his Macedonian uniform, watched with the other boys' fathers and uncles as Theron stepped up to receive his Olympic crown from the hands of Priest Rhexibius, who was determined to complete his duties despite breaking a leg in his fall from the Great Altar. Only Sosi knew there was shame, not pride, in his brother's heart. They had argued all night about how much their father should be told, and decided it would be best for everyone if Commander Sarapion believed their mother's suggested half-truth: that Theron had won the boys' sprint, and that Sosi had changed into his true shape when he found the cave where his curse originated.

Finally, the ordeal was over and they escaped into the leafy shade of the Altis, where groups of family and friends clustered around the winning athletes to admire their olive wreaths.

Commander Sarapion stood awkwardly with his two sons. Without his sword, which the Eleans had confiscated at the Altis gate, his scarred hands looked too big and rough for his body. There hadn't been much of an opportunity for a father-to-son talk, since the commander had refused a room in the Guest House in favour of camping with his men on the banks of the

Alpheos. But he seemed to believe Theron's part in the story, and that was what mattered. He reached out to grip Theron's shoulder, changed his mind, and settled for folding his arms. He cleared his throat and spoke in a gruff tone, as if giving orders to his men.

"Since you won the boys' sprint, son, you've my permission to train as a professional athlete. Your mother tells me you take your athletic training very seriously. The army will miss a recruit of your calibre, but I don't go back on my word. Congratulations." He gave Theron a brief embrace. "I'm proud of you."

Theron looked at Sosi over his father's shoulder, and his face twisted in anguish.

"*We have to tell him,*" he mouthed.

Sosi shook his head. "*No, we don't.*"

Commander Sarapion released Theron and frowned at Sosi. He shook his head as if he couldn't think of anything to say to him, and turned to leave.

Their father was still a stranger, Sosi thought sadly. A man in Macedonian armour, who couldn't wait to rejoin his men and get back to the fighting. By some miracle, it seemed their plan had succeeded, and he was pleased for Theron's sake, yet he felt empty inside.

"Father!" Theron called, a choke in his voice. "Come back! We didn't tell you the whole truth."

"No!" Sosi hissed, seizing his brother's arm. "Don't!"

His brother shook him off, removed his Olympic crown and stood bare-headed before the commander. "I've been thinking, sir, and I've decided I want to join the army, if you'll still have me. Games are fine, but they're only Games. War is real, I can see that now. Sosi used his magic to defeat the Warriors of Ahriman, but if he hadn't been here they could easily have succeeded. I want to go with you to Persia and join the army to make sure this sort of thing can never happen again."

Their father studied him for a long moment. "You genuinely want to join the army? You're not just saying that to please me?"

Theron raised his chin and stared the commander in the eye. "No, sir! I mean yes, sir, I really do. I know I'm only fifteen, but I'm fit and strong. Plenty of boys my age pretend to be older and join up. I won't be the only one."

Sosi looked at his brother in surprise. So that had been the reason for Theron's thoughtfulness of the past two days.

Their father's stern expression cracked into a proud grin. This time, he gave Theron a proper embrace, slapping him on the back. "That's my boy! But I forbid it."

Theron's face fell. "But why? I'm serious..."

"I know you are. Yet as you said, you're still fifteen, so you must obey me. I forbid it until you've run in the Olympic Games as a man. You're to continue your training as an athlete for the next four years, do you hear? You're to train hard and compete around the Circuit, and at the next Olympics I'm going to make sure I'm here to see you run in the men's foot races. *Then* we'll talk about you joining the army. Agreed?"

Theron's whole face lit up. "Oh, Father! Thank you!"

Commander Sarapion's smile died as he turned to Sosi. "Is this true? *You* stopped the Warriors? You changed your shape before all Olympia?"

Sosi avoided his accusing stare, the joy he'd felt on his brother's behalf fading fast. Feeling small again, he mumbled, "I... er... sort of..."

"Sort of, nothing!" Nike strode up and put a hand on Sosi's shoulder. She had been doing her rounds of congratulating the winners, and for the occasion her black curls had been oiled and tamed by a mass of gold ribbons that lit her face with reflected sunlight, making her radiant and almost beautiful. "Sosipolis called down Zeus' fire upon the Warrior's head! If he hadn't been here, we'd all be dead. You've no reason to be ashamed of him, commander. He didn't want the glory for himself, so he let everyone think Zeus had saved them. You ought to be very proud of him."

There was a hush. Sosi tensed. He doubted anyone had dared speak to their father like that in a very long time.

Commander Sarapion frowned at Nike. "You're the priestess who was on the Great Altar when the terrorist attacked, aren't you?"

"That's me." Nike winked at Sosi. "I saw everything, so I can vouch for how brave your son was. I expect he's changed a bit since you saw him last?"

"He's changed, all right," Sarapion muttered. His frown deepened as he noticed the colour of Nike's eyes.

He looked properly at Sosi for the first time. "Is that your true shape?"

Sosi swallowed and told the truth. "I think so, sir."

Their father looked him up and down, a muscle in his cheek twitching. "You're taller than I imagined. And you look strong. Maybe you'd make a good soldier, after all. King Alexander is generous to his officers. Soon we'll be pushing further east, where there are supposed to be mountains made of gold and creatures such as you've never dreamt of..." He gave Sosi a sharp look. "You're not going to change shape again, are you?"

Sosi glanced at Theron. "I don't know, Father," he said, which was also the truth. "But I know a lot more about my curse now, and after what happened I know I can control it, so you don't need to worry about me showing you up like I used to when Mother beat me for it. Now I've found my true shape, maybe I won't need to change so often. Can I stay at Olympia for a while? Find out more about my magic? I'm sure Nike will agree to teach me."

Nike smiled and nodded, her muscular arms folded across her breasts. A shimmer of ghostly wings surrounded her.

Commander Sarapion gave Sosi a wary look, and sighed again. "It seems you've both grown up since I saw you last. If that's what you want, then you have my permission. I'm proud of you both." He still couldn't quite bring himself to embrace Sosi, but he clapped him on the shoulder before marching from the Altis without looking back.

The brothers exchanged a glance. Theron couldn't keep the grin from his face. Sosi felt warm inside, and there were unexpected tears in his eyes.

"He's not so bad," Nike said. "I don't know what you boys were so worried about. Theron's going to be a champion athlete, Sosi's going to stay here and keep me company, Rasim's free of Ahriman, and the terrorists have gone. Even Agis seems to realize an Olympic crown won dishonestly means nothing. The only bad thing is Samos, really."

Sosi eyed the priestess. She was right. The day should have been perfect. But, like the memory of Samos and Rasim falling from the gallery, a shadow lingered over it. He blurted out the question that had been nagging him ever since Nike's dream-voice had saved him from losing the boys' sprint.

"Do you really give us victories?" he asked. "Is that the only reason we win? Because you send us dreams of victory? Does all our training and effort mean nothing?"

The others stopped talking. Eretaia, Pericles, the other boys who had drifted across when Commander Sarapion left, Theron clutching his olive wreath with white knuckles... all waited for her answer, suddenly very still.

Nike tossed her head in a flash of golden ribbons and laughed. "Is that what's bothering you? After all that's happened, you're worried about what makes some people into winners and others losers? You are dense, Sosipolis! I'd have thought you, at least, would understand. It's all to do with belief, don't you see? I could do nothing at all to help you if you didn't believe in me. If Sosi hadn't believed he was cursed when he called on Zeus to strike him, that thunderbolt wouldn't have come. But you believed it because you'd dreamt about it happening before during the battle between the Eleans and the Arcadians, and because you know Zeus throws thunderbolts at his enemies. It's exactly the same with your victories, whether they're in the Games or in battle."

She stopped laughing and gazed fondly at the knots of triumphant athletes, their muscles gleaming with oil in the shade of the olive trees. Their scented sweat filled the grove, the smell of glory and honour and human courage. Sosi's heart swelled with a pride that had nothing to do with his magic and everything to do with what he'd learnt while he had been Theron.

"I merely send people dreams," Nike said with a smile. "You're the ones who have the power to make them happen."

GUIDE TO SOSI'S WORLD

SOSI AND HIS friends competed at Olympia in 328BC at the 113th festival of the Games. At this time, Alexander of Macedon (later called "the Great") was campaigning in the East, having angered the Persians by burning their emperor's palace in Persepolis. The Warriors of Ahriman and the terrorist threat to Olympia are my own invention, although there were several groups of fanatics who united against Alexander and the Greeks under their common religion of Zoroastrianism, and it is likely that they would have used terrorist tactics against the invaders.

The poems at the start of each section are extracts from the *Olympian Odes* by Pindar, translated by G. S. Conway.

agora	Market place.
Ahriman	The "Evil One" in Zoroastrian religion.
Altis	The sacred grove at Olympia – an enclosure containing temples, altars, famous tombs, monuments, statues and the sacred olive tree.
Asclepius	God of healing.
chiton	A woman's dress.
Circuit Games	The four most important games festivals in the Greek calendar: the Olympic Games at Olympia, the Nemean Games at Nemea, the Isthmian Games at Corinth and the Pythian Games at Delphi. Of these, the Olympic Games were the most important.
dolichos	A long foot race. Twenty-four lengths of the stadium, a distance of about 4,800 metres.
double-sprint	A foot race, also called the "diaulos". Two lengths of the stadium, a distance of about 400 metres.

ephebes | Young men between the ages of 12 and 18, the "privileged youth" of the Hellenic world whose fathers could afford to let them train as athletes.

Games of Hera | Games for girls, dedicated to the goddess Hera. They took place at Olympia, but in different years from the Olympic Games.

Great Games | Another name for the Olympic Games, held every four years at Olympia.

gymnasium | Building and/or open-air yard complex used for training. Originally this was a place for boys to gain fighting skills before entering the army, but in later times was taken over by athletes training for the Games. Most Greek cities had at least one gymnasium. The Olympic training camp at Elis had three. There was no gymnasium at Olympia itself until Roman times.

Hellas | The ancient Greek colonies. To compete at the Olympic Games, men and boys had to prove they were citizens of the Hellas, though exceptions were sometimes made in the case of powerful kings and generals from other lands.

Hellenic judges	Men elected from among the nobles of Elis to run the Olympic Games. For the duration of the Olympic Truce (the Games festival and a month either side for travelling) their word was law. At the time of this story, there were ten judges. They wore purple.
Hera	Goddess of marriage, the wife of Zeus.
Hercules	Legendary Greek hero with amazing strength, who was credited with founding the Olympic Games.
Hestia	Goddess of the hearth. Her fire was kept burning constantly in the hearth of the Prytaneon at Olympia, and was used to light the Sacred Torch carried around the altars.
Hippodrome	Course used for the horse and chariot races.
House of the Lie	In Zoroastrian religion, a place of torment where the souls of those who have lived an evil life are sent after death.
hydria	Water jug.
Iskander	Persian name for King Alexander (the Great).

Nike	Winged goddess of victory. Small statues of Nike were often put in the hands of larger statues of the main gods and goddesses. For example the statue of Zeus Olympia held a Nike in his right hand.
pankration	A fierce wrestling match with no holds barred, quite different from the ordinary wrestling done by the boys (which had strict rules, three throws being a win).
Pelops	Legendary hero whose tomb lies in the Altis. The legend says King Oenomaus of Elis, forewarned by an oracle that his son-in-law would kill him, decreed that anyone wishing to wed his daughter Hippodamia first had to beat him in a chariot race. But if the suitor lost the race, he would be killed. Since the King's horses were the swiftest in the land, Oenomaus caught and killed everyone who accepted the challenge. But Pelops bribed the King's charioteer to replace his axle pins with wax, which melted during the race, causing the King's wheel to fly off and his chariot to crash. The King was killed, and Pelops won the race and Hippodamia's hand.

pentathlon	Men's athletic contest consisting of five different events: sprint, javelin, discus, long-jump, and wrestling.
Persepolis	Capital city of Persia, burnt and plundered by Alexander the Great's troops during his conquest of the East.
Philippeon	A circular monument built in the Altis by King Philip of Macedon to house the statues of Macedonians who were successful at the Games.
Prytaneon	A building housing Hestia's sacred fire, where the athletes stayed while they were at Olympia. Previous victors in the Games were allowed to eat there free of charge whenever they liked.
Rhea	A goddess, the mother of Zeus.
sprint	A foot race, also called the "stadion" or "stade-sprint". A single length of the stadium, a distance of about 200 metres.
stade	An ancient measurement – about 600 feet, or 200 metres.

stadium	Course used for the foot races, so called because it was a "stade" in length.
strigil	A scraper used for scraping sweat and oil off an athlete's skin.
throwing-loop	Short length of cord twisted around the shaft of a javelin to give the throw more power. Unlike the javelin event in modern athletics, ancient athletes used throwing-loops and aimed their javelins at targets.
unguent	Paste or lotion used on the skin, usually sweet-smelling.
Zarathustra	A Persian prophet (called Zoroaster in the West), who gave rise to the Zoroastrian religion.
Zeus Horkios	Statue of Zeus with thunderbolts in his hands that stood in the courtyard of the Council House at Olympia, before which the athletes swore their oaths. Horkios means "oath-taker".
Zeus Olympia	Huge ivory and gold Statue of Zeus seated on a throne in the Temple of Zeus at Olympia. One of the Seven Wonders of the Ancient World.

THE
Seven Fabulous Wonders

THE GREAT
PYRAMID
ROBBERY

Magic, murder and mayhem spread through the Two Lands, when Senu, the son of a scribe, is forced to help build one of the largest and most magnificent pyramids ever recorded. He and his friend, Reonet, are sucked into a plot to rob the great pyramid of Khufu and an ancient curse is woken. Soon they are caught in a desperate struggle against forces from another world, and even Senu's mischievous ka, Red, finds his magical powers are dangerously tested.

000 711278 5

www.harpercollinschildrensbooks.co.uk

THE
SEVEN FABULOUS WONDERS

THE
BABYLON
GAME

Tia's luck starts to change the moment she touches a
dragon patrolling the Hanging Gardens of Babylon.
At the Twenty Squares Club Tia wins every game –
could the dragon have given her a magical power?

But Tia discovers her lucky gift brings great danger.
While the Persian army prepares to attack her home,
she and her friend, Simeon, must fight their own
battle. Will Tia's magic save the city – or destroy it
altogether?

000 711279 3

www.harpercollinschildrensbooks.co.uk

THE
SEVEN FABULOUS WONDERS

THE
AMAZON
TEMPLE
·QUEST·

Lysippe is an Amazon princess with a mission. Her tribe has vanished and her sister is fatally wounded. Only the power of a Gryphon Stone can help, but Lysippe has a problem. She has been enslaved by the sinister Alchemist, and he is after the Stones too…

Lysippe and her friend, Hero, plan a daring escape from the slave gang and claim sanctuary in the mysterious Temple of Artemis. But can they decipher the Temple's magical secrets before it's too late?

000 711280 7

www.harpercollinschildrensbooks.co.uk

THE SEVEN FABULOUS WONDERS

‹THE›
MAUSOLEUM MURDER

Alexis has a magical gift, but it's not one he wants. It hasn't helped him find his father, who has mysteriously disappeared, or freed him from his hard-hearted stepmother. Alex's home is under seige, and he can't do anything about that either. But when Alex and his best friend meet Princess Phoebe, things start to change. Together, they must unlock the murderous secrets of Halicarnassos. Magic is the key, but there may be a high price to pay for bringing statues to life…

0 00 711281 5

www.harpercollinschildrensbooks.co.uk